PR1ME
of Life

PR1ME
of Life

P. D. BEKENDAM

WORTHY
PUBLISHING

Published by Worthy Publishing, a division of Worthy Media, Inc.,
134 Franklin Road, Suite 200, Brentwood, Tennessee 37027.

Worthy is a registered trademark of Worthy Media, Inc.

HELPING PEOPLE EXPERIENCE THE HEART OF GOD

eBook available wherever digital books are sold.

Library of Congress Control Number: 2013954253

For foreign and subsidiary rights, contact Riggins International Rights Services, Inc.; rigginsrights.com

Published in association with Les Stobbe.

ISBN: 978-1-61795-227-2 (trade paper)

Cover Design: Christopher Tobias, Tobias' Outerwear for Books
Cover Illustrations: istockphoto
Interior Design and Typesetting: ThinkpenDesign.com

Printed in the United States of America

14 15 16 17 18 LBM 8 7 6 5 4 3 2 1

for Christy

CHAPTER 1

I clean rooms in a retirement home. Four years of college, four of medical school, four more in residency, and another four training in cardiothoracic surgery, and now I spend my days scrubbing toilets and mopping floors. My shift starts at eight, when the residents are supposed to be at breakfast.

"Ben," Frank hollers as I push my cleaning cart down the long hallway of the skilled nursing facility. "Start in my room today."

Frank is a cantankerous octogenarian. I have yet to discover his pleasant side.

"Sure, Frank." I wheel my cart into his dingy room. The blinds are drawn. A crumpled potato chip bag lies open on the floor. I step over a few greasy remnants that are ground into the carpet as I make my way between the bed and the television stand, taking care not to bump the rickety plastic contraption supporting the heavy 1970s-era TV.

"Just the bathroom," Frank says as he shuffles toward his chair. He takes an unexpected detour toward his rolltop desk and rummages through a drawer. "I just remembered. I'm gonna need your help with a little project later on."

This triggers a warning bell in my mind. "Not if it has anything to do with Marvin. You know my position on that."

Frank and Marvin have been feuding for half a century. Probably longer.

"Did you hear what he did to my denture cream?" Frank's voice raises an octave and his bushy white eyebrows perform a frustrated dance.

"Yeah. Cayenne pepper and Tabasco sauce." I suppress a grin.

"Don't you want to hear my plan for revenge?"

"Absolutely not." I make my way into the bathroom . . . and shake my head in disgust. I gave it a thorough cleaning only two days ago. "Why aren't you at breakfast?"

"Nasty scrambled eggs. Hey, I found 'em!"

Curious, I poke my head out to see Frank sitting at the foot of his bed, a pair of toenail clippers in hand. His knee pops as he laboriously raises his foot and yanks off his sock. He reaches into his shirt pocket and produces a plastic bag full of wet soil. Using the cuticle cleaner attached to the clippers, he scoops up some mud and crams it under his large toenail.

"What are you doing?" I can't help but ask.

"Dr. Kentucky is coming tomorrow." He grins.

Dr. Kentucky missed her calling to become a supermodel and instead became a podiatrist.

"You're pathetic, Frank."

"Can you blame me?"

I can't. Dr. Kentucky is nothing short of intoxicating, which is why I do my best to avoid her. If she even knows I exist I'd hate to imagine what she would make of me, a thirty-eight-year-old toilet scrubber.

"Hey," Frank says, "why don't you ask her out?"

"Give it up, Frank."

"Seriously. You're not that ugly and you two are probably about the same age. What's holding you back?"

"Drop it."

"I'll put in a good word for you."

"Do you want to scrub your toilet yourself?"

"There's no need to get all riled up. I'm only trying to help." He crams more mud under his toenail. "In my lifetime I've dated more women than you've dreamed about."

I return my attention to the bathroom and remind myself that I'm here by choice. I've been doing this for three years now. I make ten dollars an hour, my job is low stress, I mostly manage myself, and nobody bothers me as long as I keep things clean. There are other perks too. I have plenty of friends. Granted, they're all forty years older than I am, but they're wonderful people—present company excluded. I'll probably stay here until I retire. I won't even have to move. In the meantime, I can enjoy all-you-can-eat Jell-O in the cafeteria whenever I want.

I make quick work of rectifying the disaster in Frank's commode and then smile with satisfaction. This is what I want. A simple life.

Eager to make my escape from Frank's company, I arrange my assorted cleaning supplies in their proper configuration on my cart: bottles organized by category and sub-organized alphabetically with labels facing outward, brushes in their holsters, mop and broom securely fastened. My cart exemplifies humankind's ability to overcome chaos and defeat the second law of thermodynamics. The universe may be a mess, but my cart is in perfect order.

As I push it out of the bathroom, one of the front wheels snags on the carpet and snaps off. My cart tilts sideways, launching a few bottles overboard.

"You should probably fix that before you spill bleach on my floor," Frank says. "I don't want any stains."

"Look who's talking. You're getting mud all over the place."

"Don't worry about that. I know just the man who can clean this up."

"Well, I'd be happy to meet him."

"I meant you, you numskull. I'll register a complaint if you don't."

"I'll tell Dr. Kentucky how the dirt got under your nails."

"Humph."

"I'll bring the vacuum by later on. I'll even plug it in for you. But mark my words, Frank: I'm not cleaning that mess."

"Humph."

"I'll see you later." I rescue my wayward bottles and carefully limp my damaged cart out the door.

Frank sends me a parting grunt.

My next stop is the Professor's room. His name is Jerry, but my private nickname for him suits him better. From what I can gather, he holds three doctorates: physics, literature, and psychology. Perhaps philosophy too, but I'm not certain. Regardless, I suspect he knows everything.

I knock.

"It's open." His voice nearly fails to penetrate the wood. Nobody seems to be at breakfast this morning. That means Frank was right. Scrambled eggs must be on the menu. I can say with confidence that this place has the worst scrambled eggs in the entire Western Hemisphere. The Professor once described them fairly adequately when he said they taste like they were fished out of the garbage disposal right before they were slopped onto the plate.

"Good morning, Jerry." I follow my three-wheeled cart into his room.

Despite his brilliance, the Professor demonstrates exceedingly poor choice in attire. Today he's decked out in orange pants and a cherry-red polo shirt. I wonder where he acquired his bright yellow socks. His entire wardrobe consists of neon garments, giving him the appearance he strayed from a tropical fish tank.

"Good morning, Doc." He pulls his reading glasses toward the tip of his nose. With grey hair in disarray and a moustache in need of trimming, he resembles the classic Einsteinian image, and what makes it most authentic is that it is completely unintentional.

I falter for an instant and hope I don't give him the satisfaction of noticing my surprise at his pregnant greeting. I glance his way as he lounges in his leather recliner, hardback book minus its dust jacket propped in his lap. He smiles as if he's solved some great mystery.

"Whatcha reading?" I ignore his triumphant grin.

"It's called *The Information*." He pauses. "It's quite fascinating— this whole subject of information. Listen to this: 'In the long run, history is the story of information becoming aware of itself.' Chew on that for a while." He stares me straight in the eye. "Say, Doc, how long have we known each other?"

"I'm not sure I follow."

"Sure you do." He pounds his chest with his fist, mimicking the rhythm of a beating heart.

A sinking feeling settles in as I realize today will mark the end of the relative peace I've managed to find at Heritage Gardens.

Heritage Gardens is a cookie-cutter retirement village located near Temecula off the I-15 between San Diego and Riverside. The sun shines 347 days out of the year here. I like the number 347 because the first two digits add up to the third, it is prime, and it rolls off the tongue. Other interesting but irrelevant facts about the number 347: it is the case number assigned to the Supreme Court ruling in Brown vs. Board of Education in 1954—the case that ended segregation in public schools; it is the area code for most telephone numbers in New York City; some models of the Boeing 747 have 347 seats; and Plato died in 347 BC.

I am annoyed by the name Heritage Gardens, as I am by most clichés. Why is it that nine out of ten retirement communities must have the word Gardens or Village or Springs in the name? I suppose this is better than an honest name like Ticking Clock or Borrowed Time, but when it comes time for me to find a place to enjoy my final days, I don't want to be patronized. I'd rather stay in a place called Heaven Can Wait a Little Longer While I Golf.

I don't golf and I've abandoned my belief in heaven, but I'd still prefer that name.

There are several levels of retirement at Heritage Gardens. The first is independent living in condos and small homes. After that, the residents graduate (or get demoted, depending on your perspective) to the nursing facility, which is where Frank and the Professor live. The last stop is the mortuary, where the residents embark on their ultimate retirement.

In all, there are approximately 126 residents here. Well, not approximately. Exactly. I'm hoping we add one more, because that would be prime. The alternative would be that thirteen residents would have to die so that the total could be 113.

I have invested the past three years in this place, learning to love it, becoming part of it, beginning to imagine how I could become a permanent fixture here.

But now the Professor has somehow managed to slap me in the face with my past.

"Did you think I wouldn't discover you're a doctor, Ben?" He closes his book with finality, as if to say, Case closed. I solved the mystery. Now what's your move?

"I'm not a doctor. I'm a janitor."

"I'm sorry." He doesn't sound very sorry. "You know I can't let this go."

"Please let it rest, Jerry." I turn to leave. I'll clean his room another day.

CHAPTER 2

Yesterday was a nuisance. Today looks promising. Tomorrow will be a blast. I'm certain it will because I just happened to meet the 127th resident of Heritage Gardens. She plans to move in tomorrow.

For several days the place has been abuzz with rumors of a potential newbie. Frank was the one who started the gossip last week, so nobody really believed it. But ten minutes ago, while I was wiring a high-speed fiber-optic Internet connection in the manager's office, Betty Boop walked in. Her real name is Betty Boestra, but I think Betty Boop will suit her just fine. She's only fifty-five years old—more than a decade younger than the next youngest resident here. And she doesn't look fifty-five. Her hair is a sleek auburn, her face virtually wrinkle free, and she has either had plastic surgery or gravity has chosen to overlook certain parts of her anatomy. Why she decided to take up residence at Heritage Gardens is beyond my capacity for deductive reasoning, but I look forward to observing the social chaos her presence is sure to initiate.

I am now standing in the foyer of the manager's office waiting for Boop to exit the inner sanctum—

But I'm getting ahead of myself. Let's back up a few minutes. As I sat inside the office fumbling with the fiber-optic cable and wondering why the manager needs such a high-speed connection,

Boop breezed in and rescued me from a train of thought that was probably going to get me in trouble.

The manager, a morbidly obese man by the name of Ross Peterson Jr., promptly commenced drooling. "Miss Boestra, what a pleasant surprise!"

"Ross, dear, I've made up my mind."

"You'll be moving in?"

"Yes."

"Well! That's excellent news!" he said, practically slobbering. "Do you have the application forms I gave you?"

She handed over a file folder, which he quickly perused.

"Oh . . . I see you missed a line here. You see this space where it asks for your date of birth? It's blank."

"Oops." Betty smiled coyly. "I must have overlooked that one."

"That's okay, I don't even know why it's on here," Junior said. "We don't really have any restrictions based on age. You could live here even if you were only forty-five as long as you pay your rent. I won't make you put down your age, but I bet I could guess it."

"I bet you can't."

"Fifty."

If he was trying to flatter her, he should've started at forty. Or at least made it interesting and picked a number like forty-one, forty-three, or forty-seven.

"Nope."

"Okay, fifty-five."

No wonder he's still single.

"Bingo!"

"I knew it! I told you I could guess your age! So when will you be able to move in?"

"Actually, the moving company will bring my things tomorrow."

"Tomorrow? Well—er—uh—yes! Tomorrow will be just fine!"

"I wanted to confirm that the corner unit—the one overlooking the koi pond—is available like you promised."

I'm sure my eyebrows rose at this. She was referring to Marvin's place. Marvin has been living there for as long as I've been around. From what I understand, his is the most coveted unit in Heritage Gardens. Frank was the previous occupant, but he had to give it up and move into the nursing facility after he broke his hip. Marvin promptly took it over, much to Frank's chagrin. Frank insists that Marvin did it to spite him, but I know this isn't true. Marvin has a passion for fish and takes great pleasure in living next to the pond. He has invested countless hours as well as a small fortune in making improvements to that little body of water. That pond is his life.

"Well . . . uh . . ." Beads of perspiration suddenly appeared on Junior's brow. "I haven't brought up the subject with the current resident because I wasn't certain of your decision." He glanced in my direction, as if suddenly realizing I was there. "Ben, would you excuse us for a moment?" He ushered me out the door and closed it.

So that's why I'm here in the foyer alone. I don't try to overhear what's going on behind that door. Not because I'm not curious, but because I would rather deduce such matters by observing the behavior that follows. Junior's actions are simple to predict. If there's an asinine way to do something, he'll find it. He took the helm at Heritage Gardens a little over a year ago, after his father's untimely death. Peterson Sr. was a saint, and I refuse to believe he intended to leave the responsibility of running this place to his incompetent son. But Junior somehow managed to weasel his way into his father's old position and I can't say I know how he keeps this place afloat.

Since I have no idea how long Junior and Boop will be in there and I am unable to be idle for more than thirty-seven seconds, I decide to spend the time ensuring that the bottles in my cleaning cart are arranged in the most efficient configuration. Part of me wants to alphabetize them, but sometimes alphabetification can lead to inefficiency. (I'm not sure if alphabetification is really a word, but it sounds good, it has seventeen letters and seven syllables, and it rolls off the tongue.) I frequently use a dust spray called Zap, but if I place it in the rear it will be hard to reach. If I resort to reverse alphabetification, Zap will be in front, but bleach will be near the rear, and I often use that as well. My solution: I'll create subcategories of cleaners based on their frequency of use and alphabetize the different products within each subcategory.

Another issue I must resolve is the fact that one of my cart's wheels is still missing. I almost ventured to the hardware store yesterday evening to buy a new wheel, but I was feeling sorry for myself thanks to the Professor's nosiness, so I didn't feel like going out. But now that I'm thinking about it again, I realize that in my cart's current state, it has a prime number of wheels. If I replace the missing wheel, the total will again be four, and four happens to be my least favorite number. Perhaps I could rearrange the remaining wheels into a triangle so the cart wouldn't be lopsided. If that fails to work, I could install two more wheels on either side of the wheel in the center, bringing the total to an acceptable five. The steering might be more difficult with five wheels, but that's a price I'd be willing to pay.

I smile with satisfaction. Another problem solved in a most agreeable fashion.

The office door finally opens and the two occupants emerge. Boop seems determined; Junior, nervous. Without a word, they walk past me and exit the building. I instantly deduce where they are headed.

Their route will take them past the chess tables, and I know a shortcut to that spot, so I abandon my three-wheeled cart and make good time without resorting to anything that involves an increased respiratory rate because I suffer from exercise-induced asthma.

Heritage Gardens sits on thirty-five acres of land. I wish it were thirty-one or thirty-seven, but we don't live in a perfect world. About half the land is taken up by twenty-eight small homes.

Or perhaps they should be called townhouses. A winding street courses through this quaint little neighborhood. Large oak trees scattered throughout the property provide shade and a sense of permanence. Aside from the independent homes, there are several larger buildings, including the skilled nursing facility, the recreation center, and the mortuary. In the middle of Heritage Gardens one will find the swimming pool, some tennis courts, a lawn, and the koi pond—which is where I am headed because the chess tables overlook the pond.

When I arrive I find the usual gang: The Professor, the Captain, el Jefe (that's Spanish for "the boss" for the glottically challenged—and yes, I'm aware that's not really a word, but if you know what it means then I've just managed to achieve my goal of inventing a new word), Jane (I don't have a nickname for her), and Frank the crank. Frank is a surprisingly good chess player, though he always plays too aggressively in his middle game and therefore sets himself up for defeat in the end. The Professor and Jane are engaged in a match. The others observe with interest. The positions on the board appear about even, but the Professor has never lost.

"What's up, Doc?" he says when he realizes I am present.

"What kind of oddball greeting is that?" Frank says.

"Just an inside joke between me and the kid." (Many of the residents refer to me as the kid. I find it endearing.)

"Well, it's not funny," Frank says.

"That's why it's an inside joke."

"He's not laughing either."

"I don't know why I waste my breath." The Professor reaches up and adjusts the collar of his neon-orange polo shirt, two sizes too large for his thin torso.

"It's your move," Jane says. Her short, white, curly hair has a bluish tint.

"Holy moly!" Frank's tone suddenly changes. "It's her."

"What?" the Captain and el Jefe say in unison.

"Over there. With the manager. It's the woman I was telling you about."

They turn their heads and squint.

"See? I told you." Frank thrusts his finger toward el Jefe.

"Wowser," says the Captain, "she's a looker!"

"Looks like they're headed for Marvin's place," I say.

"Impossible." Frank shakes his head.

"I think he's right," el Jefe says.

"Maybe she's with the IRS," Frank offers. "Or the humane society."

"Marvin doesn't have any pets," Jane says.

"I know, but I called and reported that he's hiding three unregistered cats in the attic. They said they'd be coming to investigate." Frank rubs his hands with glee.

"She's not with the IRS or the humane society," I say.

"Tell us what you know," Frank says.

"She's moving in."

"Nooo," they all say.

"With Marvin?" the Captain asks.

"I don't know about that, but she'll be living here somewhere."

"But she's too young!" Jane shakes her head.

"Apparently not."

"Holy moly," Frank mumbles. "I was right."

"Do you know when?" Jane asks.

"From what I can gather, looks like tomorrow."

"Holy moly."

It is now early afternoon. I finished wiring up Junior's office and then successfully triangulated the wheels on my cart, which is working fantastically. I feel surprisingly happy, even though I'm on my way to clean the public restroom in the mortuary.

My walkie-talkie squawks and threatens to dampen my mood. "Ben, we need your help over at Marvin's place." It's Junior. He loves bossing me around over the walkie-talkies.

"Is Marvin okay?"

"Yes. He's fine."

"Okay, I'm on my way."

I arrive in short time and find the front door ajar. Cardboard boxes litter the living room. Marvin is busy removing books from a shelf in the corner.

"What's going on?" I say.

"I'm moving." He gives me a sheepish smile.

"But—"

"I know what you're going to say. Don't worry; it's fine."

"Where are you moving to?"

"There's a room available in Building C." That's the skilled-nursing facility. There is no Building A or B. I don't know why. This mystery has caused me many sleepless nights.

"But what about the pond? What about having your own place?"

"I can always walk to the pond, and sometimes I get lonely here."

"You don't get lonely."

"How do you know?"

"Well, I know how much you love that pond."

"Listen." He lowers his voice. "The manager is giving me a good deal on my fees over at Building C, and Miss Boestra made me an offer I can't refuse. Trust me. I'm fine with this move."

A clatter outside the front door interrupts our conversation. It's Frank. Ever since he broke his hip he's been forbidden to roam the grounds without his walker. Stubborn as a mule, he refuses to use it properly. Rather than push it in front of him, he drags it along behind, creating a racket and probably endangering himself even more. So far, the nursing staff has chosen to ignore his defiance.

"Well, well, Marvin!" he says. "Are you getting evicted?"

"Try as I might, I couldn't get rid of the previous occupant's odor," Marvin says. "So I'm moving out."

"Need some help?" Frank can't think of a clever comeback.

"Sure. I have a piano in the loft. Can you please bring it down?"

"Ha-ha. By the way, did the humane society drop by?"

"Actually, they did. They inquired about the cats. At first, I didn't know what they were talking about, but then I remembered a stray I found a few weeks back. I told them I returned it to its owner. When they heard this, they gave me a fifty-dollar reward. I was pretty surprised. How did you know about that?"

Frank is speechless.

"Hey, Frank," I say. "I heard they're making homemade ice cream over in the rec center." Frank is a sucker for ice cream.

"Well, so long, Marvin. It's been a real pleasure knowing you." Frank turns to leave.

"I'm not leaving," Marvin says.

"But there aren't any more independent-living quarters available."

"I know."

"Then where are you moving to?"

"Across the hall from you, in Building C. I thought you knew."

"That'll be a real treat." Frank turns and shuffles away, dragging his walker. He offers a parting shot before he's out of range: "By the way, I got some of your mail by mistake the other day. There was a notice that time's running out for you to renew your subscription to *Woman's Day* magazine. You'd better send them a check."

CHAPTER 3

oday should be a blast. Betty Boop is scheduled to move in. Marvin's old place is vacant, so all should go as planned.

I've decided to eat breakfast in the cafeteria. I usually skip breakfast and rarely take advantage of my free meals in the caf, but I want to hear the latest gossip.

I haven't dined in many retirement facilities, so I don't know if this place is standard. If it is, retirement will suddenly become a much more depressing prospect for me.

On the surface, the dining room appears nice. Real linens adorn the round eight-seater tables, the chairs are cushioned, and the centerpieces contain fresh flowers. The food is self-serve in a buffet style, like a college cafeteria. It's all-you-can-eat. Or, I should say, all-you-can-tolerate. I've tried it all over my time here. The only thing that's remotely palatable is the Jell-O, and that's because it comes premade in little plastic containers that you peel the foil off of. If the cooking staff got their hands on it I'm sure they would figure out how to ruin it too.

I take a seat within earshot of the loudest talkers and start to choke down a bran muffin. Betty Boop is the sole topic of conversation. Even though only a few people have actually laid eyes on her, they're all talking as if they have. The men are saying things like:

"I heard she posed for *Sports Illustrated Swimsuit Edition* not more than five years ago."

"She's had plastic surgery."

"No, they're natural."

"I'll bet my social security check they're not."

"I bet she dyes her hair."

"No, it's natural."

"I hear she's filthy rich."

"No, she's probably a gold digger."

"Well, she's welcome to dig my gold."

"You don't have any."

"She doesn't know that."

The women are saying:

"She probably hasn't even reached menopause."

"I just can't figure out why she wants to live here."

"Maybe she's not right in the head."

"She's probably hunting for a husband."

"We'll have to keep a close eye on her."

I've heard enough to realize this poor newcomer doesn't stand a chance. I hide the remaining half of my muffin under a napkin and take my leave.

It is now ten in the morning and the moving truck has finally arrived. The foot traffic outside Marvin's old place has noticeably increased. I too have created excuses to pass by.

The usual crowd at the chess tables has more than doubled in size. I decide to join them, but a female voice stops me.

"Excuse me, sir, I was wondering if you could show me the way to Building C?"

I turn around.

"Oh!" Dr. Kentucky blushes. "It's you. I didn't recognize you without your uniform."

I normally wear a dark-green jumpsuit but they're all too dirty. I need to get caught up on my laundry. Puzzled, I point. "Building C is that way."

"I know." Her face turns a darker shade of red. "I've been there."

Still confused, I change the subject. "What brings you here on a Saturday?"

"A man named Marvin left an urgent message on my answering machine last night. He thinks he has an infected toenail. He said he lives across the hall from Frank. I know who Frank is, but I've never met Marvin."

"Marvin called you?"

"Uh-huh. Do you know where I can find him?"

"I haven't seen him this morning. It's nice of you to come all the way out here on a weekend."

"When duty calls I'm more than happy to answer. I'll go see if he's in his room."

"It's that way."

"Yes." She blushes again. "It's Ben, right?"

"And you're Dr. Kentucky."

"Please, call me Lex."

"Okay, Lex." Lex Kentucky. How original.

"I'll see ya." She turns and walks away.

I allow myself a lingering glance as she heads toward Building C.

So what was that all about? I'm not entirely sure, and it probably won't do me any good to try to figure it out. I don't pretend to understand women. No doubt Marvin will be surprised when she knocks on his door. I have a hunch it was Frank who called, pretending to be Marvin.

I make my way over to the chess tables. Very little attention is being paid to the pieces.

"I saw you talking to Dr. Kentucky," Frank says.

"Hello, Frank. How's the game?"

"You know we're not here to play. What were you two discussing?"

"Marvin's toe."

"Ha! It worked!"

"So you delivered a beautiful woman to his door. Explain how that's supposed to upset him."

"She'll ask to see his foot. He won't know what she's talking about. She'll get mad at him because she came all the way out here for nothing. It'll be funny."

"Seriously, Frank, do you really think she'll get mad at Marvin? Don't you think he'll tell her that he wasn't the one who called?"

"She won't believe him. Besides, I disguised my voice."

"The kid's right," the Captain weighs in.

"You guys don't understand practical jokes," Frank says.

"Sounds like the joke's on you."

"Humph."

The conversation hushes as Betty Boop makes a brief appearance. She walks from the front door toward the moving truck and gives the movers some instructions. The small crowd at the tables watches with rapt attention. Frank cranks up the volume on his hearing aids despite the fact we are too far away to overhear anything.

"Just look at what she's wearing," Jane says, breaking the silence. "I think my eighteen-year-old granddaughter has those same shorts. That woman shouldn't be permitted to dress like that around here. Isn't there some sort of dress code?"

"It's fine by me," Frank says.

"You're a dirty old fool, Frank."

"No, I'm normal."

"Well you ought to learn when to keep your mouth shut."

"Humph."

"Instead of sitting here and gawking all day, perhaps some of us should go introduce ourselves and welcome Miss Boestra to our community," offers the Professor.

"She looks busy right now; I wouldn't want to intrude," Jane says.

"I'll go introduce myself." Frank gets up and grabs his walker.

"I don't think that's such a good idea," the Captain says as Frank sets off down the walkway, dragging his walker behind. "Seriously, Frank," the Captain calls after him.

"What? Are you going to stop me from being hospitable to our new arrival? I don't think so."

"Let him go," says the Professor. "If he's going to make a fool of himself, it's probably better to let him get it over with sooner rather than later."

"I heard that."

"Man, those are powerful hearing aids," someone mutters.

"I heard that too," Frank calls over his shoulder.

I've decided to eat lunch as well in the cafeteria today. Things are just too interesting and I don't want to miss out.

The caf is especially crowded. I grab a tray and make my way down the buffet line and examine the assortment of foods available for my dining pleasure. I select a tuna-salad sandwich and potato chips and dish up some green beans (twenty-three, to be precise). I spy an open seat at Marvin's table, so I head over there.

"I had an interesting visitor this morning," Marvin says as I take my seat.

"So I heard."

"Frank's never going to get over that denture cream incident, is he?"

"I suppose not."

"Well, it certainly makes my life more interesting."

"I imagine it does." Thoughts of spoiled mayonnaise and salmonella flicker through my mind as I bite into my sandwich. "What started all this, anyway?"

"Between me and Frank? It's a long story."

"I've got time."

"Maybe later."

Some commotion a few tables over interrupts our conversation. "Quick! Somebody call a doctor!" someone yells.

Before I realize what I'm doing I'm out of my seat. The small crowd parts as I push my way over to a heap of neon garments at the center of everyone's attention. My stomach churns as I quickly turn the Professor onto his back and listen for breath sounds. I open his collar and feel his carotid for a pulse. At least his heart is pumping, but his pulse is slow and thready.

"Did anyone see what happened? Was he choking?"

"He said he thought he was having a heart attack."

I tear open his bright-green Hawaiian shirt and check his left upper chest. Sure enough, a pacemaker is implanted under his skin, which explains his slow heart rate. But why isn't he breathing?

I lift his chin and open his jaw. Just as I'm about to give him mouth-to-mouth rescue breaths, his eyes flutter open.

"Jerry, are you all right?" I say.

"What?"

"Are you experiencing any chest pain?"

"I don't think so."

"I see you have a pacemaker. What sort of heart problems do you have?"

"What?"

"Have you ever had an arrhythmia like atrial fibrillation?" I note a scar on his sternum. "Have you ever had bypass surgery?"

"What?"

"Your heart rate is slow. Your rhythm is paced right now. I think that's why you passed out. I'm trying to decide if you're having a heart attack."

"Boy, you sure seem to know a lot about cardiology." A wry smile spreads across his lips.

"I'm serious, Jerry." I look up. "Is somebody calling an ambulance?"

"There's no need for that." Jerry sits up.

"Yes, there is."

"I'm fine."

"No, you're not. You need to be checked out by a doctor."

"No, I don't." He gets to his feet.

"Jerry—"

"I have complete right bundle branch block," he says.

Immediately I understand. His rhythm is always paced. There's nothing wrong with him. This is a setup.

"But thanks, Ben. It was an interesting experiment. You're a good doctor. You never should have quit."

A murmur spreads through the crowd.

"He's a doctor?" someone says.

I want to deny it, but I'm speechless. By the time I can think straight enough to say something, it's too late. My silence has already spoken volumes.

I want to wring his neck, but I don't. I know he doesn't mean any harm. But why can't he just let it rest?

As I storm from the cafeteria, the first thought that enters my mind is that I need new shirts. My pants are fine, but my shirts are no good.

I head straight to my apartment. I don't actually live within the boundaries of Heritage Gardens. My apartment is located in a small complex next door.

If I concentrate, I can get from the cafeteria to my front door in 659 paces. I focus on this and succeed.

From my front door to my bedroom closet is another eleven (yes, my apartment is quite small). From my closet to the outside garbage bin is eighty-three—as long as I'm careful. This time I nearly misstep and take eighty-four, but I stop short and toss my no-good shirts (all twelve of them) into the bin from a short distance away. As an afterthought, I also throw out the one I'm wearing.

My shirts were no good because it has just occurred to me that they should have stripes. Not only should they be striped, but the number of stripes on each shirt should be prime. I shall find and purchase an equal number of shirts that fall into one of two categories: those with a prime number of vertical stripes and those with a prime number of horizontal stripes. Furthermore, the different number of colors within each shirt must be prime, and none of the shirts can have been made in the Dominican Republic.

This task will likely occupy the remainder of my afternoon.

Wearing one of my dirty jumpsuits, since I no longer own any shirts and my laundry still waits, I drive to Walmart to begin my hunt. I don't venture into the fourth lane from the right on the freeway, nor do I make any left turns. Not because left turns are especially hazardous, but because the word left contains four letters, and the number four is my absolute least favorite number. For one thing, it's a perfect square, and squares have four sides. I could go on, but now is not the time.

I drive a 1993 Toyota truck with an extra cab. My truck has a manual transmission with five gears. I do my best to avoid the fourth gear. When I need to shift into fifth, I make sure to stay in fourth for exactly seventeen seconds because seventeen minus four equals thirteen.

You see, there is a method to my madness. If there was no method, I would just be crazy. I'm not crazy. There is a fine line between sanity and insanity, and that line is insight. As long as I have insight, I don't qualify for the nuthouse.

I have a love-hate relationship with Walmart. The place fascinates yet repulses me. A sociologist could spend years studying people in Walmart. There is an entire Walmart subculture that has yet to be deciphered and understood. The place is woven into the fabric of American society. Walk up to anybody on the street and ask them what they think of Walmart. You are bound to get a strong opinion one way or the other. "I love that store!" they might say. "I refuse to set foot in the door," they might snarl. Very few people are indifferent to it, as they might be to Sears.

Today I love it. The friendly greeter at the door doesn't annoy me. The unsupervised kids running amok through the clothing racks don't get on my nerves. And, best of all, several different selections of striped shirts are available for my inspection. Only one meets my strict criteria, but that's a good start.

As I make my way to the cash register, the pattern on the tile floor jumps out at me. I have the sudden urge to avoid the dark squares. But no, that would be crossing the line. I force myself to ignore the random tiles. My palms begin to sweat, but I don't alter my course. This requires every ounce of my strength. A wave of anxiety stirs in the core of my being and I detect the onslaught of a full-blown panic attack. I teeter on the edge of a very slippery slope—one I have slid down before. But I refuse to let it happen to me in Walmart.

I don't remember paying for the shirt, but I must have because nobody chases me as I exit the building. I won't be doing any more shopping today, so I drive back to Heritage Gardens with only one shirt to my name. Along the way I stay in fourth gear for 444 seconds and make a total of four left turns in order to prove to myself that I am able to do it if I want to.

I triumph.

CHAPTER 4

Today I don't have much going on, but I promised Marvin I would paint the baseboards in his new room. He's been remarkably upbeat about the move, but he did seem pretty disturbed about the horribly scuffed baseboards in his new accommodations, so I immediately volunteered my services. I also need to pick up some of his books. He has to get rid of more than half his furniture and about a hundred books from his collection due to his limited space. I agreed to let him keep his books in my library until he decides what to do with them. Books don't belong in storage boxes.

I enter Building C carrying a quart of paint and my favorite brush. I pass by three residents in the foyer, parked in their wheelchairs. There are always a few here, staring blankly into space. This always depresses me a little.

Today a gentleman named Sam is part of the trio. A thin trail of saliva dribbles from the corner of his mouth as he stares at the floor. It wasn't too long ago that he was as sharp as a tack, but over the past several months he has faded rapidly.

"Hey!" His head snaps to attention as I walk by. "Do you speak Spanish?" This has been his greeting for the past few weeks. I can't figure it out. My usual response is no, and then he says that I ought to and doesn't say anything else.

Today I opt for a new response. "I used to, but I've forgotten."

There's a sudden clarity in his gaze. "Me too. I've forgotten. I think I've forgotten other things too. Why?"

"I'm not sure."

"Are you forgetting things too?"

"I hope so."

"Well, I don't like it."

"I'm sorry, Sam."

"How do you know my name?"

"I just know it."

"Do I know yours?"

"Yes. It's Ben."

He stares at the floor again. This is the most I've heard him say in weeks.

I head down the long hall toward Marvin's room. As I pass the nurses' station I quicken my pace and avoid eye contact, but I hear a magazine drop. "Ben! Is that you? Hold on for a minute. We need to talk."

I take a deep breath.

"Is it true?" Karen says. She is one of the more senior nurses on staff, fifty-something years old, one of the best nurses here.

My guilty expression obviates the need to say anything.

"But—" Karen searches for words. She looks hurt, as I expect her to be. We've talked a lot over the past three years. I've gotten to know her well. She has two kids in their late teens and another that ought to be in college—all of them handfuls. She's a breast cancer survivor. Nearly divorced her husband, but they managed to salvage things. She's planning on taking a scrapbooking cruise with her best friend next summer.

"I'm sorry, Karen. I don't know what else to say."

"You lied to all of us."

I never actually lied, but I'm not about to argue this point. "I'm still the same guy you knew yesterday. Three years ago I was living the wrong life, and now I'm not. It's as simple as that."

Her expression doesn't soften. "I thought I knew you."

"You know me as well as anybody else does."

An awkward moment of silence passes. "I thought today was your day off." She eyes the paint can.

"I promised Marvin I would touch up his baseboards."

"Well, you're not off the hook with me. I'm not gonna stop you from doing all your little good deeds for the residents because I know how much they like you, but you still have a lot of explaining to do."

"I'd better get to work," I say as I continue down the hall.

I'll explain when I'm good and ready, and that will most likely be never.

Just as I'm about to reach Marvin's room, Frank, minus his walker, appears. He's decked out in a tweed sports coat and matching pants that are several inches too short because he has them pulled all the way up to his nipples. His shoes gleam with a fresh coat of polish. One is brown and the other is black. He smells like he poured a quart of aftershave on his head.

"What's up, Doc?" he half yells. Either his hearing aids need new batteries, or he's not wearing them. "Now I know what Jerry was talking about when he called you Doc. He's right; it is kind of funny! You used to be a doctor, and now you scrub toilets! Did your license get revoked or something?"

"Where's your walker, Frank?"

"It got stolen." He scratches his backside. Thanks to his aggressive rubbing, his pants slide a merciful inch south, but they still have a long way to go until they reach his waist where they belong.

"It didn't get stolen," I say.

"Yes it did, and I know who took it." He wags his finger with enough gusto to cause his pants to drop another inch, but they encounter the top of his gut—an obstacle that will be impossible to overcome.

"Why would anybody steal it?" I don't know why I'm bothering to argue with him. Sometimes I just can't help myself.

"Ask Marvin."

"Marvin wouldn't take your walker."

"You're probably in on it too."

I finally give up. "Where are you headed all spruced up?"

"Love awaits."

"You have a date?"

"Not yet, but I will just as soon as you stop wasting my time and let me get out of here."

Waste. Waist. I can't keep myself from staring at his aberrant waistline. "Miss Boestra, I presume?" I step aside and gesture for him to get moving.

"Who else?"

"What about Jane?"

"That old prune? I can do better than that."

"I've seen how she looks at you."

"Really?"

"I thought you knew."

"Of course I noticed. There's something about me the ladies can't resist. I think it's my aftershave. It attracts them like flies. If you want, you can use some the next time Dr. Kentucky is around. Can you smell it?" He waves both hands in front of his neck to circulate more of his scent into the air. He fans so vigorously that his pants actually slip another half inch.

"I didn't realize you were wearing any." My eyes begin to water. I'm probably allergic to this stuff.

"Maybe I should put on more." He lowers his voice. "Between you and me, I never know how much is enough. I think I'm starting to lose my sense of smell."

"I think you'd better hurry over to Miss Boestra's place before somebody else beats you to the punch." I need to get him out of here before my nasal passages start to swell and I go into anaphylactic shock.

"You're right. See you later, Doc." He shuffles away.

Marvin's door is a few paces further down the hall, opposite Frank's. I'm not sure how these two are going to tolerate living so close to each other. The door is slightly ajar.

"Marvin, it's Ben."

"Good! Thanks for coming."

The room is a disaster. All the furniture is pulled away from the walls. Several boxes of books are stacked near the bed. Marvin is in the bathroom straightening his hair. "Do you think I should wear a hat?"

"What's the occasion?"

"Let's call it a social visit."

"Betty Boestra?"

"Yep. She invited me to dinner—kind of as a thank you for giving up my place."

I chuckle.

"What's funny about that? You don't think I have a chance?"

"No, that's not it. I was thinking about Frank. He's on his way over there right now. Uninvited."

"That rascal."

"He's not going to take it very well when he finds out she's already having dinner with you."

"True. This will probably surpass the denture-cream incident. What should I do? She's expecting me in twenty minutes. I'm supposed to show her the koi."

"It's not classy to be late."

"Frank will make a scene."

"I know."

"Well, that's just how it's going to have to be. Those are the books I don't have room for. Are you sure you don't mind giving them a home?"

I take one at random from the stack of boxes. It's a mint-condition first edition Steinbeck: *East of Eden*. I open to the title page and catch my breath. "This is signed by the author."

"Yeah. Most of them are."

"I can't keep these. Don't you know how much they're worth?"

"One man's trash is another's treasure."

I pick up another: *The Hobbit*. First edition with a near-perfect dust jacket. "Are you kidding me? There's no way I can take these!"

"Please, I want you to store them in your library. I've seen how well you take care of your books. You know I can't keep them in this small room. What else am I supposed to do with them?"

"I don't know what to say. Do you at least have them insured?"

"No." Marvin shrugs "Never even had them appraised. Like I said, one man's trash . . ." He puts on his coat and makes his way to the door. "Hey, thanks for painting my baseboards."

"No problem," I mumble. I still can't wrap my mind around these books.

"Well, I'd better get going. By the way, Frank was hollering earlier about me taking his walker. I wouldn't ever stoop that low. I have a theory he ditched it because he wants to impress Betty."

"I bet you're right."

As he leaves, it occurs to me that he didn't mention anything about my past. Either he is more sensitive than I thought, or he is too distracted by the thought of dinner with Betty Boop.

CHAPTER 5

I can't sleep past five. I haven't been able to since I was a medical student. I wish I could. I miss sleeping in. I miss being lazy. Every morning my alarm is set for six thirty-one, but that's just wishful thinking.

I roll out of bed, take a quick shower, throw on my jumpsuit, and walk to work. As I make my way across campus to the maintenance building—a small aluminum barn nestled in a grove of orange trees near the koi pond—I enjoy the smell of the moisture in the air. The sun hasn't risen, but the horizon glows just enough for me to notice that something is amiss with the pond. Its surface has an unnatural shimmer. When I get closer I see mounds of froth and foam spreading from a small spout that normally sprays a fountain of water in the pond's center. Somebody has filled the pond with soap.

I hurry to Building C and knock on Marvin's door.

Snow-white hair disheveled, he answers. "What's the matter?"

"There's something wrong with the pond."

"Dadburnit! I was afraid it would come to this." He bursts from his room.

"Put on your robe and slippers first," I say.

"Frank did something to it, didn't he? What did he do?"

"Looks like laundry detergent."

"Dadburnit!"

I take Marvin to the scene of the crime in an electric golf cart. He surveys the mess and mutters under his breath.

"Will the fish be okay?" I ask.

"They have a chance if we act quickly."

"What should we do?"

Marvin thinks for a second. "We need to pump fresh water into that pond as fast as we can so we can dilute the soap. There's a fire hydrant between my old place and the house next door, but we need a hose."

"There's a fire hose and an axe in the hallway in Building C."

"Well, what are we waiting for? I know how we can put the axe to good use as well."

"Now, now, let's not talk homicide."

"If he killed my fish, there's gonna be heck to pay."

I smile at his reluctance to swear. "You know, it probably didn't even occur to Frank that the soap might harm the fish."

"Frank is smarter than you think." Marvin slaps his thigh. "By golly, I'll never forgive him if my fish don't survive."

We make good time back to Building C and dash inside. I locate the case with the hose and axe. I have to break the glass to release them. Doing so activates the fire alarm. Karen comes flying down the hall to investigate. "What's going on?" she shouts.

Several doors open as the more nimble residents scurry from their rooms.

"It's a false alarm. No need to panic." I pull the hose from the case.

Muffled shouts emanate from Frank's room. He's probably fallen out of bed and broken his hip again.

My fear is short lived. His door flings open and he stumbles into the hall, water streaming after. His pajamas are drenched. "Turn it off! Turn it off! My room is flooding!"

I glance at the ceiling in the hall. The sprinklers are bone dry. "Is anybody else's room getting sprayed?" I shout. Heads shake.

"Why aren't you turning it off?" Frank yells.

"I don't know how. There must be a valve somewhere."

"It's in his closet," Marvin mutters. "I don't know why I'm telling you. We should let it run all day."

I hustle into Frank's room. Within seconds I'm thoroughly drenched by the sprinklers. I manage to find the valve in his closet and turn it off.

Back in the hall, I grab the hose and head out with Marvin.

"Hey! What about my room?" Frank yells after us. "It's flooded!"

We ignore him and make a mad dash to the golf cart. Marvin grins as we speed towards the pond. "Justice is a sweet thing," he says. "I bet that water was pretty cold. Serves him right."

"You're right; the water was cold."

"Oh, yeah. I'm sorry." He eyes my soaked clothing. "You're young. You can handle it."

We make a quick stop at the maintenance shed so I can grab a wrench. A few minutes later, I have the hose connected to the fire hydrant. The hose barely reaches the edge of the pond, but it will work. I open the valve and fresh water begins to gush into the soapy pond.

"How much do you think we'll need?" I ask.

"I say we let it run all day." Marvin shakes his head as the water begins to foam even more from the churning stream from the hose.

"What do you boys think you're doing?" Betty Boop, arms crossed, stands several yards away. Her bright pink bathrobe only reaches mid thigh. Marvin inhales sharply.

"I couldn't believe my eyes when I looked out my window just now!" Boop says. "For a glorious moment I thought I was in a chateau in the Swiss Alps!"

"She's been everywhere," Marvin whispers.

"But then I thought, that's the funniest lookin' snow I've ever seen," Boop continues in a pleasant southern drawl that sounds manufactured. "You boys want some fried chicken?"

Marvin and I exchange puzzled glances.

"Did you hear what I said?"

"Fried chicken for breakfast?" I say.

"You mean to tell me you've never had fried chicken for breakfast?" She looks at me like I'm from another planet.

"We'd be delighted to join you," Marvin says.

"Oh, my! It'll be just grand!" Boop claps her hands and bounces up the walkway to her house. "Come on in. Just be sure you don't track in any mud."

This ought to be interesting.

When we enter, she's nowhere to be seen. Hopefully she's putting on more clothing.

"Benji," she calls from somewhere inside. "You don't mind if I call you that, do you? I think it sounds sweeter than Ben. I bet you're wondering how I know your name. Well, it's on your shirt just as plain as day. Three weeks ago I wouldn't have been able to read it without my glasses on, but I got that new laser eye surgery. I swear it's the most marvelous thing. But that sneaky doctor didn't tell me I would still need reading glasses. I called him on it and he tried to claim that he did, but I remember everything. Everything. Until my dying day I'll remember that you'd never had fried chicken for breakfast. I tell you, having a perfect memory has its blessings and its curses. Did you know that I can recall every single time I've taken a sip of spoiled milk? Not only do I remember, I remember in vivid detail." She gags. "See, now look what I've done. It's like I'm drinking it right now. But never mind that. I'll be right out, I'm just tryin' to find where I stuck my spare towels. You're soaked to the skin!"

"She's a real kick in the pants, isn't she?" Marvin whispers.

"Here they are!" She emerges from her bedroom with a pink towel and hands it to me. "Why don't you boys come have a seat at the table? It'll be a while till breakfast is ready."

Marvin charges ahead. I reluctantly follow, not certain if I have the patience to endure her endless chatter and the hundreds of personal questions she is bound to ask. We sit at a small table in the breakfast nook while she busies herself on the other side of the counter.

"I swear, the worst thing about moving is getting settled into a new kitchen. I can't remember where I put anything."

I thought you had a perfect memory.

"You know how many times I moved in the past ten years?"

No.

"Twenty-three."

Hey, that's prime.

"I finally get settled in, and then a month later I'm moving again. Well, enough is enough. When's the last time you moved, Benji?"

Sneaky, but you won't get to me that easy. "It's been a while. I like to stay in one place as much as I can. Change is a bother."

"Ben is a doctor," Marvin says.

Thanks a lot.

"Well, I'll be! I would've never guessed. You know, my niece was engaged to a doctor. I never got to meet him. It was the saddest thing, what happened." She goes silent. My heart skips a few beats.

"What happened?" Marvin takes the bait.

"You don't want to know."

"Tell us."

"Oh, it's such a sad story. I just can't tell a sad story in the morning. Especially on such a bright sunny day. It would ruin our breakfast. Does it ever rain here in Southern California? I just can't get over how nice the weather is." She stirs some batter in a large bowl. "Now what on earth is a good lookin' young doctor doing cleaning rooms in a retirement center? I know it's none of my business, but I'm just dying to know." Without pausing to let me answer she turns to the refrigerator and fishes out some chicken breasts as she says, "It never ceases to amaze me how everyone I meet has an interesting story. I've never met someone whose life has been so dull that they don't have a story. In fact, if I did ever meet such a person, the very fact that they don't have an interesting story would make them interesting." She closes the fridge and continues to prattle on, but I don't hear her anymore because something has caught my eye.

A photo stuck to the refrigerator door.

Hailey.

"Benji? Are you all right? You look ill."

I need to get out of here.

"Did I say something to offend you? I'm sorry if I did. The more you get to know me, the more you'll realize that I tend to talk before I think, but I never mean any harm."

"I'm sorry. I have to go. I just remembered I have something important to do." I stand.

"But what about your chicken?"

"I'm sorry," I say over my shoulder as I drop her pink towel on the chair and make a beeline for the door.

I don't hear anything else as I make my escape from her place and that picture. This can't be happening. I can't deal with this.

I need to shut it out of my mind. I rush toward my apartment and focus all my attention on counting my paces in a specific pattern.

One, two, three, four, five, six, seven.

One, two, three, four, five.

One, two, three.

One, two.

One.

One, two, three, four, five, six, seven.

One, two, three . . .

"Ben, I need you over in Building C, stat!" Ross Jr.'s whiney voice squawks from my radio, causing me to lose count of my paces. "Do you copy?"

"I'll be right there." I resist the urge to chuck the walkie-talkie into the soapy pond. This plastic nuisance is the bane of my existence—like my pager used to be. The day I quit medicine, the first thing I did when I got home was to melt my pager over hot coals. I distinctly remember how slowly it yielded to the heat. When it was finally reduced to an unrecognizable blob of molten plastic, it still managed to emit one last beep. I think it was demon possessed. Nothing else can explain that final beep.

Now I don't even carry a mobile phone. I don't want to be easily gotten a hold of. Junior makes me carry a radio so he can boss me around. So, ironically, I'm still being summoned stat. I thought those days were over. Junior probably wants me to clean up the mess in Frank's room. I welcome the distraction.

A crowd of murmuring spectators has assembled outside Frank's door. Frank is in the center, yammering about the damage. Most of his tirade is directed toward Junior, but at times he turns and gesticulates at the rest of his audience, enlisting their sympathy. "It's like a typhoon came through here! Everything's soaked. It's only a matter of time until I have toxic mold. What are you going to do about that?"

"Ben is on his way. Don't worry; we'll have your room back in order in no time."

"Are you kidding? It'll take weeks for this to dry. I refuse to live here until you have it tested for mold. I saw a special on TV about that. Nasty stuff. It could ruin my lungs. It's a silent killer. I want a complete health inspection done. And what about my ruined furniture? Who's going to pay for that? You'd better have insurance for this sort of thing. My son is an attorney, you know. Mark my words! I'll file a lawsuit if I need to."

I walk through the crowd and enter Frank's damp quarters to assess the damage. The carpet is soggy, his bed is drenched, and a puddle sits atop his desk.

Frank and Junior follow me into the room. "I'm going to need all new carpet." Frank stamps his foot on the waterlogged floor, sending a spray into the air. "Ouch! My hip."

"Take it easy, Frank," Junior says. "Ben, can you please explain what possessed you to activate the fire alarm in the first place? Look what you've done."

"Marvin put him up to it," Frank says. "I'm sure of it. Marvin should be held responsible."

"I want to hear what Ben has to say."

I shake my head and send a scowl Frank's way. "Have you seen the pond, Mr. Peterson?"

"What's that got to do with anything?"

"It's full of soap. We needed the fire hose to pump in fresh water so we could save the fish. I assure you, had I known the sprinklers were going to be activated, I would have found another solution to the problem."

"How did the pond get full of soap?"

"Your guess is as good as mine. Do you have any ideas, Frank?"

"Humph. I don't know anything about it."

"Well, what's done is done," Junior says. "Are you going to be able to get this mess cleaned up?"

"I'm sure Frank will find it satisfactory by the end of the day."

"Very well. Carry on. I have important matters to attend to."

After Junior leaves, I turn to Frank. "What were you thinking?"

"What are you talking about?"

"You know exactly what I'm talking about."

He looks like he's about to argue, but he surprises me with his reply. "I didn't think it would hurt the fish. Honest."

"Why did you do it?"

"He had no right to do what he did. He knew I was interested in Betty. He went over there just to spite me."

"She invited him."

"It's always the same story. You think he's innocent, but he isn't. He knew exactly what he was doing."

"Marvin has dinner with a woman you're interested in, so you go ruin the pond and kill his fish?"

"I told you, I didn't think it would hurt the fish. But to tell you the truth, if the fish don't survive, I won't shed a tear. Marvin started this whole thing in the first place."

"Is that so?"

"Yeah. It was back in '44. That scoundrel crashed into my wagon with his bike and tweaked the wheel. It never rolled the same. Ever since, he's been ruining my life in one way or another."

"You knew each other when you were kids?"

"Yep. Lived on the same street until college. Imagine my surprise when we wound up in the same retirement facility. I was here first. He always was a copycat."

"So this is all over a broken wagon?"

"No, that's just what started it. You wanna know what else he ruined? Jeez, I don't even know where to start. Let's see, how about that time he stole my position as quarterback in high school? Or the time when I was going to apply for a job at the hardware store and he beat me to it? Or when he bought that used Chevy truck I had been eyeing and saving my money for? I could go on forever. Marvin has always had it out for me. Did you know he used to be a contractor? I bet he knew about the plumbing in this building. I bet he knew only my room would get flooded. He's been waiting for an excuse to break that glass and activate the sprinklers."

"I'm the one who broke it."

"That's the brilliance of his plan. He's a scheming devil."

"You're insane."

"Look who's talking, Mister I'm-a-doctor-but-I-quit-medicine-to-scrub-toilets."

"Knock-knock," a female voice interrupts. "The door was open so I . . . My goodness, what happened in here?"

Frank and I turn to see Dr. Lex Kentucky framed in the doorway.

"Well, well, what a pleasant surprise on a not so pleasant morning!" Frank turns on his charm—a phenomenon I've seldom seen.

"Broken pipe?" Lex says.

"Ben decided to test the fire sprinklers." Frank points at the ceiling. "Turns out they work. I'd offer you a seat, but the only dry place is my lap."

"Real smooth, Frank," I say.

Lex laughs. "Don't worry about him. We have an agreement. If he steps out of line, I cut his toenails too short."

"You should see my left foot," Frank says with a grin. "She almost amputated my small toe last time."

"That doesn't surprise me," I say. "You're lucky you still have feet. Seems to me that Dr. Kentucky is too forgiving."

"She can't resist my charm. Why do you think she's knocking on my door first thing in the morning? It's like I'm her morning cup of coffee. She can't start her rounds without me."

"I hate to burst your bubble, Frank, but I was actually looking for Ben."

"Oh, really?" He raises his eyebrows.

"I hate to do this in front of Frank, Ben, but there's a fundraiser tomorrow evening and I need a date. It's not black-tie or anything. The dress is semiformal. I already have two tickets, the food is good, and there's a pretty entertaining magic show. What do you say?"

"He accepts!" Frank says.

"Uh—sure." I can't think of a polite way to turn her down.

"Great! Here's your ticket." She hands me an envelope. "There are directions inside. I'll meet you there."

"Isn't this special!" Frank says as Lex turns to leave. "Two doctors on their first date."

Lex glances over her shoulder and gives me a puzzled smile as she walks out the door. "See you tomorrow night at six-thirty."

"Six-thirty," I call back.

"You owe me big-time for that," Franks says now that Lex is out of earshot.

"What?" I say, only half listening. My mind is going a mile a minute. I'm not prepared for this. What will we talk about? What should I wear? Will there be other people at our table, or will we be sitting alone? At least I don't have to pick her up or take her home. I just have to survive dinner and some stupid magic show. It's not the end of the world. I can handle this.

"Are you listening?" Frank says. "I get the credit. I hinted around that you were hot to trot."

"Great. I sincerely appreciate that."

"Hey, I just set you up with the best-looking woman within a two-hundred-mile radius! Not only is she beautiful, she's a doctor. How about a little appreciation?"

"Thank you."

"That's more like it. Now, let me show you something." He unbuttons his shirt and pulls down his collar, exposing his bony shoulder. "See that bump?"

"Yes."

"Well, what do you think it is? Is it cancer?"

"What?"

"You're a doctor. I just did you a favor, so now you owe me one. I've been meaning to have this looked at, but I keep forgetting. Tell me what you think."

"It looks very malignant. You probably only have a few weeks left to live."

"Serious?"

"That's my opinion. If you want a second opinion, I suggest you consult a dermatologist or some other physician who is actually practicing medicine."

"Come on, tell me what it is."

"Frank, do you want me to get your room back in order?"

"Jeez, it's not like I'm asking you to perform a biopsy or anything. I just wanted your opinion."

"I'm not a doctor. I'm the guy who cleans your room. If you want a medical opinion, ask someone else."

"Humph. That's the last time I do you any favors." He leaves me to contend with his soggy mess. I welcome the challenge and the solitude.

CHAPTER 6

Did you hear me? It's a dissecting aortic aneurysm. We need you in the OR stat."

"I'm aware of that. Isn't there anyone else available?" I hold my mobile phone in one hand as I glance at my watch with the other.

"You're the only cardiothoracic surgeon that can be here within ten minutes. Anesthesia already has him on the table. We can start as soon as you arrive."

"But he's my brother! I can't operate on my own family member! There has to be someone else. What about Dr. Johnson?"

"He's harvesting a donor heart in Nevada and isn't due back for a few hours. Believe me, if there were someone else we wouldn't be asking you. We're running out of time."

"Okay, okay. I'm on my way. Be there in five." I'm already in my scrubs. Within seconds I'm in my BMW, violating every traffic law as I speed toward the hospital. How can this be happening? There are five other CT surgeons in my group. How is it possible that I'm the only one available?

I leave the car parked on the curb outside the ER and toss my keys at the security guard. He knows the drill. I dash inside and take the stairs up two floors. My badge opens the doors to the operating suite, where I don a surgical cap and grab a mask from the dispenser. I secure my loupes around the back of my head as I jog down the hall. I spend the bare minimum amount of time at the scrub station and then enter Room 4, taking care not to contaminate myself.

The resident physician is already scrubbed. I give the anesthesiologist a nod and turn to the scrub tech, who hands me a towel. "Fill me in," I say to the resident.

"Classic presentation. Chest X-ray is consistent with a dissecting aneurysm. He lost consciousness five minutes before we got him up here, but vitals are currently stable."

The tech assists me with my gown and gloves.

"Okay. Let's get started." I hold out my right hand. The tech hands me a blade. "Sorry, Andrew," I say as I slice along his sternum.

"Blood pressure is seventy over forty," the anesthesiologist warns.

"I thought you said vitals were stable."

The resident knows not to respond. The tech hands me the cautery, assuming I want to cauterize the small blood vessels that I severed while making the skin incision.

"I'm not concerned about these superficial bleeders right now," I say, tossing the cautery aside. "I need to get his chest open before it's too late."

"Sixty over thirty."

"What are you waiting for? Give me the saw!"

"Fifty over thirty."

I can't see it, but I know what's happening inside my brother's chest. Blood is escaping from a weak point in the wall of his aorta, dissecting between the layers lining the artery. As the blood enters this space, it compresses vital branches that supply blood to the brain and even the heart. My brother is seconds away from having a massive stroke, a heart attack, or both.

"Forty over thirty."

There's not enough time to save him.

I know I'm dreaming, but I don't let myself wake up. I've relived this nightmare more than a hundred times, yet I force myself to live through it again and again. Nothing ever changes because the past cannot be changed. My brother's vital signs continue to fade as his heart starves for oxygen. My clumsy hands move too slowly. Finally, I get his ribs spread far enough to expose his organs, but his heart is no longer pumping. I thrust my hands into his chest and attempt to resuscitate him with cardiac massage—I squeeze his heart with my own two hands in a feeble bid to force blood to his brain. But it's too late. He's already gone.

It's over. I can wake up now.

I sit up and look at the clock. Two a.m. I won't sleep anymore tonight.

I pace around the room. My palms are damp; my heart still races. Sunrise is hours away—how should I kill the time?

Kill.

I didn't kill him. I didn't kill him. I didn't kill him.

I didn't want him to die. I tried to save him. I tried my best.

I need to reorganize my closet. Nothing is right about it.

I turn on the lights.

My new shirts are still in the shopping bags. Yesterday, after I got Frank's room back in order, I went on another shopping trip. I need to wash them before I can put them on hangers.

I've recently started to wash all my clothing by hand. It's impossible to fully monitor what goes on inside a washing machine. How can you be certain your clothes are really getting clean if all they're doing is slopping around in a tank of soapy water for a few minutes? If I wash them by hand, I can control all the variables.

As I remove the tags, I decide that while I'm at it, I might as well wash all my clothes. I've got several plastic tubs I use for this purpose on my little back porch.

I spend the next four hours scrubbing with a frenzy. All my mental energy is devoted to the task at hand. Time flies as I wash every article of clothing I own, minus the bathrobe and boxer shorts I am currently wearing.

My concentration is not broken until my doorbell rings. I dry my raw hands and make my way to the door. It's barely past six. Who could this be?

I'm surprised to find the Professor on my doorstep.

"Jerry? Is something the matter?"

"Good morning, Ben. I hope I didn't wake you." He eyes my robe.

"No. I was up."

"Do you mind if I come in?"

"Not at all," I lie. "Want something to drink? Sorry, I don't have any coffee."

"No, thanks. Mind if we talk for a minute?" He plops down on my sofa. He's wearing green pants and a yellow sweatshirt.

"Okay." I sit in my recliner.

"You've been avoiding me ever since the incident at the cafeteria," he says.

"I suppose so."

"Why do you think I did what I did?"

"Don't try to psychoanalyze me, Jerry. Just say what you came to say."

"Very well. I want to make sure you understand that I consider you a friend. Perhaps I haven't been going about it in the right way, but my intention has been to help you." He pauses, as if expecting a response. When he doesn't get one, he continues, "I don't pretend to have all the answers, but one thing I do know is that you're young and you still have most of your life ahead of you. It's not too late to get it back on track."

I pretend to ponder his words for a brief moment, but I already know what my response will be. "I appreciate your concern, Jerry. Really, I do. But I know what I'm doing."

"Do you?"

"I'm in control of my life right now. This is what I want. You're not doing me any favors by mucking around in my past. If you really are my friend, you'll let me be who I want to be."

"Who do you want to be?"

"The guy who cleans rooms at Heritage Gardens."

"This is the life you want?" He stands. "This isn't a real life. There's still time for you."

"I'm happy with this life."

"Then you don't know what happiness is."

I stand too. "All right, Jerry, I'll give you that. Maybe I don't know what happiness is. Maybe I missed the happiness boat. In fact, I know I missed that boat. I watched it sail away. So maybe it's too late for me to find true happiness or contentment or whatever it is that life is supposed to be about. But at least I'm surviving. My life—the life I have right now—is good enough."

"That's really what you believe?"

"Yes."

He looks at my raw hands. "So you're telling me you're all right."

"I'm fine."

"You don't need someone to talk to." He doesn't attempt to mask his skepticism.

"I'm talking to you right now."

"Sure you are." He turns to leave. "My door is always open."

A spider web of clotheslines encloses my back porch. It took me a while to get them all hung, but it was worth the effort. It's mid-morning. Technically, I'm late for work, but since I habitually put in more than the forty hours I get paid for, I don't feel guilty about being a little late today.

"Ben, where are you?" Junior's annoying voice squawks over the radio.

"How can I be of service?" I don't make much effort to suppress my sarcastic tone.

"Miss Boestra is having some sort of crisis with her kitchen sink."

"Do you need me to call a plumber?"

"What? No. I need you to go over there and fix it."

"I'll call a plumber." This isn't part of my job description, and that lady's kitchen is the last place I want to go.

"Say again? I didn't copy."

I hate it when he uses radio jargon. "I said I'll call a plumber."

"I'm not joking, Ben. I want to keep Miss Boestra happy. I don't think you understand how important this woman is to our facility. You are to treat her as a VIP. Do you copy?"

"Plumbing doesn't fall under my job description."

"If you aren't over there in ten minutes, you won't have a job to describe. Do you copy?"

"Yes, sir."

"Good. Report back to me on the situation within half an hour. Over and out."

Pompous moron. I guess I don't have much of a choice. Junior is unpredictable and insecure; I wouldn't be shocked if he made good on his threat to fire me. Doing so would no doubt inflate his feeble ego.

I reluctantly make my way to Boop's place. I'd rather face a swarm of Africanized bees or—even worse—have the number four tattooed onto the back of my left hand.

I ring her doorbell.

Within seconds she flings open the door. "Benji! Thank God you're here! It's horrible!"

Her clothes are surprisingly modest today—oversized blouse and black stretch pants. But when she turns to lead the way into the kitchen, I see that her shirt has an open back, revealing most of her bra.

"It was making a terrible noise, and then it smelled hot, and then it stopped working. Now my sink won't drain, and when I run the dishwasher all this foul-smelling gunk comes up."

"What was making the noise? The garbage disposal?" I follow her bra strap into the kitchen, taking care not to look at the refrigerator.

"Yes. That was last night."

I look into her sink. A few inches of brown water obscures the drain. A waterlogged noodle floats by. "Where's the switch for the garbage disposal?"

"Behind the coffee pot."

I flip it on and hear a soft buzz, but the disposal blade won't spin. I turn it off, take a deep breath, and reach into the murky water to feel around in the drain. Something is wedged between the blades. I pry it loose. "Looks like I found the problem." I hold up a chicken bone.

"Well, I'll be! It sure is nice to have a handyman around. My third husband, Jack, was that way—may he rest in peace. Can you believe I lost three husbands? I'm a widow thrice over. Jack could fix anything. Anything! He was such a sweetheart too. Your eyes remind me of him. I do declare, your eyes have the exact same shape. Let me show you a picture. I've got a photo album around here somewhere."

"I'd love to, but I've got other things to tend to."

"Nonsense. It'll only take a few minutes." She scurries off to fetch the album.

I wash my hands and test the garbage disposal. It's working fine. Now that the blades can spin, the sink drains nicely. I run the water a little while longer to make sure I'm not missing any other problems with the drain. My back is to the fridge. I can hear the cruel appliance humming. I feel it beckoning me with its picture of Hailey. I grasp onto the edge of the sink with both hands and fight the urge to turn around. But I want to. Just one small glance. I just want to see her one more time.

I know I shouldn't. It will only torture me. It will only ruin all the hard work I've done to shut her face out of my mind.

But I can't resist. My head turns, so I close my eyes, but somehow they're open again and there she is. Brilliant blue almond-shaped eyes. Perfect face framed by curls of auburn hair. Fair complexion, but not dainty. I haven't seen her face in three years, yet every detail is forever burned in my mind's eye. I squeeze my eyes shut, but still she's there. She'll always be there.

"Here it is!" Boop bounces back into the room carrying the album. "Oh, you're looking at that photo of my niece. She's a beautiful girl, that Hailey, isn't she? I need to call her. She's probably worried sick about me. She was against me moving here, bless her heart. Well, it's too late for her to try to talk me out of it." Boop sets the album on the counter and pats it affectionately. "Now what was I going to show you? Oh, yes, Jack." She opens to a page and examines a picture of her late husband. "See? There he is. The lighting isn't all that great in this shot, but you do have the same eyes."

I look at the photograph. The man in the picture doesn't look anything like me. "I see what you mean," I say.

"Let me see that again." Boop takes the album. The excitement in her voice has been replaced by consternation. "I know you remind me of somebody . . ." She flips through more pages.

"I really should get going," I say.

"Hold on for just a minute. There it is. Good heavens! I knew you reminded me of somebody. You're the spitting image of my Hailey's fiancé! I never got to meet him before he died. In fact, this is the only photo I have of him. Lord have mercy! You two could be brothers!"

I try to remain calm as I gaze at the photograph of my brother and Hailey. It was their engagement photo, taken only a few weeks before Andrew died on my table. I didn't used to look so much like him. My busy cardiothoracic surgical practice kept me out of the sun while his relaxed schedule allowed him to stay tan year round. And I was usually clean shaven. It finally dawns on me how little I look like my old self and how much more I look like Andrew these days.

"That's uncanny," I say, trying my best not to betray any emotion.

"It's more than uncanny! It's like you're twins! Are you sure you weren't somehow separated from your family at birth!" She claps her hands with glee at the thought, but then realizes the ramifications if her theory were true. "Oh, that would be so tragic. Imagine discovering that you have a long-lost brother, but then learning he had died before you ever got a chance to meet him." She pauses as she mulls this over. "Well, it was so sad how poor Hailey lost her fiancé. They had such a whirlwind romance. Poor Hailey, I really ought to call her. Once I get all my ducks in a row, I'll fly her out here to visit me. Then you could meet her!"

"I'm sure that would be nice." My heart races with panic.

CHAPTER 7

Today's a big day. Maybe it will help me forget about yesterday. I need a good distraction, and tonight's big date with Lex will most certainly fit the bill.

I think I'm more nervous about the magic show than the fact that this is a date.

I was seven years old the last time I endured a magic show. I'll never forget how mortified I was when the magician selected me from the audience and summoned me to the stage. I think I was the only kid not raising my hand. Couldn't he tell that I didn't want to go up there? I couldn't think of a way out of it. In retrospect, I should have pretended to throw up.

The spotlight zeroed in, blinding my view of the audience. I tried to find my parents in the sea of blackness, but they had disappeared along with everyone else, leaving me alone with my tormentor. He placed an empty glass pitcher in my trembling hands and instructed me to hold it tightly against my chest. He then produced a shiny faucet from his pocket. It looked exactly like the faucet from my bathroom sink. Without warning, he stuck the faucet to the center of my forehead with a suction cup. The handle squeaked as he twisted it. Cross-eyed and dumbstruck, I watched as water poured from my forehead and filled the pitcher. The audience roared with laughter. The magician poured himself a glass of water and drank it.

That brief encounter scarred me for life.

I haven't been on a date in over four years, but that's another story. I don't know what to wear. I don't have any nice clothes. All I have is striped polo shirts and button-fly jeans (I won't allow zippers anywhere near me).

And what about my hair? It's looking kind of shaggy. Lately I've been cutting it myself and hiding my hack job under a baseball cap. I probably shouldn't wear my cap tonight.

There's a barber shop on the grounds, but it's only open on Saturdays. I decide to make my way to the little beauty boutique where the ladies go. Jane runs the salon when she's not playing chess. I'm sure she'll do me a favor and give me a quick haircut.

A bell jingles as I enter the salon. I'm surprised by the number of ladies crammed into the small shop. Every seat in the waiting area is filled. So are all the salon chairs. There must be at least twenty women here. I've stopped by for various reasons in the past and I've never encountered more than two or three. I wonder if Jane is having some sort of a discount today. She obviously doesn't have time to fit me in, so I turn to leave.

"Ben? Is that you?" Jane calls from her station. She must have caught a glimpse of me in one of the dozen mirrors placed around the room. "Where do you think you're going?" She sets down her shears and walks over to greet me.

"What's going on here?" I say, nodding at the crowd in the waiting area.

Jane lowers her voice to a whisper. "I'm not entirely sure, but I think it has something to do with our new arrival." She raises her eyebrows.

"Ahhh," I say. "Competition."

"Ever since Betty Boestra arrived, business has been booming. Hair, nails, wax jobs . . . you name it." She grins. "So let me guess:

you want a haircut before your big date tonight," she says, loud enough for everybody in the salon to hear.

"How did you know about that?"

"It's only one of the hottest topics of gossip!"

"That can't be true. I didn't even know about my date until yesterday."

"Honey, everybody knew by yesterday afternoon. There aren't many secrets around here."

I turn to Maybelle Lange, a lady in her eighties who plays the piano at all the social functions held at Heritage Gardens. "Is this true, Maybelle?"

"I knew by ten in the morning."

"But she asked me at nine-fifty!" I happen to know precisely what time it was because I accidentally knocked Frank's clock off his shelf shortly after Kentucky left.

"Frank told Jim; Jim's wife called Marlene; Marlene called Shirley, Julie, and Karen; and Karen called me. That all took about ten minutes."

The ladies within earshot all nod.

"I'm sure you ladies won't mind if I give Ben a quick haircut," Jane says. "Come on over to my chair; I'm at a good stopping place with Lucy—her hair needs to set for a little while, so I can squeeze you in."

"Thanks. I really appreciate it."

"So what are you going to wear tonight?" Jane says. "I think you should definitely wear a shirt and tie, and a sports coat if you have one."

"Of course he has a sports coat," a lady named Mary interjects from the next chair over. "Every doctor owns a sports coat. By the way, are you going to explain to us what you're doing here, young man? Why aren't you out there doing what you were trained to do?"

"Mary, it's rude to pry," Jane says.

"It doesn't hurt to ask, and besides, you can't deny you're dying to know."

"Ben's past is his own business. He'll tell us about it when he's good and ready."

"Well, Ben, are you ready?" Mary asks. All the other ladies lean in our direction, not wanting to miss a word.

"No," I say.

"See? I told you to mind your own business," Jane says.

Having been denied any juicy details of my past, the ladies must content themselves with giving me advice about how I should conduct myself with Dr. Kentucky.

"Make sure you open the door for her."

"And tell her she looks nice."

"But don't get all drooly over her; sometimes it's better to play hard to get."

"Show her you know how to listen."

"If she leans in when you're saying good-bye, you're supposed to kiss her."

"No. Never kiss on the first date."

This goes on for about twenty minutes. It's nice because I'm not obligated to talk. When Jane is almost finished with my hair, she changes the subject. "Frank and Marvin are at it again."

"Yep," I say. "Seems that Betty's presence has managed to stir the pot. I still can't believe what Frank did to the pond."

"Frank does have a sweet side, you know."

"I've been around for three years and I still haven't seen it."

"It's there. It's just been hiding for a while."

Now that Jane has finished with my hair, I can make my escape. "What do I owe you? It looks real nice." I reach for my wallet.

"Nothing."

"Come on, you have to let me give you something."

"Absolutely not. It was my pleasure. I've been wanting to get my hands on that shaggy head of yours for a while now. You can repay me by refraining from cutting it yourself in the future."

"You could tell?"

"Yes."

"It was that bad?"

"Pretty bad."

"Okay. I'll be your regular customer from now on."

"Good luck tonight!"

"Thanks. I'll need it."

I'm twenty minutes early, but I only have to wait in front of the hotel for a short while. I have a sinking feeling in the pit of my stomach as I watch Lex approach in a black cocktail dress. Though modest, her dress fails to hide her curves. Her reddish curls are gathered in a classy updo and something sparkles in her hair. I'm suddenly feeling infinitely more inadequate than I did a minute ago.

"Ben! You're early. I hope you haven't been waiting long."

"No, not too long. I mean—I've only been here a few minutes." I want to kick myself for fumbling with my words. "You look very nice, Lex."

"Thank you."

"I guess we should go inside," I say. "This is a pretty nice hotel. I've never been here before." I'm not sure if I should offer my arm. I don't, but she takes it anyway.

"The Mission Inn is pretty famous. You should see it during the holiday season. It's gorgeous."

"I'll have to do that." I spent the last two Christmases alone in my apartment. Perhaps this year I'll take myself out to breakfast or lunch.

"The benefit will be hosted in one of the conference rooms. Did you remember your ticket?"

"I've got it in my pocket."

We make our way through the foyer and follow the signs. After presenting our tickets to a woman dressed in a ghastly red gown with several thousand beads haphazardly sprayed all over it, we consult the list of table assignments. I note with dismay that most of the tables seat between eight and twelve people. I hate the idea of enduring an evening with a bunch of strangers.

I'm relieved when Lex leads me to one of the smaller private tables off to the side. "I requested a table for two."

Rather than across from each other, our chairs are positioned about 120 degrees apart so that we both have a view of the stage. This will spare me from having to make much eye contact during the course of the evening.

The room fills rapidly as more guests arrive. I quickly take stock of how other men are dressed and smile with satisfaction. Somehow I managed to dress appropriately. I had to go shopping again, for the third time this week, to find something suitable. I was pleased to find a regimental tie with seventeen horizontal stripes, a blue shirt, and a navy sports coat.

"So what exactly is Shoes That Fit?" I say after we're seated.

"It's a charity foundation that makes sure underprivileged children are properly clothed—especially with shoes. My girlfriend works for the organization. I come to this every year. It's a lot of fun."

"I'm sure it is. Who doesn't like magic?"

"It's a blast. There will be three or four different magicians performing—they all have different specialties. The sleight-of-hand guy is truly amazing. There's another guy who does a good job involving people from the audience, but I'm not sure if he's here this year. I hope he is. I've always wanted to be called up on stage and sawed in half or something crazy like that."

Be careful what you wish for.

We share an awkward moment of silence—I'm sure there will be countless more of these as the evening progresses. Perhaps we would be better off at one of the larger tables after all.

"So what did Frank mean yesterday when he said, 'two doctors on their first date'?"

"Frank is a crazy old fool."

"You didn't answer my question. I'm not completely out of the loop, you know." She raises her brow and gives me a coy smile. "I have connections with the main gossip circle at Heritage Gardens. These ladies love to gab while I work on their feet. I've heard the rumors about you."

"What have you heard?"

"Mostly different variations on the same theme."

"Give me an example."

"Well, let's see. There's a theory that you were forced to leave your practice due to a malpractice lawsuit. There's also the one where you were happily married but your wife had an affair, causing you such great distress that you abandoned your life and moved across the country. And then, of course, there's my personal favorite . . ."

"I'm listening."

"That you were the personal physician for the president of the United States, but you were involved in some sort of top-secret conspiracy, so you were forced into the FBI witness protection program."

"Darn. Now they're going to have to move me again. Probably to Canada this time. I hear it gets cold there. I hate it when my cover gets blown."

"You don't want to talk about your past."

I purse my lips.

"Fair enough. So . . . what kind of music do you like?"

I smile. "I only listen to Enya."

"Really?"

"No. That was a joke." Man, this isn't going well at all. "Why don't you tell me something about you? Tell me how you decided on podiatry."

"My grandma."

"She was a podiatrist?"

"No. But she had terrible feet. I remember seeing them when I was little. I was horrified. It was so tragic how she hobbled around. Ever since, I've been on a mission to help elderly people avoid my poor grandmother's fate."

Time flies as Lex launches into a gloriously long monologue about feet and all the ailments that can affect them. Our food arrives as she expounds on ingrown toenails, bunions, flat feet, onychomycosis, arthritis, foot drop, and gout. I nod and smile all the while. Before I know it, the lights are dimming and the magic show is about to begin.

The first magician to perform is fairly young. He wears the stereotypical top hat and cape. What boggles my mind is that he keeps producing a full-grown goose from out of nowhere. Not a small dove, but a bona fide adult goose that honks, flaps its wings, and even relieves itself on stage to verify its reality. The magician pulls it from his hat, shows it to the audience, and then shoves it up his sleeve while he performs another trick. Later, he produces the goose from an empty bucket and puts it back in his hat, only to pull it out of his coat ten minutes later. The goose vanishes and reappears a dozen times throughout the performance.

Next up is the sleight-of-hand guy. He doesn't use any props—just a coin and a deck of cards. He is talented, but I feel sorry for him. It's great that he can make a quarter vanish and reappear, but the guy before him did the same thing with a live goose. They should have let the quarter guy go first.

During a short intermission Lex pays a visit to the ladies' room, giving me a chance to ponder the phenomenon of the disappearing goose. By the time she returns, it's time for the show to continue.

The final magician takes the stage. "Oh, good!" Lex whispers. "This is the guy I was hoping would be here."

The houselights dim and the spotlight illuminates the master of illusion. The curtain behind him rises, revealing several large props, including a coffin, a cage, and a rack of swords. I watch with detached amusement as the performer and his assistant proceed to execute a string of reality-bending feats. Throughout it all I notice how much the audience enjoys being misled. This magician seems to know how to defy gravity, disrupt time, predict the future, and even cheat death. If only we all possessed such power. Imagine if we all had so much control.

Before I know it, the show is over.

As I walk Lex the short distance to her car she says, "I had a good time. I'm glad I asked you."

"So am I."

I really did have a good time. A fantastic time. The best time I've had in longer than I can remember. But I can't think of a way to articulate this so we just walk in awkward silence. When we arrive at her car I realize I'm probably screwing this up pretty badly. I'm missing some sort of opportunity here, yet still I say nothing. She unlocks her door and gets into her car, sparing me the torture of deciding if I should hug her, kiss her, or something else. Before she shuts her door she says, "I'm going to leave the ball in your court, Ben. See you around."

Before I respond she shuts the door and is driving away.

CHAPTER 8

When I woke up this morning, I felt guilty. I'm not a psychologist so I'm not going to try to figure out why.

So far the day has passed pretty quickly. I've spent most of it cleaning the mortuary and Junior's office. Junior has been acting strange lately. While I was cleaning the reception area I overheard him cursing and muttering under his breath as he struggled with the paper shredder. "Blasted piece of crap. Keeps jamming up." He was working like a madman, going through paperwork, typing on his computer, and rummaging through file cabinets. Today must be the one day out of the month that he actually works.

Even though I've tried not to, I've thought a lot about Lex. She seems genuine. I admire her for that. And it doesn't hurt that she's beautiful. But who am I kidding? I have enough of a grip on reality to know that I'm in no shape for a relationship.

Now that my work is done, it's time for me to go on a different sort of date—this time with a crotchety old man. I promised Frank I'd take him to the grocery store. He doesn't have anyone else willing to take him, and he doesn't like to ride the bus that makes a weekly shopping trip from Heritage Gardens. Somehow I keep getting roped into the task, which has turned into a weekly affair.

I say hi to Karen as I pass her station. She smiles and returns my greeting, but she hasn't been the same since she we last spoke. In time she'll warm up to me again. Until then I'll give her some space.

Before I knock on Frank's door, I decide to pay Marvin a quick visit, but he's not there.

"What's up, Doc?" The Professor startles me as I stand in the hall outside Marvin's room.

"Hello, Jerry."

"How did the date go last night?" The Professor, wearing two different colors of yellow, resembles a banana dipped in lemon meringue pie.

"You knew about the date too?" I say.

"Everybody knows you went on a date."

Frank's door opens. "What are you two gabbing about? Hey, Ben, you're late."

"No, I'm not."

"You said you'd be here at five."

"And it's five."

"No; it's seven after. But I'll forgive you this time. Let's get going." He shuts his door and gestures impatiently. "I have important matters to tend to when we get back."

"Where's your walker?"

"I told you. It got stolen."

"No, it didn't." I breeze past him and enter his room.

"Hey! What do you think you're doing?"

I come back out, carrying his walker. "I came across this in your closet the other day when I was searching for the shutoff valve."

"Oh—so that's where it's been. I've been looking all over for it."

"Somehow it found its way behind a pile of clothing."

"Jeez, I wonder how it got there."

"Didn't want Miss Boestra to see you with a walker?" says the Professor.

"Put a cork in it, Jerry. You know I don't need this thing. Mr. Peterson just makes me use it because he's afraid of a lawsuit."

"I'm not taking you to the grocery store without it," I say.

"Who put you in charge? You're not a doc—" He stops himself.

"Ha!" The Professor says. "You can't argue with the doctor's orders."

"He's not a real doctor anymore. He couldn't even tell me what that growth is on my shoulder."

"You showed him that hideous thing? Listen, Frank. If you want to impress Miss Boestra, you'd better keep that monstrosity out of sight."

"That's not funny. I'm really worried about it."

"It's a seborrheic keratosis," I say.

"A what?"

"That means it's ugly but benign."

"So it's not dangerous?"

"That depends on how you define dangerous. Will it kill you? No. Will it scare women away? Yes."

"I have to get going, gentlemen." The Professor leaves, chuckling to himself. "Have a nice evening."

"Do you have your wallet, Frank?"

"Of course."

Last time he forgot it and I ended up paying for his items. He still hasn't paid me back.

"Let's get going." He starts shuffling down the hall, dragging his walker behind.

When we're in my truck and on the road, he fumbles with the radio without bothering to ask my permission. He switches from station to station, finally settling on an offensive rap song. He cranks up the volume and bops his head in rhythm with the beat.

"What on earth has gotten into you?" I shout.

"This stuff makes me feel fifty years younger! They didn't have this sort of music when I was your age."

"It's trash!" I'm barely able to hear myself over the noise.

Ignoring me, Frank continues to groove while the artist weaves an eloquent yarn of profanity and hostility. Mercifully, the store is only a few blocks away.

"You need a better subwoofer; the bass sounds weak," Frank shouts, cranking the volume even louder as we pull into the parking lot. Heads turn as our obnoxious vehicle disturbs the peace. I quickly turn the radio off as I park the truck.

"Jeez, you'd think a doctor would have a better sound system," Frank mutters as he gets out. He heads for the store entrance without his walker.

"Frank—"

"Yeah, yeah." He grudgingly takes it from my outstretched hand.

I push the grocery cart while Frank leads the way around the store. The combination of the cart's rattling wheels and Frank's walker dragging along makes for quite a racket. I guide the cart with my wrists because I hate the thought of touching the handle with my palms. I could catch anything from anywhere by exposing myself to the germs on it.

"I need deodorant," Frank says. "Jeez-a-loo! I can't ever get over how many different kinds there are." He takes one off the shelf.

"That brand is for women," I say.

"I know that." He puts it back. "I was thinking I might buy it for Marvin." He picks out another one. "What's this? It comes in cans too?"

I'm beginning to wonder how long it's been since Frank bought deodorant.

"I wonder if this stuff's flammable?" He tosses it into the cart. "I need some more shampoo too." He selects the cheapest generic brand he can find.

"Why don't you get this kind?" I hand him one that's medicated for dandruff.

"Heck, no! That stuff costs five times more than this one."

"Trust me."

"No."

"I'll buy it for you."

"I don't need your charity. I choose this one." He tosses his selection into the cart.

"Well, I'm buying this one for me then," I say.

"Suit yourself."

I glance down at the two shades of brown floor tile laid out in a perfect checkered pattern. This is the most annoying type of flooring. A completely random pattern is the second most annoying. I prefer a single color, thereby eliminating any pattern at all. If there must be more than one color, the tiles should be laid out in a complex pattern that at first glance appears random, but is decipherable with a little study. That sort of floor takes ingenuity. I once lived in a house that had a bathroom floor with three different colors of one-inch square tiles. It took me countless hours of toilet time to conclude that the tiles weren't random; there truly was a complex pattern hidden on that floor. I wonder if it was some sort of code. I would like to meet the master craftsman who laid that tile and congratulate him or her on a job well done.

"Did you hear what I said?" Frank brings me back to reality.

"What?"

"I asked what kind of aftershave you wear. I need some more 'cause I'm almost out."

"It's called Passion for Men. I don't think they sell it in a grocery store."

"Did it work last night?" He pokes me with his bony elbow and grins. "Did you get any passion?"

"That's none of your business, Frank."

He clucks his tongue with mock sympathy. "I'll take that as a no." He holds up a bottle of aftershave and squints to read the fine print. "I saw something on TV about how scientists have discovered certain chemicals that make women feel attracted to you.

They're called fare-ohms or something like that. If you buy cologne that has fare-ohms, you'll be a chick magnet."

"I think you mean pheromones."

"Well, I want a brand that has those."

"I don't know how to help you with that one, Frank."

"Maybe we'll have to go to a different store then."

"Look, why don't you get some Old Spice? They have it here and it's not too expensive."

"Does it have fare-ohms?"

"I don't know about that, but I do happen to know that it's one of Jane's favorite scents."

"Old Spice is for old geezers—that's why it has Old in its name. And who cares what Jane thinks?"

"I figured you would."

"Humph. I have my eyes set on a different prize." His eyes light up. "Speaking of which . . ."

Betty Boop rounds the corner at the end of our aisle.

"Miss Boestra!" Frank hollers as he quickly shoves his walker behind me, out of view. "What a pleasant surprise!"

Betty sees us, smiles, and waves. "Hi, fellas!"

Marvin rounds the corner and hands Betty a bag of bagels. "Found them."

"Rat-scum traitor," Frank mumbles, but not loud enough for Betty or Marvin to hear.

This ought to be interesting.

"Well, isn't this just dandy!" Betty says in her bubbly voice as she and Marvin draw near. "I just love running into people at the grocery store. You never know who you're going to bump into. Once, when I was living in Tennessee, I ran into Denzel Washington! Can you believe it? Now I bet you're wondering what he was doing in a little podunk grocery store in the middle of nowhere. Well, so was I, but I was so excited I couldn't find my voice. That's only the second time in my whole life that I was speechless. The first time was when I was invited to have dinner with the president of the United States." She pauses for dramatic effect. "I bet you're wondering which president."

"Reagan," Frank says.

"Nope."

"Bush?"

"Nope."

"Not Nixon, I hope."

"I'll give you a hint. He was only the most handsome president this country has ever had."

"I know," Frank says proudly. "It was Kennedy. People say I looked like him when I was younger."

"You had dinner with Kennedy?" I say.

"Well, I would have if it wasn't for that awful day in November. You know how people can tell you exactly what they were doing on the day he got shot? Well, I sure can. I was with my mother getting my new dress altered because I was supposed to have dinner with him the very next night. I was just a little girl, you know, but I think my life would have turned out differently if I had gotten to have dinner with President Kennedy like I was supposed to. Aren't grocery stores the most amazing places? I bet none of you imagined you'd be standing next to toothpaste and toilet paper talking about JFK. The next time we all run into each other, I'll tell you about the time I saved the life of the richest man alive and what he did to repay me."

"Perhaps you would do me the honor of telling me that story over dinner tonight," Frank says in as charming a voice he can muster.

"Oh, that would be marvelous, Frank, but I already have dinner plans."

I glance at Marvin, who winks at me.

"It was nice talking to you, boys. Benji, thanks again for fixing my garbage disposal; it's working beautifully. If things don't work out between you and Dr. Kentucky, I'll have to get you in touch with my niece. Don't get me wrong—I hear Dr. Kentucky is a marvelous woman, but I have a talent for matchmaking. The more I think about it, I'm certain you'd be just perfect for Hailey. Heaven knows she could use a good man in her life." She flashes a wide smile at me and Frank. "Come along, Marvin. Show me the way to those steaks you were telling me about."

Frank watches them walk away. I actually feel a little sorry for him.

"Who does he think he's kidding?" Frank says. "He doesn't stand a chance with that woman."

"I think both of you are asking for trouble," I say.

"Well, he's gonna pay for this."

"For what?"

"For humiliating me."

"Why don't you put your energy into a woman who's attainable? I'm telling you, Frank, I think Jane has her eye on you."

"Humph. I don't want to talk about it anymore. I need toilet paper." He starts dumping packages into the cart.

"The toilet paper is supplied for free in Building C."

"It's too coarse. I'd be better off using sandpaper."

"I've always stocked your bathroom with the free stuff, Frank. You've never complained before."

"Well, I'm changing brands. I have calluses where they don't belong." He stuffs a few dozen more rolls into the cart.

"Do you need a year's supply?"

"Mind your own business. I need some honey too."

CHAPTER 9

I wasn't planning on spending my evening with a corpse, but we don't live in a perfect world.

Sam is dead. The foyer won't be the same without him parked there in his wheelchair, asking people if they know how to speak Spanish.

I got the news while I was in my apartment contemplating whether or not I should give Lex a call. The nursing staff found Sam slumped in his wheelchair, facing his television—they thought he was sleeping. Eventually someone realized he had been asleep for an unusually long time.

One of the quirks of my job is that I occasionally have to babysit a corpse. If a resident suffers an unwitnessed death, there is a policy that the body cannot be left alone until the coroner arrives and determines whether further investigation is warranted. If the death occurs at an odd hour, the wait can be a while. Since I am one of the few employees who can stomach some alone time with a dead person, I'm usually the one who gets called.

This explains why I am sitting next to lifeless Sam instead of arranging a second date with Lex. The coroner won't arrive until morning, so that gives me approximately seven more hours with the peculiar old guy. It also gives me plenty of time to stare death in its face.

I tried to watch television at first, but that didn't seem respectful. I'm certainly not planning on sleeping. I didn't bring a book and Sam doesn't have any reading material other than an oversized Bible on his nightstand. I'd rather have a staring contest with Sam than read his Bible. I guess I really don't have much of a choice other than to sit here and ponder my own mortality. What a lovely way to spend the night.

Poor Sam. What a sad way to go. He died alone, in front of the television, and it took several hours for anybody to notice he was no longer breathing. To top it off, a janitor is babysitting his corpse because he doesn't have any family around.

I glance around his small room. Save for his library of one book and a tattered Beach Boys poster on the wall, the room is bare. Sam loved the Beach Boys.

I wonder if he would have lived his life any differently if he could have foreseen this moment.

As I study his waxy face I suddenly see myself, but I quickly shove the disturbing image back into my subconscious mind. Denial is a wonderful coping skill, but despite my best efforts, the awful notion of my inevitable death keeps clawing its way back into my awareness. Someday this is going to be me. Someday this is going to be me.

His shirt is checkered. Checkered shirts are annoying. Why don't more people wear stripes? Someday this is going to be me. Perhaps I should look in his closet and see if he has a more suitable shirt. If I were him, I wouldn't want to be buried in this. Someday this is going to be me. No, I better not change him. I would have a tough time explaining why he's half naked if someone happened to stop by before I completed the switch. Someday this is going to be me.

Since I can't stamp it out, I might as well entertain the thought.

Okay, someday I'm going to die. The way things are going, I'm going to die pretty much like Sam. Alone. Except I'll be wearing a striped shirt with a prime number of stripes, and there is a 50-50 chance that the stripes will be vertical. (I would prefer they be horizontal on the day of my death.)

If that's not depressing, I don't know what is.

Here's the really sad part: I know all this. I can see where my life is heading as plain as day. My future is literally sitting right in front of me. Dead man alone in his chair. Right there. That's me someday. And here I am in the prime of life with the full knowledge of what lies ahead.

That's right, I don't deserve any pity. I've made certain decisions, reached certain conclusions, altered my philosophy, and here is where I am. And right there is where I am headed.

As I continue to study my inevitable future, my stomach begins to churn. Another thought creeps its way into my consciousness. A nagging question taps the inside of my skull. A question so unsettling that it makes the thought of a lonely death seem insignificant.

What has become of Sam?

I used to think I knew the answer to this question, but I threw those juvenile beliefs out the window when my brother died under my scalpel. I no longer allow childish thoughts of heaven to give me any comfort. The God of my youth no longer exists. A good God wouldn't permit so much suffering in this world.

When I was in college I had a professor who loved to quote the saying that religion is an opiate for the masses, a drug to calm one's fears and anxieties, a lie to make life bearable. He was right. Religion is an opiate that I'm not willing to take. I take full responsibility for failing to save Andrew. God had nothing to do with it. I'm not prepared to say I'm absolutely certain God doesn't exist, but I do maintain that he doesn't care about us. Where's the evidence that he does?

So what has become of Sam? Is he enjoying some sort of afterlife? Is he reaping what he has sown? Is he waiting for Judgment Day? No, I don't think so. He's slipping into oblivion. He's no longer aware, and very few people are aware of him. In a short while, he'll be completely forgotten and will truly cease to exist. You can call that heaven or you can call that hell. It all depends on your perspective.

I don't much like the idea of slipping into oblivion. I can't say I like the idea of immortality either. A century on Earth is probably all I can take. After that, maybe oblivion won't be such a bad thing. It's all pointless, really.

So long, Sam. Your life is over, you died alone, and if that's not the way you wanted it, too bad because now it's too late to change anything. I glance at his Bible. You know what, Sam? For your sake I almost hope there is a heaven.

CHAPTER 10

This place really comes alive when someone dies. Everybody turns out for the memorial service, regardless of how well known or well liked the deceased was. There is a funeral committee comprised of ten people who are charged with the task of planning the event if there aren't any family or friends around who are up to the task. From what I hear, there is a waiting list of more than fifty women (that's basically all of them) who want to sit on the committee, which always strives to outdo itself by making each successive service more memorable than the last. Jane holds one of the coveted spots. They convened last night, twenty minutes after news of Sam's passing spread, to start planning.

The service will take place three days from now. Speculations about what's in store are already soaring, but members of the funeral committee are keeping their lips sealed. At the last funeral there was a live bagpipe player and a fireworks show for the grand finale. A patch of weeds caught fire when one of the fireworks failed to launch. The fire spread to an old truck that was parked nearby; the gas tank ignited and exploded. Nobody was hurt. The show had residents talking for weeks.

I ran into Jane earlier this morning and asked her how they were going to top the last service. She had a twinkle in her eye but refused to tell me what they had up their sleeves. I can't imagine what could possibly be more entertaining than blowing up a truck.

I informed Junior I was taking today off because I didn't get any sleep last night since I was corpsesitting. He hemmed and hawed, but didn't deny my request. I'm still going to get work done; I just don't want to put up with him bossing me around today.

I have a mile-long list of odd jobs that I need to do, but first I have to go to Marvin's place. He left me a message this morning requesting that I install a new lock on his door as soon as possible. I'm reluctant to find out why. No doubt it has something to do with Frank.

When I arrive at Marvin's place, I need no explanation. Garbage bags full of toilet paper are stacked outside his door. He's still inside cleaning up the last of it.

"Morning, Marvin."

He grunts a response then says, "Do you have what you need to install a deadbolt?"

"Yes. Looks like Frank broke in and had some fun."

"He didn't break in. He didn't have to. He just opened the door and waltzed right in while I was at Betty's place. That's why I need a lock." He shakes his head at the remainder of the mess. "Last night I only had enough energy to clean off my bed before I went to sleep. It's not just toilet paper; he drizzled honey all over my pillow. My bed is going to be swarming with ants."

"Classic."

"I should have seen it coming."

"Me too. I was with him when he bought the supplies. I should've known better. How was dinner last night?"

"Sublime."

"You sure are spending a lot of time with Betty."

"Don't worry; I'm not getting any foolish ideas. She's good company. She has all these plans and ideas . . . I really don't know why she's here—she should be traveling the world or writing a book or campaigning for political office."

"She does seem like quite a character."

"So tell me, Ben, what's going on with you and Dr. Kentucky?"

"Just like you, I'm not letting myself get any foolish ideas." I feel my face flush despite my effort to act nonchalant.

"You got any trash bags on that cart of yours?"

"Sure." I hand him one. I'm glad he's apparently decided to drop the subject. We both start gathering wads of toilet paper.

"Well," Marvin says, "maybe it's none of my business, but if I were you I'd be having all kinds of foolish ideas. She's obviously interested in you, and you guys seem like a perfect match."

"I appreciate your interest, Marvin, but I don't think I'm at a place where I'm ready for a relationship."

"I want you to stop and look at me." Marvin's voice has taken a serious tone. "Listen to an old man who has lived a full life. If you wait until you think you're ready for a relationship, then you'll never be ready. Don't let a prime opportunity like this pass you by." He wags his finger. "Now I want you to change my lock and get outta here and call that beautiful young lady."

"What about this mess?"

"I can handle this. You have more important things to tend to. Now get moving."

It doesn't take me long to install the lock. When I'm finished, I've talked myself into calling Lex. But first I have to run an important errand.

The hand washing has started again. I know I'm in trouble when this happens. But it's almost November and I always get sick in November. And besides, it makes me feel so much better—at least for a few minutes. I don't think of it as a compulsive act; it's more like a massage for my hands. People pay money for neck or shoulder massages when they get stressed out. There's nothing wrong with that, so what's wrong with me giving myself a free hand massage to relieve some of my tension?

This relapse sort of crept up on me. Like most people, I always wash my hands before eating, after using the bathroom, and right after I enter my apartment. This is just plain common sense. But recently I've found myself feeling the urge to scrub my palms at random times—like after I brush my teeth, or every time I see something orange. I've also slipped back into more of a ritualized hand-washing routine: heat the water nearly to the point of scalding, prerinse, apply soap, scrub between fingers first, palms next, fingers and fingernails last, rinse, scrub again, rinse, scrub again, dry hands on clean towel without a final rinse because the soap residue will act as a barrier against harmful bacteria.

The ritual concerns me, but I need it right now. I'll indulge myself for the time being, which is why I need to run an important errand. I need to purchase my favorite type of bar soap. It can't be found just anywhere. Usually I order it off the Internet, but since I don't want to wait for it to arrive in the mail, I have to drive into town where there is a soap-and-bath store that usually carries what I'm looking for.

As I drive myself to the mall, I rehearse what I might say to Lex when I call. So far all my imaginary conversations have sounded incredibly lame. I should've called her yesterday. What was I thinking?

I reach the parking lot without making any left turns. I'm not fond of malls—this one in particular. It's always crowded, and it's dirty. To make matters worse, there aren't any automatic sliding doors at the entrances. There ought to be a law that mandates automated doors for all public places—especially restrooms. Imagine how much healthier our society would be if we could eliminate all of the nasty, festering, community door handles.

I find a parking spot and make my way toward the entrance. I shudder at the thought of touching the same surface that thousands of other people have touched. I watch with disgust as someone ahead of me sneezes into their hand and then grasps the handle to open the door. I linger for a moment, waiting for an opportunity. Finally someone exits, swinging the door wide. I'm able to slip in without touching anything. What a relief.

I grimace at the checkered flooring and head quickly for the soap store. It's more of a hole in the wall than a store. Only five or six people can fit inside before it starts getting uncomfortable. Fortunately it is empty today, aside from the young female clerk. I'm bombarded by a thick conglomeration of scents as I step inside. This place always gives me a headache.

"Good afternoon, sir, are you looking for anything in particular?" The clerk fires off a friendly smile. "Doing some early Christmas shopping? We have a new line of hand lotions that most women are going nuts over. They make perfect stocking stuffers."

"Yes to your first question. No to the second."

"What can I help you find?"

"Lamax unscented bar soap."

"I don't believe we carry that."

"I bought some here about a year ago."

"Perhaps you would like to try this instead." She hurries over to a shelf and selects a bar of soap wrapped in clear cellophane.

"No, thanks. I'll just order the stuff I like off the Internet."

"Okay. Are you sure you don't want to get some Christmas shopping done while you're here? We carry a complete line of skincare products formulated especially for men—we have an exfoliator, a hydrating wash, a balancing toner, a corrective eye crème, and a moisturizer." She hands me a sample tray containing the various products.

I pick up one of the small tubes. It is priced at twenty-eight dollars. "Why would I want this?"

"Oh, it's all the rage. I have dozens of male clients who are head over heels in love with this line. It would be a perfect gift for one of your friends." She pauses for a split second before she says "friends."

"No thanks." I hand back the tray. "I'm pretty certain I don't have a single friend who would appreciate any of this."

"My boyfriend uses it," she says, as if this piece of information will convince me.

"Your boyfriend must really love you."

Her mouth twists into a pout as she places the tray where it belongs. "I just figured that if you were so particular about your soap, then you must really care about your skin."

Now I feel guilty for giving her a hard time. "You know what?" I soften my tone. "Maybe I should give it a try."

"Really?"

"Sure, why not?"

"Oh, you won't be sorry." Her cheerful grin returns. "Now, let me explain what these are for . . ."

Twenty minutes later I walk out of the small shop carrying a bag full of $139 worth of skincare products for men. This girl knows what she's doing. She probably gets a commission. I can imagine her bragging about me to her friends. And I still don't have the soap I want. What a racket. Back when I was in college majoring in biochemistry I should have stuck with laboratory science instead of taking the premed route. I could have developed my own line of facial products and made millions. Take some worthless crème, stick it in a fancy bottle, invent a French-sounding name, and turn around and sell it at a 3000 percent markup. Put the word organic on the label and add another 50 percent to the price. I could be filthy rich.

As I walk past the food court, a familiar face catches my eye. Lex is eating lunch at one of the tables. She hasn't noticed me yet. I'm about to walk over but stop when a man approaches from the other direction. Lex gets up, embraces him, and they both sit down.

He's not just any man. He's a very good-looking man. Dark, stylish hair, tanned skin, athletic figure. He probably works out several hours a day. I can't compete with this guy. Look at his complexion—he probably uses skincare products.

I turn my head the other way as I hurry past so Lex won't see me. There's not much of a chance of that. She's too engrossed in her conversation with loverboy. I scrap my plans to call her. I knew she was too good to be true. What was I thinking?

I earnestly count my paces as I walk back to my truck. My heart continues to sink as I drive home.

My mood smolders for the remainder of the day. That's the problem with my job—it doesn't require much thought, so my mind has plenty of time to dwell on random subjects. There are several subjects on which I'd rather not dwell, and Lex Kentucky has suddenly become one of them. I need to invent games to keep my mind occupied.

I just invented a new one. I take a passage or a song that I have committed to memory—like the national anthem—and alphabetize the letters within each word. For example, Oh: h-o, say: a-s-y, can: a-c-n, you: o-u-y, see: e-e-s... When I run out of songs, I alphabetize different objects in my field of view: octogenarian, rosebush, sidewalk. When that starts to bore me I begin recalling medical words—preferably those with several syllables. Enterohemorrhagic: a-c-e-e-e-g-h-h-i-m-n-o-o-r-r-r-t. Enterohemorrhagic is an especially wonderful word. It contains seventeen total letters (prime), eleven different letters (also prime), and each different letter is used a prime number of times. It's the perfect trifecta. Excited by my discovery, I search my mind for more words that meet these criteria: chondrosternoplasty. Before I know it, my day has reached its end. Thanks to trifectionary (yes, another new word).

CHAPTER 11

This place is buzzing with excitement about Sam's memorial service, which is still two days away. The energy in the air reminds me of being in high school right before homecoming celebrations.

The women are primping more than usual because it has become a common practice for residents of Heritage Gardens to attend the memorial services as couples. Frank is in ecstasy because he had the foresight to ask Betty before Marvin had a chance to, and Boop, bless her heart, said yes. Now Frank is strutting around like he landed a date with the homecoming queen, which is actually a pretty good analogy.

There has been an added dimension to the prefuneral craziness: several men, including Frank, have approached me with the same odd request. I'm not sure if I should find this humorous or disturbing, but they are asking me on the sly if I would be willing to prescribe them the "blue pill." At first I didn't know what they meant, but I quickly learned that this is a code for Viagra. Of course I refused. Like I said, this place really comes alive when someone dies.

With that lovely mental image festering in my mind, I now must answer Junior's summons and report to his office. Something's up. His voice sounded strange on the walkie-talkie. I'm not looking forward to our meeting. He better not ask me to prescribe any pills, blue or otherwise.

When I arrive, Junior's office door is closed. I'm about to knock, but I hear muffled voices from the other side. One is Junior's, the other belongs to a female. I can't make out what they're saying, but they sound earnest. As their exchange continues, Junior's voice grows louder. "Great! That will be just great! This is exactly the sort of opportunity I've been looking for! This will solve everything!"

They are approaching the door. I quickly back away and, as the door opens, act as if I just entered the building.

"Hi, Benji," Betty Boop greets me as she exits Junior's office. Her voice lacks her trademark bubbliness and her eyes seem sad. She's wearing a thin black-leather jacket and a black skirt that ends just above her knees.

"Are you all right?" I say.

"I'm okay."

"What are you doing here, Ben?" Junior interrupts in a jovial voice.

Confused, I say, "You asked me to come."

"Oh, yeah. Never mind. It's a moot point now. You can go about your business."

"So you don't need to talk to me?"

"Nope." He turns to Betty. "Alrighty, then, Miss Boestra, we'll move forward as planned."

"Good. You won't be sorry. Ta-ta, boys." She walks out the door and I notice her step lacks its usual bounce.

"Are you sure you're all right?" I call after her.

She turns. "I'll be fine, Benji. I'm just sad about Sam's passing."

"He was a character," I say. "I'm gonna miss him."

"Me too." She continues to walk away.

I have no idea what to make of this since she's only been around for about a week.

Junior chuckles and rubs his hands together.

"What's going on?" I ask.

"Exciting stuff, but I can't tell you anything more. Is Assembly Hall in order?"

"I'm heading there next."

"Good. Carry on. We have a big day coming up. Sounds like the committee is putting together quite a show in honor of good ol' Sam."

Assembly Hall is mostly used for bingo and square dancing. (If I had to make a list of ten things that annoy me most, I'm pretty sure square dancing would be on it.) Frank is the caller—the guy who tells the couples what to do while they're dancing. I hear he's quite talented in this regard, but I wouldn't know any better. I vow never to square dance.

There is enough space for about three hundred chairs. The floor is currently empty because it was being used for the previously mentioned annoying activity the other night. I figure I don't need to set up all three hundred chairs. After all, there are only 127—scratch that, 126—residents here, and not all of them are in good enough health to attend. I don't think Sam had many outside friends or family since I never noticed anyone coming to visit him. It's probably safe to set up only two hundred chairs. I don't want to overestimate because a lot of empty chairs at a funeral service can be depressing.

Of course I'm not going to set up exactly two hundred chairs. I'm going to pick a more interesting number, such as 211. I like this number. The first digit minus the second equals the third, it's prime, and it rolls off the tongue.

But wait a minute, two plus one plus one equals four. Perhaps 211 isn't such a good number after all. I'll set up 199 instead.

As I start carrying folding chairs to the center of the room an idea occurs to me. I wonder if it's possible to arrange the chairs in such a way that there is a prime number of rows with a prime number of chairs in each row, while still maintaining a total of 199. I'm up to the challenge.

"What's up, Doc?" The Professor interrupts my calculations.

I turn and say hello. Green pants, aqua shirt, and yellow rain boots. "Is it going to rain?" I ask.

"I wear these for comfort. They're convenient too. Don't have to tie them."

"Good point."

"Setting up for the big event?" He takes a seat on one of the chairs I just unfolded.

"Yep."

"Expecting a large crowd?"

"Probably average."

"Two hundred?"

"I'm setting up 199."

"Good number." He nods. "Prime."

I meet his gaze and suddenly remember why I've always liked him. This guy knows everything. Sometimes I forget that he's a heck of a lot smarter than he looks.

"Are you bringing a date?" he says.

"Hadn't considered it."

"Really? What about Dr. Kentucky?"

"I seriously doubt it."

He furrows his brow and scratches his scalp. "But I heard through the grapevine that your date went well. This would make a perfect second date."

"No. I've come to realize she's out of my league."

"So did she blow you off? Is she not returning your calls?"

"I haven't called her."

He lifts one of his galoshes and stomps it on the hardwood floor. "Forgive me for not understanding, but let me get this straight. You have a successful first date with an intelligent and beautiful woman, yet you allow nearly three full days to go by without call-ing her?"

"She's involved with someone else."

"And...?"

"There is no and. That's it. She's seeing another guy."

"She told you she's not interested in dating you?"

"No."

"Are you surprised that other men are pursuing this beautiful, intelligent, available woman? Did you two exchange some sort of prenuptial vows on the night of your first date? Did you promise not to have any contact with the opposite sex? In other words, are you crazy or just plain stupid?"

I stare at him.

He stares back.

"I see your point," I finally say.

"You're a bit out of practice, aren't you?" He clucks his tongue in sympathy.

"I guess." I unfold another chair, turn it around backwards, and sit facing him. "I don't know—I just can't picture myself with anyone. I mean, I used to. It used to be all I thought about. But things changed..." I'm surprised by how much I've just revealed. My palms begin to moisten. I quickly stand and scoot my chair to its proper place in the next row.

"See? That wasn't so bad," he says.

"What?"

"You opened up a little and it didn't kill you. But that's all for today, isn't it?" He stands to leave.

Part of me wants to stop him. I could ask him to sit back down and listen while I spill my guts. But I don't. I know exactly what he's doing. He's slowly wearing me down. He's using some sort of psychoanalytical trick to manipulate me and get me to open up. He wants to be a hero and save me.

I let him walk away.

"Hey, are we still on for tomorrow night?" he says over his shoulder as he reaches the door.

With everything else going on, I've completely forgotten about our little adventure/experiment that we've been planning. We marked our calendars for this a few weeks ago. "Oh yeah," I say. "I don't see why we can't still do it."

"Good. I want Dr. Kentucky to come too."

"We can't all fit in my truck."

"I'll drive."

"It's too last minute."

"If you don't call and ask her, then I'm going to." His eyes sparkle. "I think she'll enjoy our little social experiment."

Part of me wants to argue, but for some reason I give in. "Fine. You win. I'll give her a call this afternoon."

"Excellent!" he says as he exits the building.

Here goes… This telephone conversation is probably going to be a disaster.

"Hello?"

"Hello, Lex. It's Ben."

"Ben? Ben who?"

"Uh—"

"I'm kidding, Ben. I've been waiting for you to call."

"Honestly?"

"Yes. What took so long?"

"You want the truth?"

"Preferably."

"I was in the mall the other day and I saw you with some other guy. I figured I was no match for him."

"Well, you were right. I don't think you could ever replace him."

I can't think of anything to say.

"That was my brother." Lex mercifully breaks the silence and laughs.

"Oh. I feel like an idiot. He has great skin, by the way."

"I can't say that I blame you—for feeling like an idiot, that is—but I won't let it get in the way of a second date."

"Well, that's why I was calling. I was wondering if you would accompany me to a social experiment tomorrow evening."

"A what?"

"You know Jerry, the retired professor?"

"The one who wears the neon clothes?"

"That's him. Every few months he and I conduct what we call social experiments on unsuspecting medical students over at Loma Linda Medical School in San Bernardino. It's sort of hard to explain. Jerry says he'd love to have you along, so I thought I'd invite you."

"Tomorrow evening?" she says.

"Sorry it's so last minute." I brace myself for a rejection.

"That should be fine. I don't have any plans."

"Great! Oh, by the way, I don't have room in my truck for all three of us, so Jerry's going to drive."

"So you want me to meet you at Heritage Gardens?"

"If you don't mind. Oh, and one other thing: did you hear that Sam died?"

"The one who liked the Beach Boys?"

"Yeah. His funeral is the day after tomorrow. I was wondering if you would be my date."

"To a funeral?"

"Yeah. They're all the rage here at Heritage Gardens. It's like going to the prom. Rumor has it this one is going to be spectacular. Are you free?"

"I'm not sure."

"Okay. Well, I'll see you tomorrow evening for sure, and we can play the funeral by ear," I say, realizing how absurd this sounds.

"What time tomorrow?"

"Can you be here by four-thirty?"

"Yes."

"Okay. Bring a jacket or something because we'll be outside."

"I'm intrigued. I'll look forward to it."

That went a lot better than expected. I wonder what she sees in me? If she ever finds out what I'm really like, this thing—whatever it is—will be over in a heartbeat.

CHAPTER 12

Lex and I ride in the backseat of the Professor's massive Cadillac sedan. He claims the front passenger seat belt isn't reliable, which is why we are both in back. I feel like a fifteen-year-old being escorted by my father on a date.

Lex looks stunning as always. The Professor is a different story. His usual bright attire has been replaced by layers of ragged clothes from a thrift store. His hair is greasy, his chin stubbled with two days' growth, his skin smudged with something dark, and he smells like he hasn't bathed in a month.

"So explain to me again what we're doing?" Lex says.

"I call it a social experiment," says the Professor. "It's quite simple, really. Today I'm going to play the role of a homeless man. I'll place myself in a situation where I don't appear to desperately need help, yet am in enough subtle distress that an attentive passerby with a compassionate heart might offer his or her aid. It's a sort of test for the medical students who frequent the area. If a medical student passes the test, I'll reward them with a thousand-dollar scholarship for books."

"Man alive, Jerry." I crack open the window. "How did you manage to make yourself smell so much like body odor?"

"Ant spray."

"Ant spray?"

"I was spraying my bathroom for ants the other day and I noticed how much the spray smelled like body odor, so I sprayed these clothes with it."

"That can't be healthy."

"My skin does itch a little, now that you mention it. It certainly won't be healthy for any ants that happen to crawl on me."

The Professor is driving in the slow lane at exactly sixty-five miles per hour. At this rate it will take us forever to get to Loma Linda. To make matters worse, he claims his radio doesn't work. That leaves us with the option of engaging in conversation the whole way or enduring awkward silence. I'm not sure which would be worse. I'm starting to feel a bit squeamish. I didn't think this through before I agreed to invite Lex. It didn't occur to me that I would be trapped with her and the Professor in a confined space for such a long period of time. This could spell disaster. I need to take command of the conversation before the Professor does, so I say the first thing that pops into my mind. "Have either of you seen Mars lately?"

"Mars?" Lex says.

"Yeah. Apparently conditions have been perfect to view Mars. I was outside last night and got a pretty good look at it. I was wondering if either of you have seen it."

"I did," the Professor says.

"That's one thing I don't like about Southern California," Lex says. "The air quality is so bad here; we don't often get a good view of the stars."

"I agree," I say. "But then, on the other hand, the less I look at the night sky, the less I'm reminded how small I am compared to the vastness of space."

"Do you believe the universe is infinitely large?" The Professor glances at me in the rearview mirror.

"No. Most cosmologists agree the universe is expanding, therefore it cannot be infinitely large."

"How inconvenient for you," the Professor says.

"I'm not sure I follow," Lex says.

"I'll elaborate," the Professor says. "If the universe is expanding, then the big bang theory holds true. If there was a big bang, then there was a beginning. If there was a beginning, then there is need for a beginner. If there is a beginner, then we need God. If there is a God, then all this isn't mere chance and we cannot resign ourselves to a life with no real meaning. Most skeptics find this fact to be quite inconvenient."

"I hate to tell you, Jerry, but your little string of logic doesn't hold water," I say.

"Enlighten me."

"M-theory."

"Do go on."

"M-theory is as close as physicists have gotten to Einstein's elusive unifying theory of everything. You would need to read several books to understand it, but to summarize, if the big bang theory holds true, then at some point the universe was as small as a subatomic particle and was therefore subject to the laws of quantum physics. According to quantum physics, it is well established that quantum particles can spring into existence from nothing. Our universe is just one of trillions upon trillions that have been spontaneously springing into existence since before the beginning of time. If our universe was a spontaneous quantum event, then we don't need God. So, you see, your theory doesn't hold water. Our universe can still have a beginning without a beginner."

"You don't believe in God?" Lex says.

This is exactly what I was afraid of. "I never said that. I was simply making the point that things can be scientifically explained without invoking God."

"Then what do you believe?"

"Do you remember a few years back when there were those terrible floods in Africa?" I say.

"Yes, I remember seeing it on the news."

"One story in particular struck me," I continue. "During a break in the weather a helicopter was flying over the floodwaters, surveying the extent of the damage. As they flew over a tree, they saw a woman clinging to its branches. She was holding her newborn child in one arm and holding on for dear life with the other. She didn't know how long she had been in that tree. All she could remember was giving birth in the pouring rain and trying not to fall or drop her baby."

"I read about that woman!" Lex says. "As I recall, when she was interviewed, she thanked God for saving her and her child."

"Yes," I say. "It was quite a remarkable story. I think all the networks covered it. I remember thinking how nice it was for her that things turned out all right. You could even call her survival and rescue miraculous. So she naturally thanked God. She survived against all odds and so did her baby, so God got the credit. But what about the thousands of others who drowned or starved or died from exposure and illness or lost their homes and families? What about all those desperate souls who no doubt cried out to God but were ignored?"

"Holy smokes!" The Professor yells as he slams on the brakes. The seat belt cuts into my gut as my body pitches forward and the car screeches to a halt. I see an overturned SUV lying on the shoulder of the road up ahead. Several other banged-up cars are pointed in various directions. The accident must have happened only seconds before. The Professor pulls over to the shoulder and brings us as close to the overturned vehicle as possible. "Looks like someone might need a doctor, Ben."

In a flash I'm out of the car and running toward the overturned vehicle. The front half is crushed beyond recognition and all the windows are shattered. The driver's window has been reduced to less than a fourth of its original height because the roof is crumpled in like a stepped-on soda can. Smoke pours from the engine and some sort of fluid is leaking down the side. In an instant I'm on my hands and knees peering into the narrow opening that used to be the driver-side window. Thank goodness for modern tempered glass—the small cubes littering the ground aren't sharp enough to cut my palms.

I encounter a mass of blond hair that's quickly turning red. The upside-down head turns toward me. Eyes flutter open with a start. Before I can say anything, the thirty-something-year-old woman cries, "My baby! My baby! Where's my baby?"

"Ma'am, you've been in an accident," I say in as calm a voice I can muster. "We're going to get you out of here. Just try to stay calm."

"Don't worry about me—just get my baby. I don't hear her!" She begins to thrash around. "Dear God, please help my baby!"

Suddenly I realize Lex is beside me. "What's your name?" Lex asks as I scoot over to the backseat window.

"God, please help my baby. Please help my baby."

"Help is on the way." Lex attempts to soothe her as I peer inside the smashed passenger window. I spy a car seat on the other side of the vehicle. A little motionless body is suspended upside down. I dash over to that side of the car. A quick glance tells me that trying to open the door will be useless. Fortunately this part of the roof isn't crushed as badly. I'm able to squeeze the upper half of my body through the opening. The little girl doesn't look like she's breathing. The smell of gasoline and heat from the engine adds to my sense of urgency. I need to get her out before this death trap explodes.

I fumble with the car-seat harness for what seems like an eternity. The toddler's mom continues to moan and plead for her child. The scent of gasoline grows stronger.

I finally free the limp body and wriggle back out of the vehicle with my fragile package wrapped in my arms. "Lex, you've got to get away from the car. I'm afraid it's going to catch fire."

"No. I'm staying with her until help gets here."

I dash over to what seems like a safe distance from the wreck and gently deposit the unconscious child onto the dirt. In my peripheral vision I see the Professor rushing toward the smoking end of the vehicle with a fire extinguisher, but my main concern is the lifeless child in front of me. I don't see any blood, but her little lips are blue and her chest isn't rising. I tear open her delicate blouse and place my finger on her neck. I can't find a pulse. I hear sirens in the distance. A crowd of spectators surrounds me. Out of the blue a clear thought enters my racing mind. Ventricular fibrillation. I don't know how I know this, but I do. And I know exactly what I must do to save her.

"Why don't you do CPR?" someone says.

I close my mouth over hers and force two breaths of air down her throat. Then I sit back, carefully aim my palm at the lower section of her sternum, and thump it smartly with my hand.

"Hey!" yells a different voice. "That's not how you do CPR."

I feel her neck again.

Nothing.

I tilt her little chin up, open her mouth, and force two more breaths into her lungs.

Then I thump her sternum once more.

"That's not the right way!" someone says. "You're supposed to keep pushing on her chest to pump her blood through her heart."

"Let him be." I hear the Professor's voice. "He's a cardiothoracic surgeon. He knows what he's doing."

I feel her neck again. This time I feel a thready pulse. I give her two more breaths and then she starts breathing on her own.

The paramedics finally arrive. They place an oxygen mask on the little girl. I sigh with relief as her lips turn from blue to pink. Meanwhile, the firefighters begin the task of extracting the child's mother.

I stagger away from the crowd. Lex and the Professor come to my side. My hands are covered with blood. It must belong to the baby's mother. Lex says something and I mumble a response. The Professor asks me a question and I answer.

I want to get away from here, but they won't let me. The paramedics wave me over. They need a few answers before they leave.

"How long was the child unconscious?" asks a paramedic.

"I don't know. Between two and five minutes."

"She wasn't breathing?"

"She was pulseless and apneic," I say.

"I'm sorry, what did you say your occupation is?"

"I didn't say."

"What do you do for a living?"

"I'm a janitor."

"Well, I'm glad you knew what you were doing. The only way to get someone out of ventricular fibrillation without using an electric shock is to do what you did. You saved that baby's life. By the time we got here with the defibrillator, it probably would've been too late."

A highway patrol officer steps in. "May I please have your full name and place of residence?"

"Listen, do we have to do this right now?"

"This will only take a few minutes."

"My name is Ben. I'm living at 11265 Highland Court, Apartment 2A."

"What's your last name, Ben?"

"Smith."

"Date of birth?"

"I don't understand why you need all this information."

"It's for the accident report. I need to document testimony from witnesses in case there's any dispute from insurance companies. Also, if there turns out to be a fatality, certain details are extremely important."

"I didn't witness the accident."

"You didn't?"

"I didn't see anything. I was riding in the backseat of his car when we came upon the scene." I point at the Professor. "I simply helped the baby."

"Oh. In that case, I should probably talk to him. Thank you for your time." He heads over to the Professor.

We are finally back in the car. Our little adventure has cost us an hour. The Professor offers to turn around and go back to Heritage Gardens, but I know he really wants to proceed with the evening as planned, so I insist we carry on.

"That was something else," Lex says. "Did you hear what the mom said about you?"

"Yes."

"She said God sent you. She said you were her little girl's guardian angel."

"She didn't know what she was talking about. If I were her guardian angel, I would have prevented the accident from happening in the first place."

"You saved her daughter's life."

"I got lucky. She got lucky."

"I think it was more than luck."

"Can we talk about something else?" I look at my hands. I desperately want to scrub the blood off.

"Were you cut?" Lex says.

"It's not my blood." My voice is choked. I don't know why. I quickly turn my head and look out the window. Suddenly I feel the warmth of Lex's hand grasping mine. The tension in my body relaxes a fraction. She doesn't let go.

We ride in silence the rest of the way to Loma Linda. I count lampposts as they fly by. I don't turn my gaze from the window until I count five hundred and sixty-four. The Professor parks next to a coffee shop frequented by medical students from the nearby university hospital. Lex and I head inside. She stands in line to purchase coffees while I head to the bathroom to scrub my hands.

With our coffees in tow, we grab a table on the sidewalk, making sure we have a good view of the Professor, who is readying himself for his routine. He has retrieved a borrowed wheelchair from the trunk of his car. He has also brought along several large garbage bags filled with aluminum cans, old newspapers, and a few blankets.

The street has a slight uphill grade as it approaches the coffee shop. Lex and I watch as the Professor takes his wheelchair, now burdened with his sacks of trash, and wheels himself a hundred yards down the sidewalk. He then turns around and begins to laboriously wheel back up the incline, making frequent stops to rest along the way.

Foot traffic is light on this section of sidewalk, but soon enough two male students with backpacks slung over their shoulders pass by, giving the Professor a wide girth. Lex scoffs as they enter the coffee shop. "They didn't even slow down—they completely ignored him."

"Not completely," I reply. "They took enough care to deviate their course so they could avoid him." I pull out a notepad and scribble a few things.

"Whatcha writing?"

"Jerry asked me to keep some stats."

Pretty soon two more people pass by. This time females in their midthirties wearing jogging attire—except they aren't jogging. They too skirt around the Professor.

Twelve more people pass by before he finally reaches our table. "Guess I'll go back and start over," he says as he turns around.

"You've done this before?" Lex says to me as the Professor heads back down the street.

"Twice."

"Does anybody ever lend him a hand?"

"The first time we did this he was well dressed and played the role of an elderly man too frail to wheel himself up the hill. Ninety-five percent of passersby offered him help. The second time, he was more unkempt, but he didn't have any garbage bags. His help rate dropped to about seventy percent. The interesting thing we noticed the second time was that people were more likely to help if they were alone than if they were walking in pairs or in groups."

"Do you think they just didn't notice him because they were absorbed in conversation?"

"No. They always showed evidence of noticing him. My theory is that they felt they could justify not helping him because they could tell themselves they didn't want to inconvenience their companions, whereas the solo travelers didn't have any good excuse not to help. One guy who was alone actually got out his phone and pretended to dial as he passed by, but I'm certain he wasn't really calling anybody. He simply used his phone as his excuse."

"But today a lot of solo travelers have passed him by." Lex takes a sip of her coffee.

"That's because he's homeless and possibly not right in the head. Society views such people as voluntary outcasts. He's probably an alcoholic and it's probably through some fault of his own that he's homeless. In their eyes he's not just a helpless old man. He could have gotten help long ago but he obviously chose not to. Why should anybody go out of their way to help him now? He could even be dangerous. They have plenty of excuses not to help him. They can pass him by with a clear conscience."

"Would you have helped him?" Lex says.

"Honestly? I don't know. I'll never truly know because I'll always be biased as a result of these experiments. Whenever I come across someone in a similar situation, I'll immediately think about these experiments and I'll want to help. Even so, I'd like to think that I would've lent a hand otherwise. What about you?"

"In this case, I think I'd be afraid of him. But if he were a woman, I think I would help."

As she's saying this, a petite female medical student wearing a short white lab coat approaches the Professor. We are too far away to hear what she says as she stops and speaks to him. With some effort, she shoves the trash bags aside and takes a hold of the wheelchair's handles. Leaning into the weight of the chair and its cargo, she strains to push it up the hill. I smile and scribble some notes.

Lex takes a peek at what I've written. "Why did you write lab coat? What difference does that make?"

"The short white coat identifies her as a future doctor. She's obligated to help. How could she justify passing him by?"

"So you're assuming the only reason she's helping is because she's in uniform? That's pretty cynical."

"I'm just making an observation."

The young woman and the Professor draw near. The student's mouth is slightly twisted—as if she's in pain. "This is far enough," says the Professor. "Can you please park me next to that table?" He points to us.

"Sure," she says with a slight grimace. "Do you know them?"

"Congratulations," I say as I stand and hand her a sealed envelope.

"What's this?"

"Your reward," the Professor says.

"I'm not sure I understand."

"It's a thousand dollars. Use it as a book scholarship. It's your reward for being a decent human being."

"You mean this was a test?" The student's face turns red. "What right do you have to judge me? I thought you really needed help. I just had knee surgery a few weeks ago and pushing your stupid chair up that hill probably did some serious damage. You can keep your self-righteous reward." She tosses the envelope on the table and limps away.

The Professor raises his eyebrows and looks at me and Lex. I sit back down and scratch my head. Lex smiles coyly. "So, Ben, what are you going to write in your little notebook about that?"

A short while later, we are back in the car heading home. "I never really saw it that way before," the Professor says. "But she was right. I guess that puts an end to our little experiments."

I'm not sure if I can handle the long drive back to Heritage Gardens. I begin to wrack my brain for a benign subject that might somehow fill the void, but I can't think of anything.

"The tank's almost empty," the Professor announces as he pulls into a gas station.

"I'm going to grab something to drink," I say, thankful for the opportunity to strategize a way to survive the trip back.

"I'll come with you," Lex says.

We get out of the car and walk into the small convenience store.

"Look, they sell lottery tickets here." Lex points to a sign. "I heard the jackpot is up to twenty-three million dollars."

"Do you know what the odds against winning are?" I say.

"The chance of winning is exactly zero if you don't play." She nudges me with her elbow.

"I've never understood why more people buy tickets when the jackpot grows large like it is now," I say. "When it's small, isn't it still around seven million? I wouldn't know what to do with seven million dollars. What's the point of only playing when it grows to twenty-three?"

"Silly or not, I'm still gonna buy a ticket. It only costs a dollar."

"Do you get to choose your own numbers?"

"You can, but I usually just let the computer randomly pick mine for me."

"How many numbers?"

"Six. Between one and fifty."

"That means the odds of winning are like one in ten billion."

"I'm still buying one." She walks over to the machine, inserts her dollar bill, pushes a few buttons, and the machine spits out a ticket. Meanwhile, numbers start to race through my head.

"I think I'll get one too," I announce. "But I want to choose my own numbers."

"Just follow the instructions on the screen," Lex says. "What numbers do you want?"

"Two, three, five, seven, eleven, and thirteen."

"Why those?"

"Because they're sequential primes; their sum is 41, which is also prime; and if you multiply them all together and subtract 41, you get 29,989, which is prime as well."

"I see you have a system. Is this really your first lottery ticket?"

"I figure as long as I'm spending a dollar on it, I might as well make it worth my while." I finish punching in my numbers and the machine spits out my ticket. I examine it to make sure the correct numbers are printed on it, fold it in half, and stick it in my back pocket.

Back in the car the Professor says, "Well, you two, I don't know about you, but I had a fascinating evening. Ben saved a child's life, and I got put in my place by a student less than a fourth my age but wiser than me. I've been so discombobulated that I've completely forgotten all about dinner. Would you like to grab a bite to eat? There's a nice steakhouse near Heritage Gardens."

"Sure!" Lex says before I have a chance to object.

The Professor pulls the car out of the gas station and heads toward the highway.

"Guess what?" Lex says. "We bought lottery tickets."

"Really?" the Professor says. "Ben bought one too?"

"Yes." Lex answers for me. "Why do you sound so surprised?"

"Be careful," I say to the Professor. "I don't like being psychoanalyzed in front of other people." I say this as if I'm kidding, but I'm not and the Professor knows it.

"You're a psychologist?" Lex says.

"I do hold a doctorate in human psychology, but I was always more of an academic—I never really treated patients."

"So what did you do?"

"I guess you could say I studied people—I spent most of my life watching and observing in an effort to better understand the human condition."

"Oh, I see." She doesn't sound convincing.

"I know it sounds rather odd," the Professor says. "What was the point of learning all that stuff if I never applied it in a way to help people? Well, I have tried to help certain people. And as long as I'm around, I'll keep trying. It's funny, though. If there's one thing I've learned it's that the people who need the most help are usually the very same people who are the least likely to accept it."

"Amen to that," Lex says. "I can't tell you how frustrated I get with some of my patients. You should see some people's feet! They let all that mold and fungus grow under their toenails and they don't do anything about it. It drives me crazy."

"I hate to admit it, but I'm one of those people," the Professor says. "I know the fungus is there. I just keep hoping it will go away on its own."

This whole fungus analogy is making me lose my appetite. But I'm happy the Professor is filling the void with conversation. The drive passes quickly as he peppers Lex with questions about how to manage toe fungus. Before I know it, we're pulling into the parking lot at the steakhouse.

As we get out of the car the Professor says, "You know what? On second thought, I really shouldn't eat here. I'm trying to watch my cholesterol. You two enjoy your dinner and I'll head on back. It's not too far for you to walk, is it? We're only a few blocks away from Heritage Gardens."

"Are you sure you don't want to join us?" Lex says.

"I'm sure. They probably wouldn't let me through the door look-ing and smelling like this anyway."

"You could get cleaned up. We'll save you a seat."

"Maybe another time. You two enjoy yourselves." He winks at me, not at all subtly, and pulls the car door closed.

"He's quite a character," Lex says as he drives away.

"Yes. He likes to meddle."

We enter the restaurant and are immediately seated in a small, private booth. The waiter lights the candle in the center of our table, places our napkins in our laps, and takes our drink orders. Lex's eyes sparkle darkly in the candlelight. "You're a mystery to me, Ben."

"Am I?"

"See what I mean? So vague."

I straighten the silverware laid out in front of me and then dare to meet her steady gaze. "I'm sorry."

"You're sorry. That's all you have to say?"

"Are mysteries so bad?"

"Not at first. It's attractive at first. But I'm past that stage. I'd like to get to know this cardiothoracic surgeon turned janitor a lit-tle better."

I close my eyes for a brief moment and take a deep breath. When I open them again I see her gaze hasn't faltered. "I'm the guy who cleans rooms at Heritage Gardens." I look away.

"I see," she says. "I guess I should have met you before you built that impenetrable wall."

"I don't know if you really would have wanted to."

"Are you going to try to convince me that you're not a good per-son, Ben? Well, it's not going to work. I'm not looking for Mr. Per-fect. I see how you interact with everybody at Heritage Gardens. I saw you save that little girl's life today. I know you have a good heart. I'm willing to take the bad with the good."

"Excuse me, are you ready to order?" The waiter has returned with our drinks.

We give him our orders and he leaves. I take a sip of water and say, "I quit medicine when my brother died on the operating table." There. I said it. I can't believe I'm actually sharing this with her.

"Oh. I'm so sorry."

"I was the surgeon." I brace myself for her reaction.

Her eyes moisten as she comprehends the weight of my words. "That's tragic."

"I know what you must be thinking," I say. "What was I doing operating on my own brother? Well, I didn't want to, but it was an emergency case and there weren't any other surgeons available. Anyhow, I failed and he died."

"I'm sure you did everything in your power."

"Are you? How do you know for sure? Perhaps I didn't try hard enough. Perhaps my hands moved too slowly. Perhaps I could've been more aggressive."

"You're not being fair to yourself, Ben."

"I'm not sure of anything anymore," I say. "The only thing I'm sure of is that life isn't fair. I used to think I had it all figured out, but then everything suddenly spun out of control. I needed to simplify things, so I dropped everything and moved out here to California. You can call it a nervous breakdown or whatever, but I just needed to get away from it all. Over these past three years I've been slowly getting things back in order."

"Will you ever go back to practicing medicine?"

"No. I decided I don't like playing God. If he can't do his own job, why should I have to shoulder the responsibility?"

"What about that little girl you saved today?"

"What about her? Maybe I didn't do her any favors. Maybe she would have been better off if she died. What if some sick pedophile kidnaps her in six years and traffics her in a child porn ring? That sort of thing happens to some poor child somewhere in this world almost every day. What then?"

"What if she grows up to be a brilliant scientist and discovers a cure for HIV?" Lex counters.

"I guess we'll never know if I did the right thing."

"You did the right thing, Ben." She holds my gaze for a few seconds and then mercifully changes the subject. "What about the rest of your family?"

"I'm all that's left. My mom died from breast cancer when I was twelve, and my father had a fatal heart attack a couple years before my brother died."

"So you didn't leave family behind when you dropped everything and moved out here."

"Nope. I have an uncle floating around out there somewhere, but as far as I know, he's my only living relative. What about you?"

"Three sisters and one brother. Both parents still alive. Seven aunts and seven uncles. A zillion cousins. Thanksgiving is a zoo when my family gets together."

She tells me more about her family until the food arrives. One of her sisters is getting married in January and the wedding planning is going full tilt. Her brother has recently finished law school and is studying for the bar. Another sister is pregnant and is due in March. They all live within a fifty-mile radius of each other and the family is quite close. They get together at least once a month for dinner, and sometimes more frequently than that.

This is all foreign to me, but it sounds nice. I enjoy listening to her ramble on. It's as if she can sense that I've said as much about myself as I can manage in one night, so she's graciously filling in the void. Thankfully my lack of history is perfectly balanced by her abundance. Dinner passes in a flash.

We finish our food and I pay the check. As we walk the few blocks to Heritage Gardens, she slips her arm through mine. "That was a nice dinner," she says.

"It was," I say, "but I must admit I enjoyed the company more than the food."

"Wow, your steak must have been terrible!"

"No. It was the best steak I've ever had."

She slides her fingers down my arm and grasps my hand.

"Sorry," I say. "That was kind of cheesy. It sounded better in my head."

"It was sweet and clever." She squeezes my hand.

We walk in silence for a few minutes. "That's me over there." She points to her car.

"Are we on for tomorrow?" I ask as we approach.

"A funeral? With you? I don't know—sounds a little too romantic for my tastes…"

"I'll be the only guy without a date if you don't come."

"Well, I wouldn't want that to happen."

"So you'll come?"

"What time?"

"Ten in the morning. I'll meet you outside Assembly Hall. You know where that is?"

"Yep."

I release her hand because we're now standing next to her car. She turns and gives me a wry smile. "Hey, if you see Jerry before I do, tell him I said thanks for forcing you to invite me on this little excursion and also for ditching us at the restaurant." She opens her door and gets inside. "See you tomorrow."

As she drives away I realize my heart is racing. I can't wait to see her again, yet I'm terrified that she'll continue to peel off layer upon layer of my defenses, only to find a spoiled onion underneath all that shed skin.

All right. Enough with the lame food analogies. I'm really striking out here.

CHAPTER 13

Today's the big day. The service begins in a few hours followed by lunch and some yet to be revealed surprise that unfortunately won't involve pyrotechnics.

Right now I'm heading over to Boop's place. She needs help transporting some stuff over to Assembly Hall—she wouldn't tell me what. Apparently she weaseled her way into taking part in the service. She's been acting stranger than normal since Sam died and I can't figure out why. As far as I know, she'd never even met him until she arrived here, and that wasn't too long ago.

As I walk along the edge of the pond I see the flitting shapes of a few fish swim by. They all managed to survive the soap incident. I smile and pause to gaze at the water.

"Excuse me." A female voice interrupts my thoughts. "Can you tell me where the service for Samuel Jenson will be held?"

I turn to answer. "Over in the—" I'm stopped cold.

Hailey.

"Ben?"

Time stands still. Dumfounded, we stare at each other for what seems like a lifetime. She hasn't changed a bit these past three years. Her brilliant blue eyes are filled with conflicting emotions as she attempts to process this unexpected encounter.

"Ben," she says again.

I can't read her tone. Shock? Anger?

She sweeps aside a stray wisp of her auburn her, tucking it behind her ear—a nervous habit I remember all too well. Her lower lip quivers and she inhales sharply. She takes a step forward. "Ben—"

I feel the world dim as a tidal wave of emotions I've worked so valiantly to keep at bay threatens to overtake me.

"Hello, Hailey."

She looks like she's about to faint. "I don't understand. What are you doing here?"

"I work here," I say lamely. "I clean rooms."

"For how long?" The color returns to her face, an edge creeps into her voice, and her fists clench.

"Since I left."

"You never even said good-bye. You just disappeared. You never called, you never wrote, you just abandoned everybody. How could you do such a thing?" Her cheeks turn red. I wonder if she's going to hit me. I wouldn't blame her if she did.

I don't say anything because I have no excuse. Nothing I say can explain why I had to do what I did.

"Benji?" Betty Boop's voice floats from the direction of her house. "Is that you? Are you going to help me? We haven't much time." She bustles down the walkway in a black dress. "Who's that young lady you're talking to?"

Hailey turns around and Boop recognizes her. "Hailey, dear! You're an hour early!"

"I was able to catch an earlier flight. I tried to call to let you know."

Boop rushes forward and wraps her niece in an exuberant embrace. "I'm so glad you were able to come on such a short notice. Thanks for coming. I didn't want to face this funeral alone." Boop turns to me as if suddenly remembering I'm here. "Just look at me! I've gone and forgotten all my manners. Benji, I'd like you to meet my niece, Hailey. I told you she's lovely, although I wish you two could have met under better circumstances." Boop takes another look at her niece. "My dear girl, what's wrong? You look like you've seen a ghost."

"We already know each other," Hailey says. "Ben is Andrew's brother."

Betty's eyes widen and the color drains from her face. "But— Benji, why on earth didn't you say something before?"

"Ben disappeared after Andrew's funeral," Hailey continues in a harsh voice. "I haven't seen or heard from him since then. Nobody has had any idea where he's been for the past three years. So forgive me if I'm a bit shaken."

"Oh, my!" Boop says. "So tragic what happened." She clucks her tongue, embraces Hailey again, and then her eyes brighten. "Isn't it just amazing what a small world it is? I mean, what are the odds of something like this? I once heard that everybody on the planet is connected to everybody else through six people or less. In our case it's fewer!"

My head spins as I try to sort out Hailey's sudden appearance and her and Boop's connection to Sam. "How did you two know Sam?"

"Sam was Hailey's grandfather and my father," Boop says.

"Oh, I had no idea you were related. I'm so sorry." I can't think of anything else to say.

"You would never have guessed because we all have different last names," Boop says. "But that's easy enough to explain. My name changed when I got married, and so did my sister's. Hailey is my sister's daughter. Now, Hailey, dear, why don't you come on inside. Where are your bags?"

"I left them in the reception office. I hope that's okay. There wasn't anyone there and I didn't know where to bring them."

"That will be just fine. Benji will fetch them later. But first I need some help." She leads the way to her townhouse. I stay put. "Come along, Benji," she calls over her shoulder. "I need your help."

The last thing I want to do is follow, but I have no choice.

"I didn't know you were planning on moving here permanently," Hailey says to her aunt. "I was sad to hear you sold your house."

"That's a long story." Boop waves her hand dismissively. "I didn't have much of a choice. And besides, I really wanted to spend some time with your grandfather."

"Did you get to talk to him much before he died?"

"No. His memory was too far gone. He didn't even recognize me."

We make our way into Boop's place. I'm feeling more and more uncomfortable by the second.

"I'm sorry I haven't been keeping in touch these past few months," Boop continues. "Things have just been so hectic and I didn't want to burden you with my problems. But don't you worry—I have everything under control. Marty's come up with a plan that will solve everything."

"Not Marty! Isn't he in jail?"

"Not anymore, and that wasn't his fault, you know. You need to give your cousin more credit. He's a very intelligent boy, and he's got a good heart."

"What has he talked you into this time?"

"Costa Rica."

"You're fleeing the country?"

"No, silly. Investment properties. Costa Rica is the new Florida. Americans are moving there by the hundreds—even thousands— for retirement. Right now is the perfect time to buy land there. You can turn around and sell it for more than twice what you paid in just a few months. I sold my house and put all the money into property there. Next month I'll sell my Costa Rican property, and with my profits I'll be able to pay back all the taxes I owe and my other debts too, and I'll still have plenty of money left over to retire on."

"Aunt Betty, that property in Costa Rica is just a big scam."

"No, it isn't—Marty said it was a sure thing. He showed me this article about a couple who sold their small house here, invested in property in Costa Rica, and now they're millionaires!"

"Well, I don't trust Marty for an instant. He's always taking advantage of you."

"Honey, I appreciate your concern and I'd be happy to discuss this more later, but we have a funeral to go to. I won't deny that your grandpa was a terrible father and not much better of a grandfather, but he was blood and we need to pay our respects. Ben is supposed to be helping me get some things ready for the service and I would love it if you would help too. We can get caught up on all this other stuff later on."

Boop leads us into the kitchen and indicates that she expects us to sit at the counter while she bustles about. "I'm making your grandpa's favorite potato salad. The only thing he liked more than this potato salad was beer, but we won't be having any of that."

She already has it mostly prepared and is just putting the finishing touches on three monstrous bowls of the foul-smelling stuff.

"Hailey, dear, you wouldn't believe the places I've seen and the people I met since we last saw each other. Three months ago I was in Nepal! Oh, and I ran into Hillary Clinton in a restaurant in New York, and she signed my napkin, but I lost it. We had the most delightful conversation, and I even tried a bite of her shrimp cocktail . . ." She prattles on until she finally appears to be finished with her concoction. "There, now. Perfect!" She covers the large bowls with plastic wrap. "We can each carry one over to Assembly Hall."

It's only a five-minute walk, but by the time we get there, the bowl I'm carrying is feeling very heavy. Boop sets hers down on a table along the back wall. "We'll just leave them here for now. We'll be having the reception outside, but I don't want to leave them in the sun. Oh, drat, I forgot the most important thing. I'll be right back. You two can stay here." She rushes off to get whatever it is, leaving me and Hailey alone.

"Did you know my grandfather well?" Hailey asks, her voice a bit softer but her gaze still cold.

"I know everybody here."

"What did you make of him?"

"When I first met him, he struck me as intelligent and quick witted. He kept to himself, played a lot of pool, and every time I heard music playing in his room it was the Beach Boys."

"How did people react when he got drunk?"

"Drunk?"

"My grandfather was a raging alcoholic. He turned into a monster whenever he got drunk. It got so bad that at one point he was banned from every bar in town because he caused so much trouble. He beat my mom and my aunt when they were little. Once he even tried to hit me."

"I never saw him drink."

"Impossible."

"I'm certain of it. I never saw him touch alcohol. The only things I saw him indulge in were his Beach Boys records and his Bible."

"My grandfather owned a Bible?"

"Yes."

"Are you sure we're talking about the same person?"

"It's in his room. I'll show you if you'd like."

"I'd like to see that."

We leave Boop's potato salad to fester in the warm building and I lead the way toward Building C.

"You've really been cleaning rooms here for the past three years?" Hailey says as we walk.

"Yep."

"Don't you miss it?"

"What?"

"Your life."

"I don't think so."

"I still don't understand how you could just leave everything. You cut everybody off—even me. We were practically family." She slows her pace and stops, indicating she expects an answer before we continue.

I can't bear to make eye contact. It's hard enough for me just to be in her presence. "I don't know what you want me to say," I mumble.

She sighs. "I guess I don't know what I want you to say either. I just want things to be the way they used to be."

"Yeah. Me too," I lie. I was miserable when Andrew was alive and engaged to marry her, and I'm even more miserable now. Of course I wish Andrew hadn't died, but even if he hadn't my life would still be a mess.

Hailey's shoulders tremble and I realize she's crying. Unsure what to do, I elect not to do anything. She wipes her tears with the back of her hand. "I'm sorry. It's been a long time since I did that. It's funny—this past year I've had more and more days where I actually make it through the whole day without thinking about him. Sometimes even a week. And then, out of the blue, it all comes rushing back and I feel guilty for not thinking about him. I know I shouldn't feel guilty, but I do. He would've wanted me to move on by now."

"I'm sorry." My words sound lame because they are. She steps toward me and leans in. I wrap one of my arms around her shoulders in an awkward embrace. Against my will, my heart starts to pound. My mind screams with guilt. Unlike her, I do have reasons to feel guilty.

"I'm sorry too," she says. "It's just that seeing you—seeing your face . . ."

I let go and she steps away. We continue toward Building C in silence. I count my paces as we go.

Four hundred and thirty-nine paces later I say, "This was Sam's room." Hailey steps inside and glances around. Her gaze lingers on the Beach Boys poster for a few seconds, then she spots the Bible on the nightstand.

I remain in the doorway as she sits on the edge of the bed and picks up the oversized leather book. The pages look pretty worn. As she opens it in her lap, several loose sheets of folded paper flutter to the floor. She gathers them up, unfolds one, and reads it.

"I don't believe this," she says.

"What is it?"

"Take a look." She holds it out.

It's a letter, dated a little over three years ago, addressed to someone named Joanne. "Who's Joanne?"

"My grandmother. She died about ten years ago." Hailey looks through the other papers. "There's a letter here for every member of his family. There's even one for me."

I read the letter Sam wrote to his wife, who had been dead for seven years at the time he wrote it.

Dear Joanne,

I don't know how you're going to read this since you're already gone, but you always believed in miracles and now I do too. I'm sorry it took me so long. There are so many things I'm sorry for that it's impossible for me to fit them all on this paper. But most of all, I'm sorry that I waited to change my life until it was too late for you to see. You deserved so much better than what you got from me. You should have left me fifty years ago. I don't understand why you didn't. I finally started reading the Bible you gave me. After all those years of refusing to read it, the message finally got to me. I stopped drinking. I asked God to forgive me. And then the most amazing thing happened. I still don't understand it completely, and I wish you were here to explain it to me. Somehow I got forgiven. I don't deserve to be forgiven—not after all the pain I caused. I'm writing letters to everyone I hurt. I want them to know how sorry I am, but I don't know how to say it. I don't know if it's right for me to send the letters out. I think everybody's happy just having me out of their lives. I think the damage I caused was so great that there's no way to undo it. I was such a terrible father and husband. I just want everybody I hurt to know how sorry I am. You were an amazing woman, and I never told you. I didn't realize it until it was too late, and it's killing me that I screwed up so bad. I know you're in heaven now, and everything's all right for you. I'm glad for that. You deserve it.

"I can't believe he quit drinking," Hailey says. "He found God and he quit drinking."

"Opiate of the masses," I say under my breath.

"What did you say?"

"Nothing."

"No. I heard you. You said 'opiate of the masses.' Why are you quoting Karl Marx?"

"Karl Marx?"

"Yes. 'Religion is the sigh of the oppressed creature, the heart of a heartless world, just as it is the spirit of a spiritless situation. It is the opium of the people.'" She stares at me, blue eyes fierce. "That quote comes from Karl Marx. You're saying my grandfather turned from one drug to another—that religion is just a cheap drug. That's a pretty cynical view, if you ask me."

"I didn't really mean it in a bad way."

"Then what did you mean?"

"I don't know what I meant. I guess it all just seems like too simple of a solution to life's problems. 'Hey, I found religion now, so everything's all right. God will fix it. When things get difficult, I'll just go to church and get a dose of God, and everything will be all right again.' Maybe I'm being cynical, or maybe I'm just being a realist."

She shakes her head and carefully folds the letters. "Has my aunt seen any of this?"

"I didn't even know she was related to Sam until now."

"She needs to see her letter." She reinserts them into the Bible. "What happened to you, Ben? What happened to the Ben I used to know?"

"You know what happened."

"You know what, Ben? You're not the only person in the world who's experienced pain and suffering."

"That's exactly my point."

Assembly Hall fills rapidly as Maybelle plays the piano. Her repertoire usually consists of old hymns and a few show tunes, but today, bless her heart, she's attempting to pound out Beach Boys songs in honor of Sam.

Hailey and I take seats near the front along the aisle. Betty and Frank—minus his walker—arrive soon after and sit in front of us. Frank is sporting a pink tie.

Betty, unusually quiet, excuses herself and heads over to where the ladies on the funeral committee are sitting, leaving Frank with us.

"Wow, Frank, where did you get the tie?" I say.

"Betty had it. She let me borrow it. Isn't it great?" He beams with pride and glances around. "Have you seen Marvin?" He tries to sound nonchalant.

"Why do you ask?"

"Oh, I have something he lost and I was wondering if he misses it."

"What did he lose?" I take the bait.

"His girlfriend."

"Frank, I've got bad news for both of you—"

"Hey, aren't you going to introduce me to this beautiful young lady?" Frank cuts me off.

"Oh, yeah. Sorry. Hailey, this is Frank. Frank, this is Hailey. Hailey is Betty's niece and Sam's granddaughter."

"No kidding?"

"Nice to meet you," Hailey says.

"Holy moly," Frank says. "Sam never told me he had such a lovely granddaughter." He scratches his head. "Betty is your aunt?"

The wheels in his head are turning, but he still hasn't put two and two together.

"Hey, Ben, did you forget about our date?" Lex's voice joins the conversation.

"Lex!" I jump to my feet, nearly knocking over Frank's chair. My reaction betrays the fact that I truly did forget her. My head spins as I desperately try to think of a quick recovery. "You're early! I was just about to head outside to find you."

"No worries." She shifts her gaze to Hailey. "Hello. I'm Lex."

"Hello, I'm Hailey."

"Hailey's an old friend," I say. "We haven't seen each other in several years. She happens to be Sam's granddaughter."

Hailey scoots over, allowing me to move over so that Lex can sit next to me.

"You look lovely today, Dr. Kentucky," Frank says.

He's right. She's stunning in a simple black dress that hugs her perfect figure. Her green eyes sparkle and her fair complexion is nicely contrasted by her dark attire. "How's my favorite patient?" she asks Frank.

"Peachy." Frank grins. "I'm not here alone, you know. I have a hot date."

"Oh yeah?"

"Yep."

"Well, good for you. So do I." She pats my thigh and then leans forward and looks across my chest. "So how far back do you and Ben go?" she asks Hailey. "He's so hush-hush about his mysterious past." Her voice is playful.

"Hailey was—is—a friend of the family," I say before Hailey has a chance to answer. My palms are damp with sweat.

"Why, hello, Dr. Kentucky!" Boop has returned. "What a pleasant surprise!"

"Betty's my date," Frank informs Lex.

"I trust Benji has introduced you to my niece," Boop says to Lex.

"Your niece?" Lex says. "I'm so sorry to hear about your father."

Boy, you're quick on the uptake, I think while Frank scratches his head. "Wait a minute." Frank turns to Boop. "So if you're her aunt and Sam was her grandfather, then that makes you Sam's daughter!"

"Or I could be his daughter-in-law," Boop counters. "Or it could be that my sister married Sam's son."

Now I scratch my head.

"True, but I happen to know that Sam didn't have any sons," Lex replies. "Which leaves only one possibility."

"A very impressive display of deductive reasoning," the Professor says. I didn't notice he had taken a seat behind us. He removes his light-green sports coat, revealing a T-shirt with a picture of the Beach Boys plastered on his chest. He turns to Hailey. "I don't believe we've met."

"Hailey, meet Jerry." Lex makes the introduction. "Hailey knew Ben before we inherited him, and as you just overheard, she also happens to be Sam's granddaughter as well as Betty's niece."

"Pleasure to meet you, Hailey," the Professor says, "although I wish it were under better circumstances."

Boop, still standing in the aisle, is about to say something when Marvin and Jane arrive arm in arm. Frank quickly gets to his feet and grabs Boop's elbow. "Hello, Marvin!" he says cheerfully. "I see you managed to find a date."

"Hello, everybody." Marvin and Jane take seats next to the Professor.

Frank puts his arm around Betty's shoulders and smirks. Betty gently pulls away and says to the Professor, "Whose heart did you break, Jerry? Why aren't you escorting anybody today?"

"I couldn't make up my mind. But as it turns out, I think things are going to work out perfectly." He smiles at Hailey. "It seems to me that this young lady is without an escort, and from what I know of Ben, there's no way he can possibly handle two beautiful women. I'd be delighted if you would do me the honor."

"Of course!" Hailey says. She changes rows and sits behind me, next to the Professor. Frank and Betty also take their seats while Maybelle finishes the last few chords of "Good Vibrations." Jane makes her way to the podium to begin the service.

"Good morning, everyone. We are here today to celebrate the life of a member of our community…" She goes on to say how much Sam will be missed and relates a few humorous stories. As she wraps up her little speech she says, "And now, some people who were close to Sam will say a few words."

Frank escorts Boop to the podium, taking his sweet time to ensure that everybody in the audience—especially Marvin—has ample opportunity to realize that yes, indeed, he is Betty's escort.

When they finally reach the stage, I am surprised to see Boop step aside and Frank take the microphone.

"Uh, hello, everybody. The committee asked me to say a few things about Sam. I don't know how many of you know this, but me and Sam served together in the Korean War. I guess you could call us war buddies. We lost touch over the years, but then somehow we ended up in the same old people's—er—I mean retirement home. Anyhow, I guess there's no shame in getting old, but Sam didn't like it much. He used to joke about how his ears and nose kept growing while the rest of his body was shrinking. He even kept a chart. He would measure his nose every month and keep track of its progress. He measured other things too, but this isn't the time or the place to discuss that. You can ask me later if you want to know what his stats were.

"Before Sam started losing it—I guess it's okay for me to say that 'cause it's true—there were two things he loved to talk about. One was the Beach Boys. The other was his Bible. I tell you, I made up for about ten years' worth of missing Sunday school just by listening to Sam yack about the Bible. He sure was excited about that book. I figure I'll probably get a free ticket into heaven just for putting up with him talking about it so much.

"Sam wasn't perfect. He once told me that he made a lot of mistakes. But even though he had shortcomings, in my opinion he was a good man. I used to complain a lot about how he was always playing his music too loud, but now I think I'm gonna miss the sound of the Beach Boys coming from down the hall. So long, Sam."

Frank steps aside, allowing Boop to take the microphone. Several large easels are on stage, but they face away from the audience. Boop nods at Frank, who begins to turn the posters around, revealing several enlarged photographs of Sam taken at different stages of his life.

"Sam was my father," Boop begins.

A murmur spreads through the audience.

"When I first came to Heritage Gardens, it was because I wanted to try to make things right with my dad. You see, we hadn't spoken in years. That was partly my fault, but mostly his. Even so, for a long time that's the way I wanted it. I'm not saying I was right or wrong. Eventually I reached the point where I wanted to try to make amends, but when I got here he was so far gone that he didn't know who I was. I'm finding out, even today, that I didn't know who he was either.

"I'd like to read you a letter that my father wrote before he began losing his memory. My niece found it today, wedged in his Bible. Believe it or not, my father wrote this letter to all of you. He wanted it to be read at his funeral.

Dear fellow retirees and future honorees of Heritage Gardens Memorial Services,

I guess my turn has finally arrived. Instead of sitting in the audience wondering what the memorial committee has in store for today's service, I'm the dead guy in the casket. I knew this day was coming.

I'm writing this letter because lately I've begun to realize that my memory is fading. Pretty soon I'll be confined to my wheelchair, drooling, and randomly asking people if they know how to speak Spanish. I'm not sure why I'll do that. Probably just to mess with your minds.

But before I pass the point of no return, I wanted to take advantage of one of my more lucid moments to beg you all not to make the same mistakes I've made. I have a lot of regrets, and I don't have much to be proud of. I took me forever to realize what's important in life. I didn't invest in my relationships, and now I'm paying the price. It's too late for me, but it's not too late for all of you. Don't wait another minute. As soon as this service is over, please start making your relationships right—your relationships with family, with friends, and, most important, with God. That's all I have to say.

Betty pauses for a moment. "When I first read this, I had a hard time believing they were my father's words. But now that I've read them to you, I don't think I really need to add anything to what he wanted to say. He wouldn't have wanted a long, drawn-out memorial service. He would have been more interested in a barbecue and an outdoors Beach Boys concert." She reaches into her pocket, pulls out her mobile phone, and dials a number. "Hit it, boys."

On cue, someone opens the back doors to Assembly Hall, and the sound of live music can be heard coming from the parking lot. Another murmur spreads through the audience.

"Go on out there and enjoy!" Boop says.

"Is it really the Beach Boys?" Marvin says. "I didn't know they were still alive."

"Most of them are," I say. "But I find it hard to believe they're actually in the parking lot."

Sure enough, the sound of "Good Vibrations," this time played correctly, drifts into the building. The audience chatters excitedly as we exit and make our way toward the music. A makeshift stage has been erected in the grassy area next to the koi pond and a live band is playing with enthusiasm. A few dozen tables are set up, and it looks like a catering company has brought in several barbecues. I'm glad there will be something other than Boop's potato salad on the menu.

"How in the world did you manage to get them here?" I ask Jane, who is walking nearby.

"It's not really them, but close enough," Jane replies.

I sit at a picnic table and watch as the Professor and Hailey groove to the music. Even from this distance I imagine I can smell her familiar scent. I still can't believe she's here.

"She was more than just a friend of the family, wasn't she?" Lex takes me by surprise. I thought she was off getting something to drink.

"What? No. I just wasn't expecting to see her—that's all."

"You're not a very good liar, Ben."

"Why are you doing this?" I say.

"Because I don't like to play games. I don't like to waste time and energy either. I'm not asking you to tell me your whole life story or to reveal all your secrets, but I do need you to be honest with me. What it all boils down to is this: I kind of like you and I get the feeling that you kind of like me back. I'm not asking you to commit to a serious relationship, and I'm not giving you an ultimatum. I just want to know if I'm wasting my time." She gives me a crooked grin. "I've watched you watch her all morning. You can't keep your eyes off her. I know enough to know that you have some unresolved business with that woman, and I'm fine with that. I wouldn't want to get in the way. But please, whatever you do, don't keep me guessing."

"It's not what you think, Lex."

"Then what is it?"

"It's complicated. She's not supposed to be here. I left her in the past."

"It doesn't work that way."

"It was working. I was making it work."

"Listen, Ben. I'll make a deal with you. You obviously need some time to sort things out. I've got time. You've got my number. Give me a call when you're ready. I'm not going to wait forever. Just make sure you get back to me before someone else comes along and sweeps me off my feet. It's only happened once in my life, so you probably have several years." She stands.

I don't say anything.

"I'll see you around, Ben. Don't be a stranger."

I let her walk away. Somehow my gaze finds Hailey again. She's twenty yards away, talking to Betty. I glance back in the direction Lex is heading and discover she's looking back at me. Her expression betrays the fact that she has again witnessed my fleeting look at Hailey. She raises her brow, cocks her head to the side, and then turns away again.

The next thing I know, the Professor is sitting next to me. "If I had a snapshot of her facial expression, I could spend hours trying to deduce the unspoken message she just sent you," he says. "Women are fascinating creatures, aren't they?"

"They certainly are wired differently than we are," I say. "Somehow I think they're put together properly and we're missing some key ingredient."

"If you look at the genetic differences, we're the ones with an extra chromosome," he says.

"It is true that we have a Y chromosome and they only have Xs," I say, "but we sacrificed an X to get our Y, and a Y is actually smaller than an X."

"So you're saying our Y is a defective X?"

"It is a plausible theory," I say, "and unfortunately, it's difficult to make the same argument in the other direction. For example, I would have a hard time convincing you that their two Xs are actually two mutated Ys."

"True, but you could say that they're missing a Y."

"That argument still doesn't hold because chromosomes are supposed to be paired and similar. In other words, if a Y chromosome is so important, we should have two of them instead of an X and a Y. Women have two Xs, which are paired and similar—as they should be. Like it or not, the Y is the oddball."

"That's strangely disconcerting," he says. "So men are, in actuality, defective women."

"Pretty much."

"So how did you manage to blow it with her?"

"She can see right through me. I think she understands what's going on inside my head better than I do."

"What are you going to do about that?"

"I'm going to reorganize my books."

"What?"

"I'm going to reorganize my books."

"I heard you the first time. I was hoping for an explanation."

"I don't have one. I just know that that's what I need to do."

I count paces back to my apartment. But this time I utilize a new system. I count in sequences that end in multiples of my age. When I get to thirty-eight, I start again and count up to seventy-six. After that, I go up to 114, and so on. By the time I reach my apartment, I realize I don't much like this new system. I think I'll stick with primes. Change is seldom a good thing in my book.

Speaking of books, I'm eager to tackle the task at hand. What I'm about to undertake is by far the most challenging assignment I've managed to create for myself. I'm tempted to say it's impossible, but I cannot be certain until I try. There is one thing I do know: successful completion of this task will consume every ounce of my concentration for the remainder of the day, and a distraction is precisely what I need.

I have decided to organize my books so that there is a prime number occupying each shelf. Furthermore, all of the words in the titles on each shelf must add up to a prime number. Moreover, the sum of all the letters within the words of the titles must be prime. If that isn't enough, the grand total of all the pages contained within the volumes on each shelf must be prime.

I almost stopped at these four requirements until I realized that my number of requirements is my least favorite number. I must therefore think of a fifth requirement. Here's a good one: every fourth book on each shelf must contain a prime number of words and a prime number of letters in the title.

I tackle my chore with enthusiasm. A rush of energy courses through my nerves as the disturbing events of the day fade into the background. I must devise a strategy to accomplish my goal. First, I should isolate books that fulfill my fifth requirement. *The Mill on the Floss* by George Eliot meets it. So do *Forrest Gump*, *The Talisman*, *Pride and Prejudice*, and *Sense and Sensibility*.

Soon I have collected a small stack of books that contain a prime number of words and letters in the title. I have a total of five wide bookshelves, each with five shelves. There are millions of combinations of how I could arrange all my books. Certainly at least one will be compatible with my five requirements.

The hours pass quickly as I count, stack, rearrange, sum, and rearrange some more. I'm completely lost in my own little world.

The task becomes more difficult as the shelves fill because with each successive shelf I have fewer options for which books I can put on them. When I eventually reach the final shelf, the task will become exponentially more difficult because I will probably have to rearrange shelves that are already complete so that all the shelves fulfill my requirements.

Before I know it the sun has set and I've overlooked dinner. That doesn't matter. I'm on the second to last shelf and I sense that I will triumph. But I'm beyond exhaustion. Perhaps I can let myself take a little break. Just a short nap. I leave the remaining books where they lie and stretch out on the couch. My head hits the cushion and I fade into a dreamless sleep.

CHAPTER 14

A phone rings somewhere. I sit up and try to orient myself. What time is it? What am I doing on the couch? It rings again. I find the clock on the wall. Three a.m. Who's calling at this ungodly hour? Must be a wrong number. I stumble over to the wall and unplug the cord from the phone jack. Hopefully I can get another couple hours of sleep. I go into my bedroom and crash on the bed.

Fifteen minutes later, just as I'm almost asleep again, I'm rudely awakened by someone pounding on my door. I can't unplug that, so I open it to find Marvin.

"Marvin? What's wrong?"

"I tried to call, but it just rang and rang."

"Sorry. I unplugged it. Come on in."

"Mr. Peterson tried to kill himself."

"What?"

"He overdosed on his blood pressure medication. They took him away in an ambulance."

"Does anybody know why? Who found him?" As far as I know, Junior lives alone and doesn't have any friends or family. I can't imagine who would've found him.

"After he took the pills he panicked and called Betty. She called 911."

"Did he say why he did it?"

"He wrote a letter. Betty has it."

"Is anybody with him now?"

"Jane is on her way to the hospital."

"My goodness, I hope he pulls through this."

"I think he will. Anyway, several of us are getting together to have a meeting to discuss Peterson's letter. We would like you to be there."

"What's going on?"

"I can tell you this much. It's not good."

Six of us are gathered in Boop's living room, including Hailey, the Professor, Marvin, and don't ask me why, but Frank is here too. Boop is a mess. Hailey is trying her best to comfort her while Frank paces back and forth in the entryway. I know something's terribly wrong because he's using his walker in a proper manner. When he catches me staring at him he says, "Cut me a break. I'm feeling a little unsteady." The Professor, clothed in bright-purple pajamas and a baby-blue bathrobe, is silently reading Junior's suicide note. He shakes his head and clucks his tongue.

"What's the situation?" I say.

"We're in a pickle," Marvin replies.

"A pickle?!" Frank says. "This isn't a pickle. This is a one-way ticket to bankruptcy, foreclosure, and a big 'screw you' to all the residents at Heritage Gardens. That's what this is."

"There might be a way out," Marvin says.

"You need to wake up and smell the foul odor of harsh reality. My son's a lawyer. I know about this stuff. We're screwed."

"Somebody fill me in," I say.

"Well, it looks like our manager has an Internet gambling problem," says the Professor. "He liquidated all his cash assets and squandered it playing online poker. In order to recoup his losses, he refinanced Heritage Gardens, took all the equity, and poured it into investment properties in Costa Rica. He figured he could double his money there, but it was all a big scam. It's gone."

"How much?"

"Eighteen million dollars."

At the sound of this, Boop starts crying again. "I'm sorry," she sobs, "I didn't know. I really didn't know."

"And now Heritage Gardens doesn't have enough revenue to pay the mortgage?" I say.

"Apparently not," Marvin replies.

"We're screwed!" Frank hollers. "Screwed, I tell you."

Betty's phone rings. Hailey answers. When she hangs up she says, "That was Jane. She's at the hospital. They pumped Peterson's stomach and they're going to observe him overnight, but he's going to be okay."

"He going to have a lot of explaining to do when he gets back," Frank says, shaking his fist.

"What's done is done," Marvin says. "We need to find a way out of this mess."

"Tell me more about the Costa Rica thing," I say.

"It's all my fault." Betty is a little more composed now that she's heard Junior isn't going to die. "I didn't know it was a scam. I didn't know he was going to put so much money into it."

"What exactly happened?" I ask.

"Well, when I moved in here I mentioned the fact that I had invested my own money into this plan, through my son, Marty. Mr. Peterson asked me for my son's contact information, so I gave it to him. One thing led to another, and the next thing I knew, he had already invested. I had no idea how much. We just found out last night that it was all a huge scam involving a big drug cartel."

"That little rat!" Frank hollers from across the room.

"That's uncalled for, Frank," Marvin says.

"Why don't you shut your piehole," Frank says. "Your girlfriend helped swindle all of us."

"She didn't know."

"I think we're straying from the subject," says the Professor, who has been pretty quiet. "We need a plan."

"Anybody got eighteen million dollars?" Frank says.

"Maybe we could raise it," Marvin says.

"Yeah, right." Frank kicks his walker, winces, and then kicks it again.

"We probably don't need to come up with that much cash," I say. "We just need to have enough money to pay the creditors before somebody decides to shut this place down and sell the real estate."

"I wonder how much cash we're talking about?" the Professor says.

"Only Peterson would know."

"You mean there isn't a board of directors who runs this place?" Hailey says.

"Nope. Peterson pretty much runs the show. He makes all the decisions and handles the finances."

"Which is exactly why we're in such deep you-know-what." Frank shoves his walker against the wall with a clatter.

"Careful, you're going to scuff up the walls," Marvin says.

"Assuming the only source of income is from monthly fees paid by residents here," Hailey says, "you'll just have to figure out how much more income you need each month, and raise everybody's rent accordingly."

"But the rent is already pretty steep," Marvin says. "I don't think the residents can afford an increase."

"Finally he says something that makes sense," Frank mutters. "How much more a month are we talking about?"

Everyone looks at me.

"You expect me to know?"

"Give us a guess," the Professors says.

"We need Peterson," I say. "I don't have the foggiest idea."

"How many residents live here?" asks Hailey.

"One hundred and twenty-six."

"And what's the rent?"

The Professor gives her a rundown of the different fees paid by the residents.

She thinks for a second then says, "This is just a loose calculation based on very little information, but assuming it's a standard thirty-year loan with a good interest rate, you're probably looking at an additional five hundred dollars a month per resident."

"Holy moly!" Frank says. "There's no way anybody here can afford that!"

"Like I said, that's just a guess based on very little information," Hailey replies.

"Are you a CPA?" says the Professor.

"No. Nothing like that. I just like to run numbers in my head. Ben is right. We need Peterson to provide us with details so we can get a better idea how deep this hole is and how quickly it might cave in."

CHAPTER 15

The past twenty-four hours were painful. As soon as Junior got back from the hospital Hailey and I began the arduous task of sorting through the mess he's made. Her knowledge of financial issues has been a godsend. We also had several powwows with Marvin and the Professor. Frank was around too, but he mostly wore on nerves that were already frayed. When we finally reached the point where we figured we had a pretty good handle on the true nature of the current state of affairs, we decided the next step should be to hold a community meeting at Assembly Hall, which is where we are now.

Somehow I got elected to lead this meeting. The rumor mill has been working furiously, and as a result, I'm facing a room full of geriatrics whose blood pressures are off the charts. The purpose of this gathering is to set the record straight and hopefully brainstorm a solution to the problem at hand. Everybody healthy enough to be here is present, including Boop, who is determined to do everything within her power to undo this mess because she feels responsible—although I'm certain Junior would have found a way to get us to this point without Boop's involvement.

The excited chatter quickly abates as I approach the podium. The feedback from the cheap microphone echoes through the hall. I clear my throat.

"Ladies and gentlemen, I'm sure you are all aware that as a community, we are in a bit of trouble. The purpose of this meeting is not to place blame or to vent anger, but to inform you all of the nature of the problem and hopefully begin the process of finding a solution."

"I heard that Peterson stole all our money!" someone yells from the audience. "Is that true?"

"Mr. Peterson doesn't have access to your personal accounts and he hasn't stolen any money from any of you," I say. "What he has managed to do is misuse the finances of his business to the point where he can no longer afford to run Heritage Gardens. Unless we can find some alternative source of income, Mr. Peterson will be forced to sell this facility."

"Fine by me!" someone shouts. "We could use better management."

The crowd murmurs in approval.

"If Heritage Gardens is sold, it probably won't be to an entity that wishes to run a retirement facility," I respond. "This property would be more valuable to developers. If Mr. Peterson is forced to sell, you will all lose your homes."

Approval now turns to angry chatter.

Speaking above the noise, I continue, "In order to save this facility, we project that Heritage Gardens will have to increase its monthly revenue by close to sixty thousand dollars."

The audience gasps.

"I know that sounds like a lot," I say, "but we figure that with cost-saving measures we can bring that figure down to fifty thousand. Since our only source of revenue is the monthly rent paid by residents, it looks like the deficit can be overcome by a raise in monthly rent in the amount somewhere between four and five hundred dollars."

"That's crazy!" someone shouts. I glance over and see that it's Frank. He's shaking his fist in the air. "We can't afford that!"

"That's why we're having this meeting. We need to brainstorm and come up with creative ways to earn money." I glance at my watch. "It's nine o'clock. I'd like you all to divide into discussion groups of no more than six people. Each group should appoint one person as a spokesperson. Jot down your ideas. We will reconvene here in an hour and each spokesperson will present their group's ideas. I think that will be a good starting point."

I retreat from the podium as the crowd breaks into a confusing mass. Slowly they filter out of the building to find private places to hold their discussions. Hailey approaches me from the side of the room, where she had been standing during my speech. "You did well," she says.

I shrug my shoulders. Out of the corner of my eye I think I see the back of Lex's head as she exits the room, but she's gone before I can be certain it was her.

"It will be interesting to see what they come up with." Hailey takes a seat in the front row. "Come sit." She pats the chair next to her. "You look exhausted."

I collapse into the folding chair. She's right. I haven't felt this drained since my days in general surgery residency.

"My aunt feels terrible about all this," she says. "I'm worried about her. She's always been on edge, so to speak. I'm afraid she's on the verge of a nervous breakdown."

"Yeah."

"Well, I promised my aunt I would stick around until we get this mess ironed out. So what I'm saying is I'll be around for a while. Maybe we could get together and really talk."

"What about your job?"

"I'm not in pharmaceuticals anymore. I couldn't stomach the greed so I started a wedding photography business. I have a partner now. She can run things without me just fine. I can take as much time as I want."

"I'm glad you can be here to support your aunt," I say. "It's good to have family around at times like these."

"Yes, it is." She rests her hand on my forearm.

A chill runs up my arm. "I need to use the restroom before these people all come back." I pull my arm away and stand.

"And I need to find my aunt." Hailey stands as well.

"I'm sure you'll find her with Marvin and Jerry," I say over my shoulder as I head for the door. "They're good guys. I'm sure they're looking out for her."

The restroom in Assembly Hall is one of my least favorite restrooms at Heritage Gardens, but I desperately need to wash my hands. My Lamax bar soap arrived in the mail the other day. I carry a sliver of it in a Ziploc bag in my pocket.

I burst through the swinging door and make a beeline across the ghastly tiled floor toward the sink, fumbling to open my bag of soap along the way. I don't wait for the water to heat up. I vigorously scrub the spot where Hailey just touched my arm, but despite my efforts, I can still feel her soft touch. No matter how hard I scrub I still feel it. Somewhere in the back of my mind I know this is an exercise in futility, but I scrub even harder. I continue to scrub until my soap is completely dissolved away.

I turn off the water and stare at myself in the mirror. I shake my head at the pathetic man staring back at me. Get a grip. Look at yourself. You're a mess.

I know I'm a mess, but I don't know what to do with myself.

Just let it go. Let the past stay in the past.

But it's not right. The way I feel about her isn't right.

You can't change your feelings.

Yes, I can.

No, you can't.

Yes, I can.

Look at me. I'm talking to myself. I really need to get a grip. How long have I been in here? I need to get back to the meeting.

I'm again onstage holding the microphone in my clean hands as the residents find their seats. "All right, everybody, it's your turn. Please do your best to be brief so that each group has an opportunity to be heard. This is not the time for debate, but rather a chance to get our ideas out in the open. Who would like to go first?"

"I would!" Frank is already out of his seat and heading toward the stage. He's in such a rush to be first, he doesn't bother to bring his walker with him.

"Okay, Frank. Which group are you representing?"

"I'm representing myself," he says as he's halfway up the stairs.

"You weren't part of a group?"

"I don't need a group to have ideas." He snatches the microphone from my hand.

I shrug and step aside.

"Hello, everyone. I'd like to start by saying that even though this idea wasn't exactly my own, it's still a good one. I know it's good because I saw it in a movie once. I don't remember all the details exactly, but I'm pretty sure it was a true story. The movie took place in England or somewhere over there in Europe where they all have funny accents. There were all these old ladies and they needed money for something—I don't remember what—so they got this idea to pose nude for a calendar. Now, I know what you're thinking. Everybody in the movie thought they were nuts too. I mean, who wants to look at a bunch of naked old ladies? But they made the calendar anyway, and it sold like hotcakes. They made a ton of money. Now maybe we don't really have to do naked pictures. Maybe we could do a swimsuit edition or something. But we need the money, and if nudity sells, then by golly, I say we go for it!"

A murmur of disapproval spreads through the audience.

"It's a good idea, I tell you. I saw it in a movie!" Frank hollers.

I step in and take back the microphone. "Thanks, Frank. Remember, this isn't a forum for debate. All ideas are welcome as long as they are legal and meet with the general approval of the residents here at Heritage Gardens. I suppose that when the time comes to take action, we will take a vote to settle any disputes. A simple majority will rule."

Frank mumbles something as he makes his way back to his seat. Meanwhile, Maybelle takes the stage.

"My group came up with several creative ideas. The one we were most excited about was the creation of a gift shop on campus. Many of the residents are quite talented and crafty. We have quilters, painters, sculptors, basket weavers, potters, furniture makers, and I'm sure there's even more than what I just mentioned. People could donate their crafts and artwork to be sold in the store, volunteers could staff it, and all the income could go towards paying off our debt."

"That's a fine idea, Maybelle," I say.

Next, a woman named Jackie approaches the podium. I don't know her very well, but I've heard she was quite a successful business woman before she retired. Usually she keeps to herself, so I am surprised she is stepping forward.

"Good afternoon, everyone. I believe Maybelle's group was on the right track. Believe it or not, so was Frank. Since we don't have the financial means as a group to fund the repayment of this debt, we need to find some sort of goods or service that the public desires and that we can provide. While the gift shop is a wonderful idea, how many people can we expect to come through there on a daily basis? We need to find a way to reach a broader market, and there is a tool that is pretty simple to use. I'm talking about the Internet.

Frank's idea with the calendar is good too. Those calendars didn't sell because they were sexual; they sold because they were humorous. Perhaps we could find a way to merge these ideas. Something like handmade greeting cards that we could sell over the Internet. Everyone could contribute. Our artists could do the printing and artwork. Anyone could contribute the subject matter for the different cards. And there would be a lot of sorting and shipping that would need to take place. It wouldn't be easy to pull off, and I'm not sure how profitable it would be, but it might just work."

Sounds of approval spread through the audience.

"Thanks, Jackie," I say. "Who's next?"

Nobody stirs.

"Come on, I know there must have been other ideas out there. Anyone?"

Still no response.

"This isn't the time to be shy, people."

"The only idea my group could come up with was to have a bake sale," someone shouts from the back row.

"All we could think of was a rummage sale," someone else says.

"Well, those ideas are a good start," I say, trying to sound enthusiastic, "but Jackie is right. We need to come up with a strategy that will provide a steady, and hopefully growing, income. Something beyond just a one-time sale or event."

"Hey, I got another idea!" Frank is on his feet and heading toward the stage again.

"You already got a chance," someone yells.

"I don't see anyone else up here," Frank says over his shoulder as he climbs the steps. I reluctantly yield him the microphone again.

"Maybe we could earn it all in one shot," he says, slightly short of breath.

"Now you're talking crazy," someone yells.

"Well, there is a way we could earn a bunch of money all at once. I say we all pitch in ten bucks and play the lottery. We could greatly increase our chances of winning with such a large pool. You never know. If we won, it would solve the problem and we could all have hot tubs installed in our rooms!"

"Sit down, Frank," another voice calls. "That's not a good idea."

"Hey, this is supposed to be a friendly exchange of ideas," Franks snaps. "As a matter of fact, we don't even need to play the lottery. We just need to track down the yahoo who won it last week. The bozo still hasn't claimed his prize. What a jackass. They're holding a ticket worth twenty-three million dollars and they haven't cashed it! If they don't want the money, then at least they could give it to us. It's probably one of you morons. Go back to your rooms and look at your tickets again. I know you all play. This time use your magnifying glasses and make sure you're reading the numbers right."

"Okay, Frank, that's enough," I say. "Let's try to be polite." I take the microphone back and usher him off the stage. "Anyone else have anything to contribute? This is your last chance."

Nobody responds, but I don't care. Something has just clicked in my memory. I never even bothered to check if my numbers won. In fact, I'm not even sure where my ticket is. It's probably still in the back pocket of the pants I was wearing the night I bought it.

"Okay, if that's all, then I guess we can end this meeting."

"Wait." Betty stands. "I have something I'd like to say."

"Certainly, Miss Boestra," I reply. A barely audible murmur of disapproval rumbles through the audience. By now, every single resident of Heritage Gardens has heard about Boop's role in Junior's downfall. It's unfortunate that she's shouldering this much of the blame.

Boop takes the stage. "As you all know, it was I who told Mr. Peterson about the investment opportunity that turned out to be a big scam. I don't blame you all for being angry with me," Betty says into the microphone, trying valiantly to maintain her composure. "I feel just terrible for what happened. If you all lose your homes on account of me, why, I think I'll just die with despair. I've been trying to think of some way that I could help undo what I've done. If I had any money I'd gladly donate it all, but you see, I lost all my savings in this scam too." She wipes a tear from her cheek.

"Anyway, if there's any way I can help any of you, please let me know."

The audience is silent as she leaves the stage.

I rush to my apartment in such a hurry that I forget to count paces. I breeze past the stack of yet to be shelved books on my floor and head straight for my basket of dirty laundry, which, thank goodness, I haven't had a chance to wash since I purchased that lottery ticket. I thrust my hand into the back pocket of the pants I wore that night, certain I put the ticket there, but it's empty. I check the other pockets, but they're empty as well. I dump the contents of my hamper on the floor and meticulously go through all the pockets of all my clothes, but my search yields only the Walmart receipt from the purchase of my first striped shirt.

Before I waste any more time searching, I decide to log onto the Internet to find out what the winning numbers were. I don't actually need my ticket because I remember exactly which numbers I chose: two, three, five, seven, eleven, and thirteen.

I scroll down the page on the California Super Lotto website and finally find what I'm looking for.

My heart skips a few beats and then slams into gear like a racecar.

After the adrenaline rush subsides enough for me to once again put two coherent thoughts together, I sit down on my couch, close my eyes, and focus all my mental powers on recreating every single move I made after that ticket came into my possession. I distinctly recall folding it in half and slipping it into my back pocket between my wallet and my right butt cheek. I'm certain that's what I did with it.

Maybe I actually somehow crammed it into my wallet.

I take out my wallet, give it a thorough search, sigh in frustration, and continue to mentally retrace my steps. The next event that involved my twenty-three-million-dollar butt cheek was when I got my wallet out to pay for dinner. And later, when I got home, I took my wallet out again and set it on my nightstand. My ticket could have slipped out of my pocket on either of these two occasions.

I keep my apartment in meticulous order, so I would definitely have encountered my stray lottery ticket if it were lying around here. Rather than waste my time searching my apartment, I decide to go to the restaurant. I walk so I can retrace the exact route Lex and I took that night when we came home. I scan the ground as I go, just in case it slipped out of my pocket along the way.

When I reach the restaurant, I head straight for the booth Lex and I shared. To my dismay, it is occupied by a middle-aged couple. Their drinks look fresh and I don't spy any appetizers on the table yet. They could be here for another hour or two. There's no way I'm going to wait for them to finish their entire meal while my ticket sits under their table. What if they spill something and destroy it?

"Pardon me; I hate to disturb your lunch, but I was wondering if you would mind if I checked under your table for an item I might have left behind."

"Sure, no problem," the man says.

"Actually, we do mind," the woman says.

"Honey—"

"Don't you 'honey' me." The woman raises her voice. "I've had it up to here with this narcissistic, instant-gratification mentality everybody has nowadays. Here we are, trying to enjoy a nice meal away from the kids, and some impatient guy comes along and interrupts our private conversation so he can conduct a search. Why can't he wait until we're done? The world doesn't revolve around him."

"It'll only take a second," the man says.

"Well, I'm not moving. And if he looks under our table while I'm sitting here, I swear I'll press charges for sexual harassment."

"You'll have to excuse my wife's behavior," the man says with an embarrassed laugh. "She's never like this. You just happened to pick the absolute worst moment to interrupt our conversation."

"Don't talk about me like I'm not here!" The woman's voice gets louder. Heads begin to turn. "You men are all the same. All of you! Egocentric, thoughtless pigs."

I mumble an apology and begin to back away.

"What are you looking for?" the man says as he feels under the table with his foot.

"Don't you dare ignore me!" the woman shouts.

"Don't make a scene, honey."

"I don't have a choice! If I don't make a scene, I'll never get the message through your thick skull that things are not okay with us. Did you hear that? Our marriage has been on the brink of ruin for months! Stop pretending like everything's all right!"

"Please forgive me," I say. "I'm sorry. I'll come back later." I make a hasty retreat to the parking lot and sit on a brick retaining wall in view of the restaurant entrance. I wonder if they will stay for their meal. Probably not. It seems I just managed to serve as the catalyst that is going to propel yet another troubled marriage to its final destruction. Why is it that so many married couples are unhappy?

I suppose if I knew the answer to that question I wouldn't need my winning lottery ticket. I could make a fortune selling the secret to marital bliss.

I don't have to wait long for the couple to emerge from the restaurant. The woman first, followed soon after by her bewildered husband. I dash inside and head straight for the booth despite angry rumbles from patrons who recognize me as the cause of their recent disturbance.

I get down on my hands and knees and thrust my head under the tablecloth. Stale crumbs and halfway decomposed bits of salad

leaves serve as evidence that the floor underneath the table probably hasn't been swept in over a week.

My heart jumps into my throat when I spot a piece of paper
folded in half. It's the right size, and nothing else catches my eye. I
snatch it up and scoot out from under the table. I don't even cringe
when my left hand splats in something slimy.

I stand erect and examine the paper in the dim light. The words
Super Lotto scream at me. I nearly pass out from all the noise in my
head. Somehow I manage to make my way outside.

The walk back to my apartment is a blur. Or did I run? It doesn't
matter. I'm here. With the ticket still clutched in my right hand. I
need to find my inhaler because I'm starting to wheeze.

Just as I find it, my doorbell rings. In my excitement, I didn't
shut the door all the way. Frank views this as an open invitation
and lets himself in. "Ben, I'm glad you're home. We need to talk."
He shuffles across my entryway and heads for my kitchen. "You got
any booze?"

"Now's not a good time, Frank."

"What—you got a woman here or something?" He chuckles and
opens my fridge. "Hey, there's nothin' in here! What's the point of
having a refrigerator if you don't keep anything in it?"

"Seriously, Frank."

He slams the refrigerator door and looks at me. He's about to
say something but his jaw snaps shut and he examines me closely.
"Something's up," he says. "I used to be real good at reading people.
Back when I was selling encyclopedias I could always tell within
two seconds whether someone was gonna say yes or no. I might not
be as sharp as I used to be, but I know something major is going on
inside that strange head of yours."

"Could you come back tomorrow?"

"I'm not going anywhere till you tell me what's going on." He
shuffles over to my kitchen table and plops down on one of my
chairs. In the process of doing so, he scoots the chair so that one of

the legs rests on the grout line of the tile floor. I hate that. Either all of the legs need to be on a grout line, or none of them.

"It's none of your business, Frank."

"What's that in your hand?"

"Nothing." I move it behind my back.

His nostrils flare and his eyes narrow. "I'm no Sherlock Holmes, but it seems to me that you've got a death grip on what appears to be a lottery ticket."

"What's so important that you walked all the way over here to talk to me about?" I try to change the subject. "Why didn't you just call?"

"Let me see that thing." Frank is out of the chair.

I back away.

"That's it! Isn't it?!" Frank shouts. "Holy guacamole! You've got the winning ticket! Why the heck didn't you cash it in yet?"

"Calm down, Frank. The last thing I need is for you to burst a brain aneurysm right here in my apartment."

"Let me see it."

"I already lost it once. I think I'll hang onto it."

"Well, did you at least sign the back of it?"

"What do you mean?"

"Jeez, don't you know anything? There's a place for you to sign your name on the back. That way, if you do lose it, nobody else can claim it because your signature is on it."

"Oh. I guess I'd better sign it then."

"You're darn right you should!"

I grab a pen from next to the phone and carefully sign the ticket.

"Holy moly," Frank says. "Watcha gonna do now?"

We both stare at the twenty-three-million-dollar piece of paper as it lies face down on my kitchen table.

"I don't know," I say, halfway in a trance. "I bet there's some sort of hotline I'm supposed to call or something."

"I wouldn't do that if I were you. As soon as you call, the media will find out and then you'll have the paparazzi chasing after you and it will all be a huge mess. You need to keep this as quiet as possible." He peers intently at me as I read the fine print on the back of the ticket.

"It says here that all cash prizes over six hundred dollars need to be claimed at this address in Sacramento. Am I supposed to mail this in?"

"Are you insane?!" Frank throws his hands in the air. "What are you gonna do? Send it by certified mail and insure it for twenty-three-million dollars just in case it gets lost?"

"I guess I need to bring it to Sacramento myself."

"Now you're talking. When do we leave?"

"I'm pretty sure I can handle this myself, Frank. But please, try to keep your mouth shut while I'm gone. I don't want the rumors to start flying until I cash this thing in."

"I want to come too."

"Sorry, Frank. It's a long drive."

"If you don't let me come, I'm gonna tell everyone. I'll call the media and tell them that the guy who won the jackpot is a janitor who lost his medical license. They'll go crazy over a story like this. They'll never leave you alone."

I sigh with resignation. "Fine. You win."

"Great! We'll take Jerry's car because your truck is a piece of crap. I'm gonna invite Betty too. This will be a blast!" He scurries out the door.

"Don't forget your walker, Frank."

"Oh, yeah. Shoot. When do you wanna take off?"

"First thing in the morning. I hardly slept at all last night and it's a long drive to Sacramento."

"Great!"

I shut the door, then head to the phone and dial Marvin's number.

"Hello?"

"Hey, Marvin, it's Ben."

"What's going on?"

"Would you like to take a road trip?"

"What?"

"I'm holding a winning lottery ticket in my hand and need to go to Sacramento to cash it in."

"You're not serious."

"I wouldn't joke about this."

"It wouldn't be a funny joke," he says. "Count me in."

"Do you want to hear what else isn't funny?" I say.

"Tell me."

"Frank is coming too."

"You're right, that isn't funny."

"I think Betty might join us as well," I say.

"Now that might turn out to be a little funny. When do we leave?"

"I figured I'd try to catch some sleep before we leave. How about five-thirty?"

"Sounds like a plan. I like the idea of hitting the road early."

I also call the Professor, who jumps at the opportunity for a road trip. He's happy to let us all ride in his car.

CHAPTER 16

My alarm goes off after what seems like five minutes. I double check the time on my watch to be sure my clock isn't malfunctioning. I throw on some clean clothes, grab a plastic grocery bag, and shove a change of socks and underwear along with a clean shirt in it. I add a few toiletries. I suppose I can afford to purchase whatever I need if I've forgotten anything essential.

Next, my thoughts turn toward how I should transport my winning ticket. I suppose I should probably keep it in something waterproof. Like a Ziploc bag. But it should have some weight to it so it won't blow out the window or something like that. I don't feel comfortable keeping it in my pocket. Maybe I should strap it to my body in a fanny pack.

An old thermos I own comes to mind. I fetch it from the back of a cupboard, check the inside to make sure it's completely dry, and then carefully place my ticket inside a Ziploc bag and drop the bag into the thermos. I screw the cap on tight. It has a handle, so I fashion a loop of twine large enough to allow me to carry the thermos around my neck. This way it should be next to impossible to lose or damage my precious cargo.

I'm ready to go. I take a deep breath and try once again to comprehend the magnitude of what's happening.

I make the ten minute walk to the parking lot outside Building C and forget to count my paces along the way. The Professor and

Marvin are standing next to the Cadillac. I join them and we wait for Frank and Betty.

"I don't know what amazes me more," says the Professor, "the fact that you won the lottery, or the fact that you actually purchased a ticket."

"What do you mean?" says Marvin.

"Ben doesn't strike me as the type of person who plays the lottery. He knows the odds of winning are exceedingly small, and he doesn't believe God would ever let him win anyway. So why would he waste a dollar on a sure loss?"

"I honestly don't know why I bought it," I say.

"Let's see," the Professor says. "If I remember correctly, you bought it that night with Dr. Kentucky. You were under the influence of a woman. Strange things happen when you're with the right woman."

"I'll say," Marvin says.

I'm not in the mood to argue with the Professor, but I do agree that God didn't have anything to do with me winning. I bought my ticket on a whim and selected, of my own accord, a very specific set of numbers that just happened to beat overwhelming mathematical odds. Besides, I'm not the only person who has ever won the lottery. It happens dozens of times a year.

"Hi, fellas!" Boop's shrill voice echoes across the parking lot. "Isn't this so exciting?"

She, Frank, and an unexpected Hailey have arrived.

"What's he doing here?" Frank points at Marvin.

"I invited him," I say. "Where's your walker?"

"I'm not bringing it. Besides, there won't be any room for it with all this excess baggage." He nods at Marvin.

"Now, now, boys," Boop says. "This is a time for celebration! I won't tolerate any bickering."

"Don't worry about the space," says the Professor. "I've got seat belts for six, so we'll all fit."

"I thought your front seat belts weren't reliable," I say.

"I got them fixed."

"Where's the ticket?" Frank says.

"In here." I show him my thermos.

"I got something better than that. Check this out." He hands me an old briefcase with a handcuff dangling from it.

"Why on earth do you have one of these?" I take it from him and examine it.

"It came in very handy on several different occasions."

"Why?"

"Wait!" says the Professor. "Don't tell us. We can take turns guessing. It'll make the drive more interesting."

"Fine by me," Frank says. "Just put the whole thermos in there. That thermos is a pretty good idea, by the way. It's probably fire-proof and waterproof. My briefcase can serve as an extra layer of protection."

I place the thermos in the open briefcase and snap it shut. Frank spins the combination lock and slaps the handcuff on my wrist as Marvin chuckles.

"What's so funny?" Frank says.

"Nothing."

"This is serious business." Frank turns to me. "I don't see why we need this jackass along. I don't see how he'll contribute anything worthwhile to this trip."

"Let's get going." The Professor cuts off the argument.

We all pile into the car. Hailey and Betty share the bench seat up front with the Professor, who insists on driving the first leg of the trip. I'm stuck between Frank and Marvin in the back. This is going to be a long ride.

"I just can't believe this is happening!" Boop says for the ump-teen-billionth time. She's been prattling nonstop since we started driving, which was about fifteen minutes ago. "I mean, seriously, I just about died with despair when I found out everyone at Heritage Gardens was going to lose their homes on account of little old foolish me. I didn't know what else to do, so I prayed and prayed and prayed. And what do you know—the good Lord answered my prayers! Doesn't the Lord work in mysterious ways, Benji?"

I'm not sure how much longer I can take this.

"Did you hear what I said?" she says when I don't respond.

"Mysterious is a perfect word," Frank chimes in. "One mystery I'd like to know the answer to is: when's the good Lord finally gonna decide to take old Marvin home to eternity?"

"If He's smart He'll try to keep you out for as long as possible," Marvin replies without pause.

"Do you believe in heaven, Jerry?" Hailey asks. She's been quiet up until this point.

The Professor thinks carefully before he answers. "I don't like the word *believe*. I prefer the word *hope*. I hope for heaven."

Silence reigns for several glorious seconds.

"I like that," Hailey says. "'I hope for heaven.'" She tests the words as if trying on a pair of questionable denim jeans. "I guess there's a lot of truth to that."

"Well, I know there's a heaven." Betty weighs in with her opinion. "I just know it. A while back I saw this thing on *Oprah*, you know. It was this special on people who had actually died for a few minutes, but then they were resuscitated. These people actually saw heaven with their own eyes."

How do you see something with your own eyes if you're dead? I want to say, but I hold my tongue.

"They all described the same thing in separate interviews, so it proved they weren't making it up," she continues.

"What did they see?" Marvin asks.

"Well, they all described the same thing, and sometimes they even used the exact same words. They felt warm and comforted, like they were wrapped in a warm blanket, and something was carrying them toward a beautiful light. They all said it was the most beautiful and comforting thing they had ever experienced. They weren't afraid at all. The only thing they wanted was to get to that beautiful light. They were heading closer and closer, but then they were rudely brought back to life so they didn't get all the way there."

"That's what everybody says when they think they've died," Frank says. "Everyone knows they're supposed to see some sort of light. I bet those people on *Oprah* were all just saying they saw the light because if they dared to admit they didn't see it, everyone would think they were heading down instead of up, if you catch my drift."

This is the first intelligent thing I've ever heard Frank say.

"Wait a minute…" Marvin says. "Didn't you almost die in the Korean war?" He leans forward and stares across my chest at Frank. "That's right—isn't it? If I remember correctly, you took a piece of shrapnel in the neck and practically bled to death." He pauses for effect, then says, "And I bet you didn't see the light."

"I didn't see the light because I wasn't all the way dead." Frank slaps his knee.

"Or…" Marvin's voice trails off.

"I'm going to change the subject," the Professor says. "Who would like to hazard the first guess as to why Frank owns a hand-cuffed briefcase?"

"I'll give it a try!" Betty says.

"Okay, shoot," Frank says.

"I think you needed to transport some precious jewels across the country, and this was the only secure way to do it."

"Sorry, not even close."

"Let's try to narrow down our theories by asking yes or no questions," the Professor says.

"Good idea," Hailey says. "How many times did you use it?"

"That's not a yes or no question," Frank says.

"Okay, I'll rephrase. Did you use the case many times?"

"Yes."

"Did you travel with it?"

"Not exactly."

"You're supposed to just say yes or no," Marvin says.

"Well, then ask better questions," Frank says.

"Did you use it to transport a valuable object?" I say. I can't keep myself from joining the game.

"No."

"Did you use it to transport anything?"

"No."

"But you did use it."

"Yes."

The car becomes silent as we all ponder this mystery.

"I just can't figure out why someone would carry around an empty briefcase handcuffed to their wrist," Betty says after a long silence.

I've come up with a pretty good theory, but I don't say anything in order to give the others a chance to solve it on their own.

"What time is it?" Frank says.

"Quarter after six," the Professor replies.

"Can we pull off at the next gas station? I need a snack."

"Why don't you just admit why you really want to stop," Marvin says. "You need to pee."

"I've got a bladder of steel," Frank insists. "You're the one with incontinence issues. We'll probably have to pull over to change your diapers every few miles."

I'm beginning to regret I invited Marvin along. I was hoping he'd be able to resist getting sucked into Frank's little catfights.

"Well, I'm not afraid to admit that I have to use the bathroom," Boop announces. "So that settles it. We'll stop on account of me and I'll encourage you all to use the restroom."

We pull into a service station and gratefully extricate ourselves from the vehicle. We've been on the road for less than an hour, yet it seems like an eternity. Everyone except for me and Hailey enters the convenience store. We stretch and then lean against the car. "This is going to be a long ride," Hailey says with a laugh. "How far is it to Sacramento?"

"It will probably take eight or nine hours at the rate we're going."

"I'm glad I'm not stuck between those two in the backseat," she says.

"I know. I'm thinking about drugging them. You don't happen to have any Benadryl with you, do you?"

She chuckles. "This is quite an adventure. How much is that ticket worth?"

"Twenty-three million dollars before taxes."

"That will certainly solve the problems at Heritage Gardens." She gazes at the sky. "Quite a coincidence—don't you think?"

"Stranger things have happened."

"Yeah—like how you and my Aunt Betty both somehow wound up clear across the country at the same retirement home even though neither of you have actually reached retirement age."

Yes, and like how my brother and I were both madly in love with you but I never had the guts to act on it so he seized the day. And then after I failed to save his life I did my best to run away, but somehow, here you are.

"Quite a coincidence," I say.

"Well, I'm glad it's all working out." Hailey looks me in the eye. Her expression is hard to read. "For a while there I thought my aunt was going to fall apart. I didn't know what I was going to do. But now that I know she'll be all right I guess I can head back home."

I choose to ignore the emphasis she places on the word home and say, "They probably miss you at work."

"No, I don't think they do. My partner has everything under control."

"Oh, that must be nice."

"It is and it isn't. It's nice to have freedom, but it's also nice to be needed."

"Yeah, I know what you mean."

"Do you?" Her gaze is too intense. I look away. I don't know what she wants from me. She has every right to be angry with me. I should have at least dropped her a line to let her know where I was.

"Look, Hailey, I don't know what to say except that I'm sorry." I still can't look her in the eye. "I'm sorry I left like I did after Andrew died. I'm sorry he died. I'm sorry about everything."

"I'm not looking for an apology, Ben." She touches my arm.

"Then what do you want me to say?"

"This isn't you, Ben. This life isn't you. This isn't who you were meant to be. You were one of the best surgeons around. Andrew always said so. He admired you. I can't tell you how many times he said he wanted to be like you—the way you interacted with your patients, the way you comforted their family members, the way you encouraged your colleagues. You're an amazing doctor. Everybody misses you." She pauses. "I miss you."

My heart begins to pound. I take a step back. "I can't go back, Hailey." I shake my head. "I just can't go back."

"Hey, everybody!" Frank shouts from across the parking lot, "Let's get going before Marvin gets out of the bathroom."

This is one of the few times I'm actually glad to hear Frank's voice.

We're back on the road. Here I am, rubbing thighs with Frank and Marvin but wishing I was up front next to Hailey. I quickly try to shut this thought out of my troubled mind by alphabetizing the words in the lyrics to the Righteous Brothers' song "You've Lost That Lovin' Feeling."

"I'd like your opinion on something that's been bothering me," Marvin says to nobody in particular. "I was watching a movie recently—I forget the name of it. Anyway, it was more like a character study. It was about this pretty, middle-aged woman who struggled with alcohol and never had any meaningful relationships. The movie kind of just dropped us in the middle of her troubled existence. We got to learn about all her conflicts and struggles. And then it just ended. Nothing got resolved. I couldn't figure it out. What's the deal with that? Who wants to get involved in a story that doesn't have an end?"

"Maybe you fell asleep during the important part," Frank says.

"Or maybe the DVD was broken and you didn't get to see the end," Betty says.

"No," Marvin says. "The credits rolled. I even looked through the scene index to make sure my DVD player didn't somehow skip some scenes."

"I know exactly what you're talking about," says the Professor, who's quite a movie buff. He watches just about every movie that gets released. "This is the latest trend—mostly for those artsy-fartsy independent moviemakers. They want to make movies that shed light on the human condition. They're sick of Hollywood-style happy endings where everything turns out all right. I saw the movie you're talking about. We get to see a snapshot of this person's life, and we get to live in their reality for a short while, but just as in real life, we don't get to find out how it ends."

"Sounds like a lame chick flick to me," Frank says.

"I wouldn't want to watch that movie," Hailey says. "I like happy endings."

"They should put some type of warning on the DVD cover," Marvin says. "'Warning: this movie is all about conflicts but there are no clear resolutions. If you want a complete story, please rent something else.'"

"Sometimes you can't package the whole story in a ninety-minute flick," Boop says. "Reality is more complicated than that."

"That's my point!" Marvin says. "Stories are supposed to be a way to escape reality. That's what a good story does. It takes us on a journey away from our own depressing reality and provides some sweet relief. If reality was so great, we wouldn't need to waste time watching movies because we wouldn't want to miss any reality. Just like when you're watching a great movie you don't want to get up and go to the bathroom because you don't want to miss anything."

"You should just hook yourself up to a condom catheter," Frank says.

"What?"

"A condom catheter. It's exactly what it sounds like. They're much more comfortable than the type you have to jam all the way up into your bladder. You just slip one of those babies on, hook it up to a urine bag, and then you don't have to get up to use the bathroom. I'm pretty sure they make them in your size, but you might have to special order extra-small off the Internet."

"On a more serious note," the Professor interjects, "if any of you want to be entertained by a good story you should read the novel *The Storyteller.*"

"A story about a guy who tells stories?" Frank says. "How original."

"Tell us about it," Boop says.

"In my opinion, the best stories are true stories," the Professor begins. "This particular tale is written as a novel, but I believe it is based on something that actually happened. It's about a wandering storyteller who makes a meager living telling stories to anyone willing to pay. What his customers don't know is that his stories always come true. Days, weeks, months, or even years down the road they find themselves living the story he told them. Some of them are even different characters in the same story and as their lives interconnect they begin to realize they all share a common connection: the mysterious storyteller."

"Oh, wow!" Boop exclaims. "I would just love to read that. What makes you believe it's true?"

"Because I met the storyteller once."

"And what was the story he told you? Did it come true?"

"I'm not permitted to say. That was one of his rules. The story he told me was for my ears only."

"Sounds like a con artist to me," Frank says. "How much did he charge?"

"His fees were a dollar for a short amusing tale, or twenty dollars for a story that would change your life."

"Ha! What a rip-off. I'll tell you a story that will change your life for only five bucks. It goes like this: Once upon a time there was a sucker who paid twenty dollars to a con artist. Don't be like that sucker. The end."

The hours pass slowly as we make our way up Interstate 5. I keep hoping everybody will fall asleep (except the Professor, of course, since he's still driving) but everybody is too excited. My precious cargo rests safely in my lap, although the handcuff is starting to chafe my wrist.

"Hard to believe there's twenty-three million dollars sitting in that briefcase," Frank says, breaking a long, luxurious silence.

"I know," I say.

"Mind if I ask what you're going to spend it on?"

"Well, from what I understand, I can either get my money in one lump sum, or I can choose a twenty-year payout. If I take the lump sum, and if I subtract all the taxes, I'll probably walk away with somewhere between 13 and 16 million dollars. That still leaves us a couple million short."

"You mean you're gonna donate all of it to Heritage Gardens?" Frank says.

"Of course. What else would I do with it?"

"I don't know. Maybe buy a couple beach houses, a yacht, and a few women. You're nuts to give it all to Peterson."

"Well, I don't think I'll give it to Peterson. The way I see it, whatever percentage of the debt I pay off will be the percentage of Heritage Gardens that I own."

"That will probably be more than half," Marvin says. "You'll own more of it than Peterson. Will that make you his boss?"

"I don't want to be anybody's boss," I say. "But I will have the power to hire some competent management so nothing like this ever happens again."

"Sounds like a good plan to me," Frank says. "But I still think you're crazy."

We stop for lunch at an In-N-Out Burger, and then press on in hopes of reaching the California Lottery Headquarters before it closes. Frank dozes off after lunch and the remaining hours of the drive pass mercifully fast.

I glance at the clock in the dash as we pull into the parking lot. It reads 4:44 and I shudder. We rush into the lobby before they have a chance to lock the doors. We make an odd group—the Professor dressed in a lavender polo shirt and orange pants, Frank leaning on his good hip and pretending like he doesn't miss his walker, Betty Boop perky as usual in a hot-pink sundress, Hailey a silent beauty, Marvin keeping his distance from Frank, and me with a battered old briefcase cuffed to my wrist.

"Hey, Frank, you got the key for this thing?" I say as we look around for a receptionist.

"What?" He rubs his hip.

"The key to the handcuffs."

"I don't have a key."

"That's not funny, Frank."

"I'm serious. I don't have a key. Never did. I never actually locked the cuffs all the way. Don't worry though; it shouldn't be too hard to get it off."

"I don't understand," Betty says. "You never actually locked it?"

"Figures," Marvin says. "I'm guessing he only ever used that briefcase to try to pick up women. Probably fed them some line about being a secret agent or some such nonsense."

"That's right," Frank chimes. "Worked like a charm."

I smile to myself. My theory was right. "Well, at least tell me what the combination is to open the lock so I can get the ticket out."

"I don't have that either. I used to, but I don't remember it."

"Then why on earth did you lock it?" Marvin yells.

"I don't know. I was a little overexcited I guess. It shouldn't be too hard to bust it open or pick the lock."

A receptionist finally appears from an inner office. Frank charges forward, surprisingly quick despite his delicate hip. "Where do we go to cash in our jackpot?" he asks the petite woman.

"Have a seat over there and someone will be with you shortly." She indicates some plastic chairs against the wall.

I sit down and place the briefcase on my lap. I examine the combination lock. It consists of four dials, all of which are rusty.

"Here, let me take a look at that." Frank snatches the case from me.

"Easy, Frank. It's still attached to my wrist."

"Sorry about that." He stands it up in my lap so that the lock is facing upward, and then he places his ear next to the lock while he fumbles with the dials.

"How're you going to hear anything?" Marvin says. "You're as deaf as a doornail."

"Not with these hearing aids in. I can hear a mouse fart in the attic when the volume is cranked up on these babies."

Betty clucks her tongue at his vulgarity. Hailey stifles a laugh.

A stout balding man in a poorly altered suit appears from nowhere. "I understand you are in possession of a winning ticket."

"Yessirree!" Frank says. "It's in here." He pats the briefcase.

The man looks at my handcuffed wrist without betraying any emotion. "Very well. Why don't you accompany me to my office and we'll take a look."

I stand to follow him. Frank is still clutching the handle of the briefcase. "You can let go," I say.

"Oh, okay."

The man leads the way down a short hall, through a series of doors, and finally to a nicely appointed office. He positions himself behind his desk and with a wave of his hand indicates two chairs opposite. I take one. Frank takes the other. The rest of our party is forced to stand against the wall. The man gazes at me expectantly.

"There's a slight problem," I say.

He nods his head in understanding and picks up his phone. "Get Jim on the line, please." He waits. "Jim? Can you please bring your toolbox to my office."

A brief pause.

"Yep."

Another brief pause.

"Yep." His final yep is laced with a hint of mirth. He hangs up the phone. "He'll be here shortly." He leans back in his chair, obviously not in the mood to make any small talk.

"We've got the twenty-three-million-dollar winning ticket in there!" Frank can't keep his mouth shut.

"Well, then, I guess congratulations are in order," the man flashes a polite commercial smile.

"He had the winning ticket and he didn't even bother to check if he had won. What a numskull!" Frank laughs and slaps his knee. He's the only one laughing. "He never would've known if I hadn't said anything!"

Jim finally arrives with a large toolbox in tow. He glances at the briefcase and immediately deduces the problem at hand. He examines the lock first, and then the hinges. "This thing is pretty old," he says. "It was made back when they made things right." He produces a hacksaw from his toolbox. "I'm going to get the cuff off first."

I feel my face flush as he attacks the chain with his saw blade. He must think I'm a real idiot.

He makes short work of it and has my wrist detached from the case in a matter of minutes. Next, he takes the briefcase, sets it on the floor, and using a large flathead screwdriver and hammer, proceeds to pulverize the front latches. "Did I mention I'm probably going to have to destroy your briefcase to get it open?" he says as he hammers away.

After he finally busts the latches off, he opens the case and extracts my thermos. "Let me guess..." He hands the thermos over to me.

I'm sure my face becomes redder as I unscrew the cap and peer inside. The plastic bag is plastered to the side near the bottom. I turn the thermos upside down and give it a few shakes, but this fails to dislodge the bag. The nameless bald man releases a barely audible sigh.

"I think a metal coat hanger might do the trick," I say.

"I'll be right back," Jim says as he dashes out the door.

"You remind me of Alfred Hitchcock," Betty says to the man behind the desk. "I met him once, you know. He was quite a character. A genius, you know. He knew everything about everything. Or at least he made it seem like he did."

Jim is back. He hands me the hanger, which I bend to the appropriate shape. I successfully fish the bag out of the thermos and hand it over to Hitchcock's outstretched hand.

Hitchcock carefully extracts the ticket from the bag, unfolds it, and gives it a cursory examination. He then waves it in front of a barcode scanner attached to his computer. He reads something on the screen and then turns his expressionless eyes toward me. "I'm sorry, Mr..."

"Ben. You can call me Ben."

"All right, Ben. Which jackpot were you under the impression you had won?"

"The twenty-three-million-dollar jackpot," Frank answers for me.

"Do you perhaps have another ticket in your possession?" Hitchcock says.

"I don't understand," I say.

"I scanned this ticket, and there is no prize attached to it."

"That's impossible," I say. "I checked the winning numbers myself. In fact, I have them memorized. Two, three, five, seven, eleven, and thirteen."

"You're correct. Those are the winning numbers for the unclaimed twenty-three-million-dollar jackpot. Those numbers, however, are not on this ticket." He hands it to me.

My body deflates as I look at the numbers. Four, eight, twelve, sixteen, twenty-eight, and forty-four. I stare at them in shock. Is this some kind of sick joke? Not only are these not my numbers, they're all multiples of four. Somebody changed my ticket, or switched my ticket, or something.

It is dead silent in the car. The Professor is spent from the long drive, so I am behind the wheel. Our original plan had been to find the nicest hotel in town and spend the night before driving back, but that plan was quickly tossed out the window.

"I still don't understand what happened," Betty breaks the silence.

"Let me summarize," Frank says. "Mr. Smarty-pants-doctor-surgeon-janitor over there bought a winning ticket, lost it, found a different ticket but never bothered to check the numbers to make sure it was his, and dragged us all to Sacramento to make fools of ourselves."

"Frank, be nice," Betty says.

"We didn't need to come all the way to Sacramento to discover he's a fool." Marvin nods at Frank.

"I'm sorry, everybody," I say. These are the first words I've spoken since we left Hitchcock's office.

"You're sure you had the winning ticket?" asks the Professor.

"I'd bet my life on it. I chose the numbers myself and double checked the ticket before I folded it and stuck it in my pocket."

"And you lost it while you were in the restaurant?"

"I'm not sure when I lost it, but when I found a folded ticket under the exact same table where Lex and I sat, I naturally assumed it was mine. I didn't even bother to check the numbers."

"Strange coincidence," he mutters. "I wonder what the odds are of this happening? Well, no matter. The good news is that your ticket is still out there somewhere and nobody else has found it because if they had, they would have cashed it in by now."

"Well, then, let's go find that ticket!" Frank says. "Step on it, Ben. You're only going seventy. I'm sure this baby can handle eighty-five or ninety."

I compromise and settle on a speed of seventy-three miles per hour. My head spins as I replay the sequence of events over and over again in my mind. Disbelief gradually turns into anger as a strange realization begins to set in—the realization that I'm being toyed with. There are just too many coincidences to allow any other logical explanation. The universe is messing with me.

It's kind of sad how cynical I've become, but the more I think about it, I wonder how anybody makes it through life without becoming this way. The way I see it, after you make it past the innocence of youth you have one of two choices: you can either become cynical or delusional. I tried delusional for a while. It was sort of nice while it lasted—mainly because I didn't realize I was delusional. But then I woke up. So now I'm cynical. And the universe is once again having its way with me.

I've driven four hours and we're not even halfway back to Heritage Gardens. I'm tired, hungry, and depressed. I talk everyone into stopping for dinner and a couple hours sleep at a cheap hotel. I offer to pay for everything. Nobody puts up a fight, so that's what we do.

CHAPTER 17

The mood is still grim this morning. Even after coffee and donuts.

"What's your next step?" asks the Professor as we start out on the final leg of our journey with the Professor behind the wheel.

"I'm going to ask Lex if she remembers anything that might help me find my ticket. Maybe she'll be able to think of something that I'm not remembering."

The next three-and-a-half hours are uneventful other than some small talk. Boop is unusually quiet, and Hailey seems concerned about her. Even Frank and Marvin manage to refrain from their usual bickering.

When we finally arrive at the parking lot outside Building C, I notice a large crowd gathered outside the building. Several residents hold a large banner that reads, "Hip-Hip-Hurray, Ben Has Saved the Day!" There's even a van from one of the local news networks parked nearby.

"Shoot," I say. "How'd they all find out?"

"I might have said something to Jack," Frank says.

"I thought we were keeping this a secret," I say.

"Well, he saw me packing my things. He's a nosy old fart, always peeking in my room if I leave the door open. What was I supposed to do?"

"What's done is done," says the Professor. "The question is how are we going to handle this?"

"The media probably already knows we didn't cash a ticket," I say. "See the smirk on that reporter's face? She's probably already got the story from the lottery headquarters."

"We can't let the word get out that the ticket is missing," Marvin says. "Otherwise everyone will be looking for it."

"So we'll just pass it off as an error," says the Professor. "We'll say Ben thought he had the winning ticket, but just got confused about the numbers. Are we all in agreement?"

"Nobody's going to buy that story," I say.

"Sure they will," Frank says. "If you're dumb enough to quit your high-paying job as a surgeon to become a janitor in a retirement home, then you're dumb enough to do just about anything."

"There's nothing wrong with Ben's job." Boop tries to defend me. "He's good at it. He's the best janitor I ever met."

"Sure, there's nothing wrong with being a janitor," Frank replies. "But everything is wrong if you're a janitor and you have a medical degree."

The Professor parks the car and turns off the engine. The crowd surges toward us, cheering all the while. The reporter and her camera crew push through the crowd, ready to pounce on us as soon as we exit the car. The crowd hushes when I get out, affording the reporter the perfect opportunity to attack.

"Is it true that you drove all the way to Sacramento to cash what you thought was a winning lottery ticket?"

I glare at her but don't reply.

"Is it true that this facility is on the brink of financial ruin and you were hoping this ticket would save it?"

A murmur spreads through the crowd as they begin to catch on.

"No comment," I say.

"How much debt is this facility in?" the reporter continues her relentless questioning.

I glare at her again and begin to walk away. Someone from the crowd quotes the eighteen-million-dollar figure.

"How did you manage to allow this facility to get into so much financial trouble?" the reporter continues questioning the back of my head.

"It wasn't his fault!" Frank shouts at her. "He's just the janitor here. He was going to donate all of his winnings to save this place." He shakes his fist at her. "You vultures are all the same—just looking for a story. Never mind that real people are involved!"

I glance over my shoulder to give her a parting glare. I see her expression soften, and perhaps even a look of shame emerges as the true nature of our situation finally seems to strike home. Her crew turns off the camera when they realize they aren't going to get a newsworthy story out of this one.

I turn to the Professor. "I'm going to leave the explaining up to you. I need to get out of here."

I trudge away from the crowd and head toward my apartment, counting my paces as I go.

Back in my apartment, I feel lonelier than I've felt in a long time. And I've spent a lot of time alone. This feeling rarely hits me, but when it does I hate it more than anything. I don't quite know how to put it into words. There's a gnawing at the core of my being—an emptiness so vast that it feels like nothing could possibly fill it. It is so heavy and so intense that it makes me want to just give up and stop breathing. And this scares me more than anything. I'm scared I might do the unthinkable. When I get like this, I need to be around somebody—anybody. I'd even welcome Frank's company just so I wouldn't feel so alone.

I pick up the phone and dial Lex's number. Telephone numbers are easy for me to remember. In fact, I can't forget them—even if I want to.

"Hello?"

"Hello, Lex, it's Ben."

"Hi." Her tone of voice is difficult to interpret. "I saw you on the news a few minutes ago."

"Great." So they decided to run the story after all.

"Actually, it was a sympathetic segment. I've got it recorded on my DVR if you want to see it."

"Do you mind if I come over?" I jump at an excuse to get out of my apartment. "I need to talk to you about this whole situation."

"Come on over." She gives me directions on how to get to her place.

It turns out she lives in a townhouse on a golf course not too far from Heritage Gardens. My breath feels short as I stand outside her door. I should've brought my inhaler. I usually don't leave home without it.

I ring the doorbell. She answers wearing thin, mint-green cotton pants and a matching long-sleeved shirt. "Hey, there, you caught me in my comfort clothes and I didn't feel like changing," she says unapologetically. "Today's a lazy day at home for me. Come on in."

I follow her into her living room. I sort of feel like an idiot in my blue jeans and striped polo shirt.

"Would you like something to drink?" She indicates for me to take a seat on her couch.

"No, thanks," I say, even though my mouth suddenly feels dry.

She plops down in a large cushioned chair situated at a slight angle next to the couch and picks up a remote that was sitting on the armrest. She turns on the television and navigates through a menu until she finds what she's looking for. "Here it is."

"And Martha has been following the developing story about that twenty-three-million-dollar lottery ticket that has not yet been cashed in," says an anchorman sporting a tasteful regimental tie.

The reporter who accosted me earlier appears on the screen. "Thank you, Mark. We are here at Heritage Gardens, a local retirement community, where residents are sadly disappointed after their expected fairy-tale ending just developed an unexpected twist." The camera pans from her face and zooms in on the crowd in the background. The celebratory banner lies abandoned on the ground and several of the distraught residents of Heritage Gardens are in tears. "It seems that a janitor named Ben who works at this facility was under the impression that he was in possession of the winning ticket. He drove all the way to Sacramento to cash it in before he learned he was mistaken.

"There is an added dimension to the disappointment here at Heritage Gardens," she continues. "We have learned that this facility is on the verge of closure due to serious financial troubles. The janitor was going to donate all of his winnings to save the homes of the retirees you see gathered behind me. Now they will have to find some other recourse before the land is sold from under them. Sources tell us that a prominent developer has had his eye on this property and wishes to acquire the land in order to build a shopping mall."

Lex turns off the television and looks at me with sad eyes. "What happened with that ticket, Ben?"

I recount all the events starting from the moment I purchased the ticket. She nods when I ask if she remembers seeing me put it in my pocket. "I do remember that. You folded it in half and slipped it in your back pocket. Are you certain, beyond a shadow of a doubt, that your ticket had the winning numbers?"

"You saw me choose them."

"I remember that you had some sort of system where the numbers all added up to something."

"That's right. That's why I'm so sure I know exactly what numbers were on my ticket. And this ticket I found in the restaurant—the one I brought all the way to Sacramento . . . When I finally looked at the numbers on it I saw that it contains numbers I never would have chosen in a million years."

"Dare I ask why?"

"Because they are multiples of four and I absolutely despise the number four."

"What's wrong with the number four?" she asks, feigning insult. "I absolutely adore the number four."

I chuckle and allow my eyes to wander the room. I usually don't pay much attention to details of interior design beyond tiled floors, but I'm suddenly intrigued by Lex's apartment. This is her personal space. In a way, it's part of her. I can't remember the last time I was in such a place. A nicely framed print of water lilies by Monet is displayed on one of the walls. Opposite that, there's a bookcase containing a small DVD collection (mostly romantic comedies) and several books (mostly nonfiction). Some pictures of family and friends are placed here and there. I notice a deluxe edition of Scrabble resting on the bottom shelf.

"I see you're a Scrabble fan," I say.

"I've never lost," she says with a hint of pride.

"Neither have I."

"Is that a challenge?" Her eyes narrow.

"Just a statement of fact."

"Sounded like a challenge to me." She snatches the box from its place, scoots the magazines off the coffee table, and slaps the box down. "You're on."

I glance at my watch. Part of me wants to continue my search for the ticket, but another part of me longs to stay.

"What? Are you afraid of losing to a girl?" Lex taunts.

"No, I was just debating whether or not I should go easy on you because you're a girl."

She sets up the game and we start to play. She hits me with words I wouldn't have ever dreamed of while I find myself having to resort to my vast knowledge of esoteric medical terminology to prevent myself from getting completely clobbered. We play right through the afternoon. She teases me relentlessly, but I enjoy it. She makes small talk and tells me funny stories from her childhood, and I soak it all up with pure joy. She makes me pasta for dinner. Before I know it, I've lost to her four times in a row and I'm forty-five points behind on our fifth round, but enjoying myself more than I can remember in the longest time.

It's getting late. It's my turn to make a word. The board is pretty full and only a few letter tiles remain in the bag. If I don't make a move quickly, I'll lose again for sure. I stare at my seven tiles and carefully study the board.

"Are you going to make me start the timer?" Lex snaps her fingers. She's pretty strict on the rules.

"I don't know why I'm even trying," I say. "You're so far ahead I don't think I'll ever catch up."

"Would you like to resign?"

"Never." I go back to studying my tiles. Then it hits me. If there's an open T on the board I can form a word that will use up all my tiles. If I use them all in a single turn I score an extra fifty points. That would be enough to take the lead. I grin in triumph as I spot an open T.

"What are you smiling about?" Lex says.

"You'll see." I slowly place my tiles on the board. "L-O-N-L-I-E-S-T. That's fifty bonus points for using all my tiles in a single turn, isn't it?" My grin falters as I realize the irony behind the word I just formed.

Lex gives me a sympathetic smile. "That's pretty sad, Ben."

"What do you mean?" A wave a fear courses through me. Am I that transparent? Is it obvious that I'm desperately lonely?

"You spelled it wrong," she says. "You're missing an E after the N. Your word is worth zero points." She removes the tiles from the board and hands them back to me.

"Oh."

She gazes at me again, but this time her eyes pierce right through me. "Ben, would you like to stay? You could sleep on my couch."

I stare back at her, paralyzed with fear.

"Ben?"

"Uh—yeah, actually. That would be nice."

"I'll get you a pillow and a blanket."

"Okay. Thanks."

CHAPTER 18

I awake with a start from the same nightmare I always have—the re-enactment of my brother's death. But this time it was slightly different: I dreamt the whole thing from my brother's perspective—lying face up on the operating table, watching myself frantically try to save his life. And after the heart monitor flatlined and I had given up on the cardiac massage, I watched myself tear off my mask and throw it on the floor. What I saw next horrified me. I saw myself smile.

I sit up and wipe the sweat from my brow. Where am I? This isn't my apartment.

Then I remember. It's still dark outside. Lex's bedroom door is shut. I've got to get out of here.

I tiptoe over to the kitchen counter. In the darkness I locate a tablet and pen near the phone. I scribble a quick note of thanks and leave it where I'm sure she'll find it. Then I quietly let myself out the front door.

It wasn't on purpose. It wasn't on purpose. It wasn't on purpose. I hurry to my truck in the predawn light. I never deserve to be happy. I never deserve to be happy. I never deserve to be happy.

I've got to find that ticket. There's no two ways about it. It must be somewhere in my apartment. At first, this theory seemed implausible because my apartment is in perfect order. Everything has a place, and everything is in its place. I won't tolerate it any other way. Since I know exactly where everything is, I would certainly know where my lottery ticket is. But perhaps it somehow fluttered out of my pocket and escaped underneath a piece of furniture or something like that. I can't be certain unless I perform a thorough, comprehensive search. I speed toward my apartment and welcome the distraction that a thorough search is bound to provide.

I step through my front door with a sense of purpose. I need a strategy. Something systematic. I carefully consider my options before I settle on my line of attack. Scenes from movies where FBI agents ransack an apartment in search of evidence come to mind. I never understood this method of search. They are just creating a chaotic disaster in which nothing will ever be found. I need to be more organized than that.

I head to the point in my apartment that is farthest from the front door. I shall start here and systematically examine every single square inch.

If the ticket doesn't turn up, I won't have to waste my time looking through my apartment again because I will be certain that I looked in every feasible spot.

The farthest point from my front door happens to be the southwest corner of my bedroom. Here, in the ceiling, there is an air conditioning vent. This is where I begin. I grab a chair so I can examine the air duct behind the vent. Logic dictates that it would be physically impossible for my ticket to wind up here because the air blows out of this vent rather than being sucked in, yet I still perform the task. Of course the ticket isn't here, but if I hadn't checked, my search wouldn't be complete.

In this manner, I gradually cover ground. I lift the alarm clock from my nightstand and examine it from all angles. I take the National Geographic magazine from its place and leaf through every page. I remove the drawer from the nightstand and look inside the housing. I take the pillow off my bed and even remove the pillowcase. I even go so far as to remove the plastic dust-mite protector from my mattress, just in case my ticket somehow found its way under here.

At first I'm careful to put everything back in its place, but soon I begin to realize that this is taking more time than I thought. Also, a sense of urgency is coming over me, becoming more intense with each passing minute. What if the ticket isn't in my apartment? What if I'm just wasting my time in here? What if it's still in the restaurant? What if somebody else finds it first?

I decide I need to finish searching my apartment before morning so I can get over to the restaurant before it opens to the public. I'm sure someone will let me inside to do a quick search there. I increase my speed. I'm still being as thorough as before, but in the interest of time I'm no longer putting things back in their place.

My earnestness continues to intensify. I am now in my closet, yanking out clothing. I thrust my hand in the pockets and then toss each article in the general direction of my bed.

After my closet has been completely disemboweled I turn my frenzied eyes toward my next victim: my carefully organized library.

After I unshelve every last book I move around the living room, throwing couch cushions, overturning my recliner, ripping window shades off their brackets. Then I move into the kitchen. Somewhere in the fringes of my consciousness I realize I'm spinning out of control, but I'm finding a sort of sick pleasure in this orgy of destruction. I lose track of time as I relish in the creation of pure, unadulterated chaos.

When I finally return to my senses, I find myself panting on my living room floor, surrounded by a perfect disaster, no lottery ticket in sight. My ecstasy quickly wears off as the horror of what I've just done begins to set in.

"Holy moly." Frank's voice interrupts my despair. I must have left the front door open because I don't remember hearing him knock. "What happened in here?"

"I didn't find my lottery ticket," I say. "Don't you ever use the phone?"

"I did, but it just rang and rang."

I must have unplugged it during my rampage.

"So you're sure it's not here," Frank continues.

I don't respond. I hear the faint sound of my walkie-talkie squawking from somewhere in the midst of the disaster.

"Sounds like your boss is trying to get ahold of you."

"Did you need something, Frank?"

"I want to know what the plan is."

"I'll tell you what," I say. "Let me go find out what Peterson wants and then I'll meet you back at your apartment. We can have a little meeting and you can invite whoever you want, okay?"

"Why don't you just ask Peterson what he wants over the radio?"

"Because I'll never find it in this mess." I turn and walk out the door.

Ross Peterson Junior, a different man now, sits behind his desk. He looks at me with sorrowful eyes. "Please, Ben, have a seat."

I actually feel a little sorry for the guy, even though it was his selfishness and greed that created this whole mess.

"I was sorry to hear that the lottery thing didn't pan out." He lets loose a sad sigh. "It would have been very generous of you to help us out with your winnings." He appears utterly defeated.

"What's your next move?" I say.

"Well, the bank is holding firm on this one. If I don't make a payment within the next nine days they're going to foreclose. On the other hand, I have a developer who is very eager to purchase the property. They want to buy it from me ASAP. I'll admit that I don't understand the politics behind all this, but they're offering me a premium price. If I sell it to them I'll have enough to pay off all the debts, plus I'll have money left over to compensate the residents and help them with moving expenses."

"How much money are we talking about?"

"If I did the calculation correctly I'll be able to refund everyone their last month's rent as well as give them a thousand dollars apiece for moving expenses."

"When do you have to decide?"

"That's why I called you in here." His mouth twitches nervously. "I don't feel comfortable making this decision on my own. Everyone here seems to respect you."

"You want me to decide what to do?"

"If the bank forecloses, I won't be able to help any of the residents relocate. If I sell to the developer, there will be no turning back because they plan to bulldoze this place and turn it into a mall."

"But if we make a payment to the bank within nine days we'll be able to buy some time?"

"Yes, but the developer says they need a decision within forty-eight hours."

"How much money do we need to make a payment to the bank?"

"Sixty thousand dollars."

I whistle. "That seems pretty steep."

"That includes some back payments and some penalties. They're playing hardball."

"I see."

"So what do you think?" He raises his brow and his mouth twitches some more.

"Stall," I say. "We don't want to burn that bridge with the developer, but we shouldn't give up yet. Maybe we'll still find a way to come up with the money."

His gaze shifts from me to his lap and then back to me. "Yeah, that's what I was thinking. I think that's a good plan. I really don't want to have to sell this place."

I feel a bit guilty for the contempt I used to hold for him. I used to think he was the most selfish person I knew, but right now his true colors are showing through. Deep down, he truly does care for this place and the people in it.

Next I go to Frank's place. The usual gang is assembled. I'm a little surprised to see Marvin here. I doubt Frank invited him—he probably found out about our little meeting some other way.

Frank's small apartment seems even more cramped with all six of us packed inside. My eyes immediately find Hailey. Concern is etched on her face. I wonder how much longer she plans to stick around. I've got enough trouble without the added torture of her presence.

"So what's the skinny?" Frank says.

I give them an update that includes the details I just learned from Junior. When I'm through, they silently ponder the impossibility of our situation.

"Well, I guess we should formulate a plan," the Professor says.

"I have an idea," Frank says. "We could try to win the lottery."

"That's not funny," Marvin says.

"I don't remember inviting him to this meeting," Frank says. "Who let this guy in?"

"I asked him to come," Boop says. "He was with me when you called."

Frank's mouth snaps shut. Marvin tries to hide a grin.

"I'd like to get over to the restaurant and give it a good search," I say.

"I'll come with you," Hailey says.

"I'm gonna call my son," Frank says. "He's a lawyer, you know. Maybe he can help us take some sort of legal action that could buy us some time."

"And maybe the rest of us should call a meeting to inform the other residents about what's going on," Boop says. "I bet we could come up with the sixty thousand dollars if we all put our heads together."

"Sounds like a good start." The Professor claps his hands. "Let's get moving."

Heading outside, I lead Hailey through the grounds of Heritage Gardens in the direction of the restaurant. I figure it would be just as much work to walk all the way to my apartment to get my truck, so we might as well just walk straight to the restaurant.

"So we're going to the place you had dinner on the night you bought the ticket?" Hailey says.

"Yes."

"You were having dinner with that woman I met at the funeral. What's her name again?"

"Lex Kentucky—Dr. Lex Kentucky."

"It was date?"

"I wouldn't call it a date. The Professor manipulated the situation so that we wound up having dinner alone with each other."

"The Professor?"

"That's my nickname for Jerry."

"That fits him perfectly."

The sun is behind us, rising in its meridian. I notice our shadows side by side, leading us forward. It makes a nice image but I quickly shut it out by counting the fallen leaves on the sidewalk.

"What kind of doctor is she?" Hailey breaks the silence.

"A podiatrist."

"Well, good for her. That would've been my last guess. My first impression was that she should be a supermodel."

I don't respond.

"I haven't seen her around since the funeral," she says.

I don't like the direction this conversation is heading so I change the subject. "How's your aunt doing?"

Hailey sighs. "She's managing to stay optimistic in her own peculiar way. I'm worried about her, though. She's suffered from bipolar disorder for many years but she doesn't like to take her medication. For the most part she does fine, but every so often her illness gets the better of her and she makes a string of poor decisions."

I notice that Hailey carefully avoids the cracks in the sidewalk as we make our way along a fairly busy street outside the bounds of Heritage Gardens.

"She's usually able to keep the manic part of her personality under pretty good control," she continues, "and that's good because some people wind up in jail when they go off on a manic episode. The thing that worries me the most is that she might hit a low, which isn't very often at all but can get really bad. That's mainly why I'm staying with her through this whole ordeal. I'm afraid she might become horribly depressed."

"That's tough," I say. "Your aunt always seems so happy. I have a hard time picturing her in the throes of depression."

Hailey glances at me. "Why are you smiling?"

"The cracks." I point at her feet. "Not your aunt, the cracks."

"Oh. It's just this thing I do." She blushes and looks away.

"Yeah, I know what you mean."

"You'd better be careful," she says. "I know about some of your little secrets."

"Oh, yeah?"

"Yeah, your brother told me some things."

"Like what?"

"Let's see… There's the phone thing—how you have to tap each button three times before you press it down all the way to dial it. And there's the toothbrush thing—how you refuse to brush your teeth with a blue toothbrush." She snickers. "Oh, yeah, and there's my favorite one of all."

"I'm dying to hear."

"The zipper thing." She bursts into laughter.

I can't believe my brother told her about the zipper thing.

"Let me see your fly," she says, still giggling.

"No."

"I bet your pants don't have a zipper." She sings the words like kids do when they're making fun of each other on the playground.

I feel my face flush. Everyone has their phobias. Mine happens to be of zippers. It's a perfectly legitimate fear and I'm sure that hundreds—even thousands—of other people suffer from this same affliction. I'm not certain if there's an official label for it, but I propose the term metallofasteniophobia. Zippers are dangerous devices. Don't be fooled by their apparent usefulness. Once they get stuck, they're stuck. And if something delicate is stuck in them— say, a sensitive piece of your anatomy—you are in for a world of hurt. Furthermore, I submit that zippers can be deadly. Suppose, for instance, you are on a ferry, crossing a strait. You are bundled up in your nice warm zippered coat when suddenly, to your dismay, you fall overboard. You hit the water with a splash and your oversized coat quickly becomes waterlogged, turning into a twenty-pound weight that's dragging you to the bottom. You struggle to take it off but, alas, the zipper is stuck.

Zippers can kill. Zippers can maim. I'll never allow one near me.

When Hailey and I arrive at the restaurant we discover that it won't be open for another two hours. We pound on the front doors, but to no avail.

"There has to be somebody in there," I say. "Come with me."

I lead the way around to the back of the building, and sure enough, we find an employee entrance into the kitchen. The door is ajar. We cautiously enter.

"Can I help you?" says a man in a heavy Spanish accent. He looks us over, then his eyes widen with recognition. He quickly fumbles in his pocket, whips out a hair net, and places it on his head. "La Jefe is not here," he says nervously. "She say you might come."

"Your boss is expecting us?" I say.

"Oh yes, yes, of course. You want for me to show you around?"

"We were hoping to do a quick search," I say, masking my confusion. "We're in kind of a hurry."

"Okay, okay, follow me," he says, eager to please. "Where you like to look first?"

"How about under the tables?" I say.

He leads the way through the kitchen and into the main dining area. I'm still trying to figure out how he knows why we're here. He must have seen me on TV. But that still doesn't explain how he knows I'm looking for the ticket. The wheels in my head start spinning. The only way he could know we had lost it would be if he had found it. My heart quickens. What sort of game is this guy playing?

Now that we're in the main dining area, I pull Hailey over to the far corner and stoop down, pretending to look under a table. The worker remains a respectful distance away, but he's keeping a wary eye on us.

"I think he found my ticket," I whisper to Hailey.

"What?"

"How else could he know why we're here?"

"But that doesn't make any sense," she whispers back. "If he had it he would have cashed it in by now."

"But you saw the way he looked at me. He recognized me. I don't know why he hasn't cashed it yet. Maybe he was afraid to. Maybe he thought he might get accused of stealing it. Something's up with this guy, I can feel it."

Hailey shakes her head. "I think you've got it wrong. He's mistaken us for someone else."

"No, I'm telling you, that guy has my ticket."

"So what are you going to do?"

"I don't know. Let's just keep pretending to search and I'll come up with a plan."

My mind races as I make my way around the room, inspecting the floor under the tables and chairs. Maybe he wants to make some sort of deal. I wouldn't have a problem giving him some sort of reward for finding my ticket and returning it to me.

By the time Hailey and I have circled the room twice, I've convinced myself this guy is up to no good. I signal to Hailey that I want to go.

"Everything okay?" asks the employee.

"Fine," I say, checking his nametag. Javier. "I think we'll be leaving now."

"Don't you want to look in the kitchen?"

"No. We'll just let ourselves out the front door." I head in that direction, motioning for Hailey to follow. Javier shrugs as we leave.

"Mind if I ask what happened in there?" Hailey asks when we are outside. "We didn't do a very good search."

"That's because that guy has the ticket."

"Then why didn't you ask him about it?"

"I plan to. But not until his boss is there and we have some witnesses of our own."

An hour has passed. Our little group has reconvened in Frank's room, of all places. I bet we could find a more comfortable location if we put a little effort into it. Now there are seven of us because Jane has joined us too. She, Boop, Marvin, and the Professor have arranged for the whole community to meet in Assembly Hall after lunch. Frank wasn't able to get a hold of his attorney son, but he thinks he'll be able to sometime tonight.

"So you didn't find the ticket at the restaurant?" Marvin says.

"We didn't find the ticket," I say, "but we found the guy who has it."

"What?" Frank says. "Somebody's got it?"

"Yep."

"Well, why didn't you get it back from him?"

"He doesn't know that I know he has it, and I didn't want him to get scared and disappear."

"You should've walloped him and snatched it while you had the chance!" Frank says. "That's what I would've done."

"Hold on a minute," the Professor says. "Why don't you back up a bit and explain who this person is and how you know he has the ticket."

They all listen intently as I replay the events from the restaurant. When I'm almost finished, Frank cuts me off. "What are we sitting around here for? I say we all go down there and demand he give it back to us. Maybe we should call the police too."

"I'm not convinced that this all adds up," the Professor says.

"That's what I tried to tell him," Hailey says.

"Well, it makes perfect sense to me," Frank says. "Javier found it when he was cleaning up. I bet nobody else was around to witness it. Instead of throwing it in the trash, he thought to himself, 'Hmmm, maybe this is worth twenty-three million dollars; I should probably check before I throw it away.' And then, when he got home, he found out it really was worth twenty-three million dollars. He didn't know what to do. He held on to it thinking that eventually he would come up with a plan. But then he found out that the person who bought the ticket is looking for it. I bet he's scared to death that he did something wrong. Who knows what's going through that mind of his. I say we pull him aside and offer him a hundred bucks to hand it over."

"A hundred dollars?" Marvin says. "That's all?"

"I think that's a pretty good reward," Frank says.

"Maybe I should talk to him," Boop says. "I speak Spanish almost fluently, you know. I learned it while I was in Madrid. I almost became Spanish royalty."

"He spoke nearly perfect English," Hailey says. "We don't need an interpreter."

"Spain has a king?" Marvin says.

"I don't care whether it has a king or a donkey," Frank says. "We're getting off the subject here." He heads for the door. "I'm gonna get our ticket back. You people are welcome to come along, or you can sit around and yack about which countries have kings and which don't."

"We can take my car," says the Professor.

"But there's seven of us," Marvin says. "Maybe we should leave Frank behind."

"If anybody shouldn't come, it's you!" Frank says.

"I'll stay back," Jane says.

"Nonsense," says the Professor. "We can all fit. It's only a short drive."

I'm in no mood to argue, so we all head to the parking lot. Frank doesn't have his walker and I don't feel like arguing about that either. If he falls and breaks his hip again it will just keep him out of our hair.

"Ladies can sit in the front," Frank says. "That means you, Marvin."

"It's my car, so I'll assign the seating," says the Professor. "I think it would be best if Jane and Betty sit up front. The rest of you can squeeze in the back." He unlocks his door and gets in.

Hailey and I eye what's left of the back seat after Frank and Marvin squeeze in. "You first," she says to me. I'm about to argue but I realize that either she's going to have to sit partially in my lap or I'm going to have to sit in hers.

"Watcha waiting for?" Frank says. "She won't bite."

I take a gulp of air and somehow force myself into the car. The next thing I know, Hailey slides in and shuts the door.

My body stiffens. I can't breathe.

"Am I hurting you?" Hailey says.

"No." This isn't right.

She shifts her weight and repositions herself. Her left thigh rests squarely on my lap and both of her legs cross over mine. The only way she can keep herself from sliding forward is by wrapping her left arm around my neck and leaning her body sideways into my chest. This maneuver brings us practically cheek to cheek, though her head is a little higher than mine since she is in my lap. If I were to lean my head toward her, I could bury it in the nape of her neck.

This is ridiculous. We should have walked. I'm afraid she can feel my heart pounding. In fact, in this position it's probably impossible for her not to.

"Step on it, Jerry," Frank says, bringing me back to reality.

"I'd rather we all get there in one piece," says the Professor as he slowly navigates through the parking lot.

As we turn a corner Hailey places her free hand on the center of my chest. She cocks her head as if listening, but I know what she's doing. She shifts her weight again, this time maneuvering her body slightly away from mine so she can swing her head around and find my gaze. I turn my head to the left, making it impossible for her to see my face. She presses her hand firmly against my chest, allowing my heart to pound against her palm.

She knows.

The Professor glances in the rearview mirror. I think I see the trace of a smile on the corner of his mouth.

I don't remember the remainder of the short drive to the restaurant. I've had blankouts like these before. I call them blankouts because I don't know what else to call them. I know I'm still awake and breathing, but I can't remember what happened during them. I find them very disturbing, but thankfully they don't last very long and they happen very infrequently. They occur when I'm overwhelmed with a stressful situation. Usually I'm able to maintain some sort of grip on reality by employing one of several techniques—most of which involve counting. But every once in a great while I either forget to use these mental tricks or don't have a chance to, and somehow I lose track of time. I don't know where I go, and I don't know what makes me come back. This frightens me. What scares me the most is the thought that one day I might leave on one of these little excursions and never return.

This time I do return, and I find myself outside the restaurant with everyone else. Frank leads the way through the front door. I don't know who put him in charge, but I'm too frazzled at the moment to do anything about it. The rest of us follow him to a hostess who is at her post behind a small podium. "Seven for lunch?" she says.

Her quick count impresses me.

"No," Frank says. "We need to speak with your manager."

"May I ask what this is concerning?"

"Sure. One of your coworkers is a thief."

"Why do we let this guy open his mouth?" Marvin says. "Don't pay him any mind. Please tell your manager that we need to inquire about an item that may have been found by one of the employees."

"Certainly." She disappears.

"What's wrong with what I said?" Frank says.

"It was inflammatory," Marvin says. "It won't do us any good to come in here like a posse. We're not a lynch mob."

"Seems to me that lynch mobs usually get the job done—and in pretty good time," Frank says.

"I think it would be best if we let Ben do the talking," Marvin says. "After all, it's his ticket."

"Fine by me," Frank says. "If he wants to talk then he should speak up instead of skulking around in the background."

The hostess returns. "If you would please follow me, the manager will see you in her office."

Frank motions me ahead with a sarcastic flourish. We follow the hostess through a side hall and into a spacious office. There aren't enough chairs for us all, but there is plenty of standing room. The manager is already on her feet, ready to greet us. She appears to be in her mid-thirties and is dressed in a business suit. I'm relieved to be dealing with someone professional. "Hello," she says. "I'm Sharon. I understand there's an issue involving one of my employees."

Out of the corner of my eye I see Frank's carotid artery flopping around in his neck like a freshly caught fish in a net. He's dying to say something, but he's somehow managing to hold his tongue.

"Yes," I say. "We believe that one of your employees found a lost item and was perhaps afraid to turn it in."

"I see."

She doesn't say anything else, so I continue. "We have good reason to believe that Javier found a winning lottery ticket that I dropped on the floor. We would like to question him regarding this matter, and we would also like him to know that when he returns it we will give him a much deserved reward."

Her eyes suddenly widen with recognition. "Hey, I saw you on TV. You're the janitor from the retirement home."

"Yes."

"Javier is one of my best employees. He would never keep a lost item for himself."

"People do strange things when twenty-three million dollars is at stake!" Frank can't contain himself any longer.

"What makes you think he has it?" the manager says, her gaze still on me.

"I came here earlier today with her." I point at Hailey. "Javier let us inside. He immediately recognized me, like you did just now. He seemed to know that we were here to look for the ticket. How would he know we were searching for it unless he had found it? My guess is that he found it and kept it. When he discovered how

much it was worth, perhaps he got scared that he had done something wrong."

"You were here earlier today?"

"Yes. Before the restaurant opened."

"Ohhh . . . that explains everything." She smiles and chuckles. "I
was wondering what Javier was talking about. This is all a big misunderstanding."

"I'm not sure I understand," I say.

"Javier thought you were with the public health department. I've
been telling all my employees that we are due for an inspection and
that they should be prepared at all times. It keeps them on their
toes. Javier thought you were here to inspect the restaurant. When
he told me about your inspection I thought it was strange that you
barely glanced at the kitchen. I've never heard of a food-service
inspection that was limited to just the space under the tables."

"How do you know for sure he doesn't have our ticket?"
Frank says.

"Now it all makes sense," Hailey says. "When Javier first saw me
and Ben, he immediately put on his hair net. He was acting just
how I would expect an employee to act during a restaurant inspection."

"Well, I don't buy it," Frank says.

At first I want to side with Frank, but this is my first clue that
something is wrong with my line of thinking. I have to admit that
the manager's explanation fits the facts much better than my own.

"What do you say, Ben?" says the Professor.

"I think I jumped to the wrong conclusion," I say.

"So that's it?" Frank says. "We're not even going to question
the guy?"

"I don't think we should do that." Betty speaks up. "It's such a
horrible thing to be falsely accused. I was once accused of stealing
a goat. Can you believe that? A goat! Such a silly accusation, yet
when I tried to explain I was innocent I felt like nobody believed

me. It was such a stressful ordeal that I developed a stomach ulcer and almost died. I don't think we should question him."

"So are we all in agreement?" says the Professor.

"Yes," we all say, except for Frank.

"I can't believe we're just going to let this guy walk away with our ticket," Frank says.

"Thanks for your time," I say to the manager. "Sorry about the misunderstanding."

"Would you like to look around the restaurant some more?" she says. "Perhaps it's still in here somewhere."

"We've already looked in all the places it might be," I say. "If it was here, somebody would have either found it or just thrown it away by now."

"Okay. If it turns up at least I'll know where I can find you," she says. "Have a nice day and good luck with your search."

Back outside, the mood is low. Another failed attempt at locating my ticket. I look at the Professor's car and it occurs to me we haven't searched it yet. Perhaps my ticket slipped out of my pocket during the ride from the gas station to the restaurant. I mention this to everyone and we make quick work of searching every square inch, including under the floor mats and in the cracks of the seats.

Our search turns up nothing. "I think I'll walk back to the facility," I say.

"Mind if I join you?" Hailey asks.

"Not at all," I lie.

"Don't forget about the community meeting after lunch," Boop says as she gets into the car.

Hailey and I watch as they drive away.

I turn and head in the direction of Heritage Gardens. "It's probably buried in the county landfill by now."

Hailey walks by my side in silence for a while.

After we've walked a couple blocks she says, "Do you remember when we first met?"

"Yes." I don't elaborate. Of course I do. How could I forget?

"Tell me what you remember."

"It was at a Christmas party. Andrew forced me to come. I was standing in the corner, wishing I wasn't there, and then I saw you slip. You hit the floor pretty hard."

"You were the first one to my aid. I hit my head so hard I think I passed out for a few seconds."

"I remember that. I thought you had a concussion. I wanted you to go to the emergency room."

"But I refused." She laughs. "I always was a little stubborn."

"I know. I asked you, like, three times but you wouldn't."

She suddenly stops walking. We're in front of a small park. "I want to rest a minute." She heads over to a bench a short distance away under the shade of an oak tree. I have no choice but to follow.

I sit next to her and she levels her gaze at me. "How come you never asked me out?" She rests her hand on mine, sending a shockwave up my arm. "Don't try to convince me that you didn't want to."

"Because my brother did." I pull my hand away.

"I gave you several opportunities. But you never took advantage of them. I didn't start dating Andrew until after I was convinced you weren't interested in me." She pauses. "And then I fell in love with him. I really did love him more than anything. But now he's gone and I'm wondering, what if…"

"Don't do this," I say. "Not now."

"Why not? I see the way you look at me."

I drop my gaze to the ground. I can't stand to look into her sad eyes. "It's too late." I get up and start to walk away.

I don't know what I'll do if she calls after me, but she doesn't.

I head straight to my apartment, counting my paces in prime sequences along the way. It's not until I arrive that I remember the state I left it in—complete and utter chaos. At first my heart sinks, but then I recognize what a blessing this is. If there's anything I need right now, it's a distraction such as this. I dive in with vigor.

I like the word *vigor*. It's almost as good as *verve*. The problem with *verve* is that it has two *v*'s and two *e*'s, and two plus two equals four, and two times two equals four. Two isn't a bad number (after all, it's prime) but when there are two pairs of something, the number four begins to crop up, and four is trouble. I suppose *verve* could possibly be salvaged if the two *v-e*'s were separated by some letter other than *r*. Unfortunately, *r* happens to be the eighteenth letter of the alphabet and eighteen is not prime. And to top it off, *r* is the fourth letter in the word *four*, making it perhaps the worst letter of all (although the letter *d* is in close contention.) The more I think about it, *verve* isn't a good word at all.

I wade through the mess in my living room. I wonder how some of my books made it clear across the room. I certainly hope I didn't throw them. That would be such a heinous crime.

I'd better put them back on their shelves in their newly assigned places. I wish the task were more difficult, but unfortunately their new order is perfectly engrained in my memory. Perhaps I should devise a new system. But what could possibly be better than the system I recently employed?

Then it hits me. I can maintain my same system but impose a new rule that will force me to reorganize them all. I can keep the criteria involving the prime numbers of words and letters in the titles and total number of pages and so on, but the additional criterion will be that any book with the letter *r* in the title shall be confined to one of the bottom shelves.

This task keeps me occupied for the next six hours.

I skip lunch. I ignore the rest of the disaster in my apartment. The reorganization of my books becomes my entire universe for the time being. I cannot move on with life until they are once again in order.

"What's going on in here?" The Professor's voice interrupts my progress. "Why weren't you at the meeting?"

I ignore him and continue with my assignment.

"Ben? Can you hear me?"

"Not now, Jerry."

"Why aren't you answering your phone?"

"Come back later."

"Are you all right?"

"I'll be fine. Let me finish this."

"How much longer?"

"Don't know. A few hours."

"Okay, I'll come back later."

It is now dark outside. It would be dark inside as well, but a lamp in the corner happens to be on. I'm still sitting on the floor next to my bookshelves. Four final books are spread in front of me. They all contain the letter *r* in their titles, but my bottom shelves are full. These last four books will not fit. I've been staring at them with dismay for an unknown period of time.

"Ben?" The Professor is back. I need to be more careful about locking my door. "How's it going?"

"I can't do it," I say.

"Can't do what?"

I bury my face in my hands. I want to cry. For the first time in three years, all I want to do is cry.

I hear the Professor make his way through the mess. He finds a clear spot on the floor next to me and sits. He picks up one of the volumes, inspects it, and sets it back down.

"The other day at the funeral, after you had that encounter with Lex, you told me you were going to reorganize your books."

I don't respond.

"Is that what you're working on?"

I still don't say anything.

He gazes at the shelves and then again at the four volumes on the floor. "I was wondering something, Ben."

I still don't speak. I'm afraid I'll burst into tears if I try to talk.

"I was wondering if I could borrow these four books. You know how much I like to read. I was wondering if you would let me take them out of here for a while. I promise I'll take good care of them."

I finally meet his gaze and nod my head.

"Good." He gathers them up and stands. "I'll take these to my place. I want you to get some sleep. I'll check on you in the morning."

A burden is lifted as he carries the offensive books out of my apartment. In doing so, he has made it possible for me to move on—or at least get some sleep. I'm beyond exhaustion.

I pick myself off the floor and force my way into my bedroom. I don't bother to push aside the denim jeans and striped polo shirts strewn all over the bed. I collapse on top of them and instantly fall asleep.

CHAPTER 19

The Professor wakes me. When my eyes flutter open, the reflection of the morning sun off his pink shirt jolts me to full consciousness.

"Rise and shine!"

I sit up and rub my eyes. On the side of my face I can feel the imprint from the button fly of one of my pairs of jeans.

"Glad to see you got some rest," he says.

I nod.

"Want to talk about what happened in here?"

I rub the side of my face again. "I missed the meeting yesterday."

"Yes, you did. It was productive."

"Oh, yeah?"

"Yes. We came up with enough cash to make the first bank payment."

"How did you manage to do that?"

"An unlikely source. It turns out that Frank has a rather lucrative stock portfolio and a healthy savings account—none of which he knew about until he had a conversation with his son."

"That's good news."

"It certainly is. And Frank is rather enjoying his role as hero for the moment."

"So when exactly will Peterson be able to make the payment?"

"Probably tomorrow."

"And that will buy us another month?"

"At the least. And it looks like we have other possible sources. Marvin told us about his books—most of which are now in here. He wants to sell some of them at auction. Sounds like they have a lot of value. We might be able to buy a few more months that way." He waves his hand at my room. "It looks like it's going to take you about that long to clean up this mess."

"Yeah, I sort of lost control in here."

"How does it feel?"

"How does what feel?"

"To lose control. Doesn't it feel just a little good to let loose?"

"I don't think so."

He sits next to me on the edge of my bed. "I'll admit I was pretty worried about you last night—with the books."

"Yeah, that was pretty bad." Part of me wants to put a stop to this conversation right now, but I must admit that he did perform a huge favor for me. The least I can do is be polite.

"You know what?" he says. "I think you're putting too much pressure on yourself to find that ticket. Maybe you should stop looking for it altogether."

"It wasn't the ticket that was bothering me."

He turns to face me, eyebrows raised. "I'm surprised you're willing to admit that." He shakes his head. "I'm really surprised. I knew it wasn't the ticket, but I wasn't going to say anything unless you brought it up."

"Is it that obvious?" I say.

"It's obvious to me. But I've had years and years to study people. You're not exactly an open book, but I can put two and two together."

Don't do that. That would make four.

"There's a lot more to it than you think," I say.

"There always is."

I shift my weight on the bed. I link my fingers and crack my knuckles. I can't do this. I don't operate this way. Operate. There's an *r* in the fourth spot in this word. I don't operate. That's right, I don't operate. Literally and figuratively. I'll never perform surgery again—not after what I did to Andrew.

Andrew. There's that *r* again. It's haunting me.

"Had enough for now?" The Professor stands.

I don't reply.

"Very well." He turns to go, but halts. "If you want some advice, here it is: you need to relinquish control of your life. Put your faith in something bigger than yourself."

I don't say anything as he exits my bedroom. "Oh, I almost forgot," he calls from the living room. "Peterson was looking for you. He wants you to come to his office as soon as you get a chance."

I change into my work clothes and brush my teeth. It has just dawned on me that I've seriously neglected my work duties over the past several days. True, this place wouldn't fall apart if I disappeared for a week, but Junior has probably started to notice. I bet this is what he wants to talk to me about.

I think I destroyed my walkie-talkie during my rampage through the apartment. Junior is going to want me to get a new one.

I make quick time getting over to his office. His door is open, so I enter and sit opposite him at his desk.

"I've decided to sell to the developers," he says, dispensing with any sort of greeting.

"But we have the money for the payment!"

"We have enough to make the first payment, but we still don't know where we're going to find money next month or the month after that," he says.

"We'll come up with something, and there's still a chance my ticket could turn up."

"You know that's not going to happen." His gaze flicks from side to side and he wrings his pudgy hands. "Listen, Ben, the developers sweetened the deal quite a bit. I don't know why, but they really want this place. If I don't sell now, we'll all regret it in a few months when we're dead broke and out of options. Then everybody will blame me for not taking action when I could have."

"What did they do to sweeten the deal?"

"They added four—I mean two—hundred thousand dollars cash." He dabs the sweat off his brow.

"Wow," I say.

"Yeah. I'd be crazy to turn them down."

"But what about all the residents? They'll all lose their homes if you sell."

"They'll be fine. Places like this are a dime a dozen. Besides, with all this extra cash I can afford to be more generous with helping to subsidize the cost of their relocation."

"Sounds like you've already made up your mind."

His cheeks bloat and turn red. "It was my decision to make. I own this place and I can sell it if I want. I thought you would see the wisdom of such a move. I'll never get an offer this good again, and if the bank forecloses, I'll be penniless. This way we all can leave with some cash in our pockets." He stands and glances at the door.

I take my cue and stand as well. "You already signed the papers, didn't you?"

"I didn't have a choice."

I shake my head with disgust. "When does everyone need to be out of here?"

"They wanted an expedited escrow, but I demanded thirty days."

"Thirty days! That's all?"

"That should be plenty of time."

I feel sick to my stomach. "Exactly how much of this extra cash are you planning to pass on to the residents?"

"Just what are you insinuating?" His face turns a deeper shade of red. "If I wanted to, I could keep all of it. There's no law that says I have to help out with anybody's moving expenses, but I'm still going to anyway. Most people would consider my actions extremely generous."

"Yeah, your generosity astounds me," I mutter as I walk out the door. I pause in the hall and call over my shoulder, "If you were hoping I would make the announcement to everybody, you'd better think again. You can tell them you're a sellout yourself."

"Sellout!" he hollers back. "Look who's talking! You think I don't know about your past? I hear the gossip too, you know. At least I have the guts to seize an opportunity instead of running and hiding and becoming some loser who scrapes by in a dead-end job that pays barely above minimum wage."

I spin and almost lunge at the selfish jerk, but stop myself.

He flinches and then smirks when he realizes I'm not going to attack him. "Don't worry," he says, "I'll write you a good letter of recommendation for your next job. I saw a help wanted sign for a cleaning person at a motel in town. Maybe you could work there."

It takes all my energy to maintain my composure. "You're not your father's son," I say. "He was a good man. He never would've let it come to this."

I head straight to Building C and knock on the Professor's door. We aren't able to reach Marvin at his room, but he does answer his mobile phone. He happens to be over at Betty's place having lunch, so they invite us over.

"Think we should let Frank know?" says the Professor as we walk out his door.

"It'll just upset him when he figures out that Marvin was having lunch with Betty," I say.

As we exit the building, Frank's voice calls after us, "Hey! What are you guys up to?"

I can't think of a good lie, so I turn to tell him the truth. I'm surprised to see Jane by his side. I catch the Professor's eye and he winks.

"We're headed over to Betty's place for an emergency meeting," I say. "Would you two care to join us?"

"Seems like we've been having a lot of these emergency meetings lately," Frank says. "What's it about this time?"

"Let me put it this way," I say, "make sure you take your blood-pressure medication before you come."

"But my doctor says I have to wait for at least two hours after I pop a Viagra," Frank says and then guffaws.

"Frank!" Jane slaps him playfully. "You're a dirty old man." She looks at us and blushes. "Don't believe a word he says. He didn't take any pills."

"You're darn right I didn't," Franks says. "Don't need it. Everything's working fine in my tool department. Hey, is Marvin gonna be at this thing? Because if he is I'll bring some samples I swiped from the doctor's office last time I was there. I thought I might be able to sell them on the street, but I'd be willing to donate them to Marvin out of charity."

"Are you coming or not?" I say.

"Jeez, Mr. Sour Pants. This must be bad. We're coming."

Boop bustles about her kitchen. We don't all fit around her small table, so the Professor and I perch on barstools at the counter while Frank, Marvin, and Jane sit at the table. I'm not sure where Hailey is.

"My, my, I wasn't expecting such a large crowd for lunch." Boop's head is buried in her fridge. "Now don't get me wrong, there's nothing I love more than having company. I just wish I was more prepared." She clucks her tongue as she rummages around. My heart skips a beat as I catch yet another glimpse of the photo of Hailey on the refrigerator door.

"Well," Boop says, "I'm sorry to say all I have to offer in the way of sandwiches is turkey, ham, pastrami, roast beef, or chicken breast. The only types of bread I have are whole wheat, white, rye, sourdough, or rosemary. And unfortunately my cheese selection is limited to Swiss, provolone, sharp cheddar, mild cheddar, Monterey jack, mozzarella, or American. And if you want veggies all I have is lettuce, tomato, cucumber, red onion, pickles, olives, or avocado."

"You mean you don't have any bologna?" Frank says with genuine disappointment.

"I'm terribly sorry, but I don't."

"What about salami?"

"Come on, Frank," Marvin says. "Don't be rude."

"Jeez, it doesn't hurt to ask. Maybe she missed it in there with all that other crap."

"I'm sure there's something you like out of all those options," the Professor says.

"How about onion dip?" Frank says.

"I do have onion dip!" Boop bobs her head and smiles.

"Good. I'll take onion dip on sourdough, please." Frank turns to Marvin, "Did you hear that? I said 'please.'"

"Onion dip on sourdough?" Marvin says.

"That's right."

"It's a wonder you're still alive."

"Usually I put bacon on it too, but I didn't ask because I wouldn't want to be rude."

"What kind of sandwich would you like, Marvin?" Betty says.

"I think I lost my appetite. Maybe you should come back to me later."

Boop proceeds to take the rest of our orders.

"Aren't you going to write any of this down?" Frank says. "How're you going to remember it all?"

"Don't you know?" Boop says. "I have a perfect memory. Did I ever tell you I remember everything? Everything. The good and the bad, and in vivid detail. Why, I can remember every time I ever

took a sip of spoiled milk—" She gags. "I do that every time!" She
gags again. "I've got to start using a different example." She assembles a sandwich with turkey, Swiss, avocado, and mayo on rye and
hands it to me. "Here you go, Benji. Enjoy!"

I requested roast beef and cheddar.

I despise avocado. I've never actually tried it, but I know I'll hate
it. It doesn't look right. It's green and slimy—like those worms that
live on tomato plants.

"Thanks," I say. I'm not the least bit hungry and I was already
feeling sick to my stomach before I even got here. I'm afraid the
avocado is going to push me over the edge.

Boop is still watching me, waiting for me to take my first bite.

I pick up the sandwich with both hands and look at it. It gives
me an evil smile and then sticks out its green tongue. Bile churns in
my stomach and creeps up into my throat. It's now or never. There's
no use delaying the inevitable. I open my mouth, and then…

"Hey, everybody!" Hailey's voice rescues me from that fateful
bite. "What's going on?"

All eyes turn toward my savior. I set the sandwich down, a move
that goes unnoticed.

"We're having lunch and an emergency meeting," Boop says.
"Would you like a sandwich?"

As Betty turns back to her ingredients I deftly scrape the offensive avocado off my sandwich and bury it in my napkin, which
quickly disappears into my pocket. Disaster averted.

"What's the emergency?" Hailey says, avoiding eye contact
with me.

"Yeah. When are you going to tell us?" Frank says.

"Don't you all want to eat first?" I say. "This news is sure to make
you lose your appetites."

"I think we should eat first," Boop says. "My father used to say
that one should never find out bad news on an empty stomach. Of
course, when his stomach was full, it was usually full of beer."

"Hey, that's a good idea!" Frank says. "Got any booze?"

"I'm not a fan of alcohol," Boop says. "I think the world would be a better place without it."

"I was just kidding," Frank says. "I don't like it either. Is my sandwich ready yet?"

"I'll make yours next." Boop opens the tub of onion dip.

Hailey wrinkles her nose as her aunt spreads the dip on two slices of sourdough bread and then slaps the pieces together.

I sigh as my thoughts turn towards the news I'm about to break. I don't want to be the one who has to tell them. I glance down at my sandwich again, giving it a quick inspection for any residual traces of green. I take a bite. I'm barely able to choke it down, and not because there used to be avocado on it.

"Is it that bad, Benji?" Boop says.

"I'm sorry, I'm just not hungry," I say.

"I didn't mean the sandwich."

"Oh. Yeah, I'm afraid to say that it really is that bad."

"Come on," Frank says, "the suspense is killing me."

"No, your sandwich is killing you," Marvin says.

"Just get it over with and tell us." Frank crams a massive bite into his mouth, leaving a dollop of onion dip on his nose.

"Peterson sold to the developers," I say. "We have thirty days to vacate the premises."

"What?" Frank is out of his chair. The blob of dip on his nose dislodges and splats on the floor.

"It's a done deal," I say.

"But that doesn't make any sense!" Jane, who has been quiet, speaks up. "Why would he go and do a thing like that?"

"Because he's a selfish ratfink traitor!" Frank shakes his fist in the air. "I bet those developers offered him a truckload of cash and he couldn't resist the offer. I'm right, aren't I!"

"That can't be true," Jane says. "I was with him in the hospital after he took all those pills when he thought he was going to lose this place because of his mistakes. He seemed like he really cared. Why would he suddenly change and sell this place out from under us like this?"

"I thought the same thing," says the Professor. "But I think the real reason he tried to kill himself was because he thought he was broke. I don't think it had anything to do with the possibility of losing Heritage Gardens. I think Frank hit the nail on the head with his analysis of the situation."

Boop is standing frozen in the middle of the kitchen, loaf of bread in one hand, jar of mayonnaise in the other. She bursts into tears. "This is all my fault. All my fault. All these wonderful people are going to lose their homes because of me. I just don't know what I'm going to do."

Frank, still on his feet, shouts, "By golly, I know what to do. I say we declare war on the developers. They're going to have to drive their bulldozers right over the top of my cold, dead body if they want to tear this place down!"

"Where will I move to?" Marvin says. "I don't know where to go. How am I going to find another place so soon?"

"You're not gonna have to," Frank says as he grabs his walker. "I'm gonna put a stop to this right now."

"Where are you going?" Jane says.

"I've got a few phone calls to make," Frank says. "Don't worry, I'll come up with something. You people stay here."

Hailey tries to calm her aunt while Marvin and Jane remain at the table, still in shock. The Professor leans over to me. "How much money is Peterson going to make on this deal?"

"I'm not exactly sure. He said it was an extra two hundred thousand, most of which he claims he's going to give back to the residents. But I have a hunch the developers are giving him more."

"Why would they do that?" he says.

"I really have no idea."

"It would make more sense for them to wait for the bank to foreclose. Then they could purchase the land for a killer deal." He scratches his chin. "They must have some sort of timeframe they have to stick to or something like that."

"All I know is that they got their way. Peterson signed the papers. He probably did it a week ago but was afraid to tell anyone."

"So what are we going to do?" Marvin says.

"Start packing," I say.

"So that's it?" Hailey says, making eye contact with me for the first time. "You're just going to give up?"

"What do you want me to say?"

"I don't know." One of her arms is wrapped around her aunt's shoulders. "There must be a way we can put a stop to this legally."

"It's been a while since I looked at the contract for my lease," says the Professor, "But I'm sure there's some sort of provision about how much notice I'm supposed to be given if Peterson wants to terminate my lease."

"Even if that's the case, I don't think it will stop the sale," I say.

"But at least we could delay it for a while," Hailey says.

I don't respond. It seems like a hopeless battle to me.

"What we need to do is find a way to get the developer to back out of the deal," Marvin says.

"From what I gather, they're pretty intent on purchasing this place," I say. "They're willing to pay more than they have to, and they're doing everything in their power to expedite things."

"Exactly," Marvin says. "They must be in some sort of a hurry. If we find a way to stir up trouble or delay things, they might back out altogether and purchase a different property rather than get bogged down in some sort of legal battle."

"Well, I don't have any bright ideas," I say. "But I'm willing to go along with whatever you guys want to do. If there's a way to save your homes and put a stop to Peterson, I'll do whatever it takes."

"We need an inside man," Marvin says. "Someone close to the enemy so we can sniff out any weaknesses. You're the closest person to Peterson. Try to find out everything you can about the deal and the developer."

"That might be difficult," I say.

"Why?"

"Because I sort of chewed him out earlier today."

"Well, then you better go make nice."

"How am I supposed to do that?"

"I don't know—do what he would do. Kiss up. Be a weasel. Butter him up. I'm sure you'll think of something. But you'd better act quick. Seems like we don't have much time at all."

I'm back in Junior's office. He's busy at his paper shredder. I wonder what sort of evidence he's destroying.

"What do you want?" he says when he notices me.

"I came to apologize," I say in as meek a voice I can muster without making myself vomit.

His eyes narrow. "Why?"

"I reacted rather harshly earlier today. I said some things I shouldn't have."

He crosses his arms. A smug expression slowly overtakes the suspicious look on his face.

"Now that I've had a chance to think about it some more," I say, "I see the wisdom of the move you made. You made a choice that will benefit everybody in the long run." I almost say that I even think it's exactly what his father would have done, but I can't force myself to.

"I knew you would come around," he says, still smirking.

"Yes. I owe you my sincerest apology. You've done a lot to help me and you've been a good boss. I know there's probably a lot to be done over the next several days and I was wondering how I could help you."

"Now that you've finally seen the wisdom of my decision, the way you could help me most is by convincing everybody else that this really is the best thing," he says. "Can I count on you to do this?"

"Certainly. I'll make the announcement tonight at dinner. Is there anything else?"

"I'll let you know." He returns his attention to the shredder. "I won't be able to be there this evening, but I would like a report on how it goes."

"I'll do that." I turn to leave. Big surprise. I'd hide at home too if I were him.

CHAPTER 20

I awoke this morning from a new nightmare. One that held a terrible truth. A truth that has been trying to worm its way into my head over the past several months. A truth that I keep beating back into my subconscious mind only to have it reappear. This time it used a new tactic. A better one. Now I have to do something about it; I have to disprove it or else I cannot go on. This truth gave me a chance to repudiate it once and for all—it challenged me with a test. A test that I must complete before I'll once again be able to tolerate living with myself.

I think I can steal myself away for a few hours this morning in order to accomplish this task. I really don't have a choice.

It's probably best to stay away from Heritage Gardens this morning anyway. After my announcement last night, I'm sure the place is in an uproar. I'll give the storm a chance to calm a bit longer. In the meantime I'll take care of what I must do.

It involves my wrong lottery ticket—the one with the multiples of four. I still have it. Something inside me wouldn't let me throw it away. It's still in the plastic bag, folded and stuffed in my wallet where I should've put my first ticket before I lost it.

With grim resolve I dress myself, shave, brush my teeth, and step out the door. My apartment is still a total mess, but it will have to wait until later.

My destination is the police station downtown. When I arrive I feel like an accused man awaiting the jury's verdict. There's no escaping it. I must find out.

It's a small police station, basically an open room with several desks scattered about. There are two or three closed doors that lead to private offices. The only person in the main room is a secretary behind a desk close to the front door.

"Can I help you?" The fluorescent lighting doesn't help her poorly colored hair.

"I'd like to speak to somebody about fingerprints."

"That would be me. It's a fifty dollar fee if you need to be printed."

"That's not exactly what I need."

"Then why don't you tell me exactly what you need." She taps her fingers on her desk.

I fish the plastic bag out of my wallet. "I need to know how many sets of prints are on this ticket."

"Do you wish to report a crime?"

"No, nothing like that."

"We don't offer forensic services as a convenience. We are here to fight crime."

"Listen, ma'am. I know you're probably very busy and I'm probably going about this all wrong. I don't want to waste your valuable time. Could you please maybe tell me how I should go about finding out who has touched this ticket?"

"You would need to get it fingerprinted and have the fingerprints matched against the national data base." She gives me a curt smile and then turns to her computer.

"And where would I go to do this?"

"A law enforcement agency." She doesn't turn her gaze from her screen.

"I see." I stand there, plastic bag dangling from my fingers.

"Did you need anything else?"

"I don't know how to explain how important this is to me." I'm trying not to sound too desperate.

She finally turns her cold stare back at me. But her gaze softens when she sees my expression. She sighs and holds out her hand. "This counts as my random act of kindness for today. You're lucky that I also double as lab technician here."

I give her the bag.

"It'll take a little while," she says. "You can sit over there. If the system is running slow it can take over an hour to get a match."

I take a seat on an uncomfortable wooden bench near the door. Each passing minute is an excruciating century. The weight of the suspense is unbearable, but I must know. I must know the truth.

Finally, after what seems like an eternity, she returns. "Only two different sets of prints could be identified on this piece of paper. Due to privacy issues I cannot tell you the names of the individuals, but I can tell you that one of them resides in Sacramento, and the other's last known residence was in North Carolina but he was registered as a missing person about three years ago." She hands the bag back to me. "Strangely enough, that missing person looks a lot like you."

"I see," I say. "You're certain there aren't any other prints?"

"Yes."

"I see."

"Now, Mister, I've gone above and beyond the call of duty. If you would excuse me, I have some real work to do."

"Okay, thanks," I say. I walk out the door and stand outside the building in a state of shock. I need to talk to the Professor.

"Thank goodness you're here," I say when the Professor answers his door. He appears about to reply but he remains silent when he sees my face. He ushers me inside and takes a seat in his well-worn recliner. The only place for me to sit is on the side of his bed, so I do. He gazes at me expectantly.

Words fail me.

He folds his hands in his lap and waits.

"I don't know where to start," I say.

"Just say what you came to say, and try to use as few words as possible."

"Okay." I think for a few seconds, then say, "I'm crazy."

"That's a good start, but I think you're going to have to use a few more words than that."

"Okay. How about insane, nutcase, loco, mad, mental?"

"Those are all good words too, but I understood your first one. I was hoping you would explain why you think you're crazy—a task which crazy people are usually unable to perform."

"There are only two sets of fingerprints on my lottery ticket," I say, expecting him to immediately understand the horrible implication behind this fact.

"You found the missing ticket?"

"No. I'm referring to the incorrect one."

"You had it fingerprinted?"

"Yes."

"Why?"

"To prove to myself that I'm not crazy. But instead, I managed to secure undeniable proof that I've lost my mind—or at least part of it."

"Go on."

"Give me a second." I wipe my palms on my pants. "This isn't easy for me. I'm used to having it all figured out." Part of me wants to get up and run out the door and never come back. I don't know where I'll go, but it will be far away from here. I could start a new life and leave this one behind. I'm more scared than I've ever been. Scared of the worst thing I could ever be afraid of. Scared of myself. "Sometimes I have these blankouts," I finally say.

"You mean blackouts?"

"No, blankouts. You know, like when you're driving and then suddenly you realize you're home and you can't remember for the life of you whether or not you stopped at all the red lights because you can't remember the last ten minutes of your drive."

"Those are quite common."

"I know. That's not what I'm worried about. I'm having episodes of something similar. Or at least I've become more aware of them. Anyway, whatever they are, it's more than just some sort of hypnosis." I gulp. "I think I'm splitting."

He furrows his brow. "Splitting? What makes you think this?"

"I've noticed some minor clues here and there, but mostly I've been plagued just by the thought of it. One day, about a month or two ago, the thought just popped into my head. Ever since, it keeps coming back at random times. I've tried to reason it away but it keeps coming back. And then, this morning, it challenged me to a test. I was happy to accept this challenge because I figured it would give me a chance to make it go away once and for all."

"And what does any of this have to do with the lottery ticket?"

"I now have undeniable proof that only two people have ever touched that ticket." I pause to allow this to sink in. "I was one of them, and the lottery official in Sacramento was the other."

He thinks this over for a moment. "So you never had the winning ticket?"

"No, that's not what I'm saying. I did have the winning ticket. I saw it with my own eyes. Lex saw it too. In fact, I don't think I ever lost it. I think I still have it somewhere but I won't tell myself where it is."

He rubs his chin.

I take the plastic bag containing the losing ticket out of my pocket. "This is the ticket with the nonwinning numbers. As you know, I found it under the exact same table where Lex and I had dinner. And I have now confirmed that it was never touched by

anyone but myself and the lottery official. The only logical explanation is that I purchased this ticket myself and placed it under
the table where I knew I would eventually look for it." I pause. "If
the fingerprints aren't proof enough, I also have another piece of
evidence. The numbers on this ticket are all multiples of four. I'm
the only person who knows that I despise the number four. I chose
these numbers to taunt myself."

"The only problem is that you have no memory of actually performing any of these actions," he says.

"Exactly. That's how I know I'm splitting."

The fire behind his eyes tells me his mind is working furiously
to process my revelation. He wants to poke a hole in my theory, but
it's watertight. I've already tried to debunk it myself, but to no avail.
The irrefutable fact is that there is more to me than just me. There's
a part of me that has broken loose, and it's playing games with me.

He finally speaks. "I once studied a patient who had multiple
personalities." He slowly shakes his head. "I don't think you're
splitting."

"It doesn't matter what you think," I say. "I have proof."

"There's another theory that could explain everything," he says.
He gazes at me as if he expects me to know what he means.

I have no idea.

"Come on, Ben," he says. He glances at the ceiling.

I look up as well, but don't find the answer. Then it hits me. "You
can't be serious," I say.

"Of course I'm serious. Perhaps you're dealing with some sort of
supernatural intervention. Perhaps nobody had ever touched that
ticket until you picked it up from under the table. And then, of
course, the lottery official touched it. That would explain how there
are only two sets of prints on it."

"That's not a plausible theory." I shake my head with disgust.
"That's a copout."

"No, it's a choice."

"A choice?"

"Yes. A choice."

I storm from the Professor's room. Choice? What kind of sick choice is this? I thought for sure the Professor would help me. He only made things worse.

I'm too distraught to count my paces as I head to my apartment. It's come down to one of two options: either I'm mentally ill or God is trying to get my attention. Which one is it going to be?

If I decide I no longer have control over my mental faculties, I don't know how I'll go on. On the other hand, if I decide God really does care about what I'm up to, the implications will turn my world upside down. I'll have to start caring about him. And then I'll have to figure out what my purpose is. And then I'll have to put my faith in something bigger than me.

I'd rather just put my faith in me.

But I can't trust myself—not if I'm splitting. I'll never be able to trust myself again if that's the case.

Or maybe I can. It's possible to recover from a mental illness. Perhaps with the help of some intense psychotherapy and maybe even some heavy-duty medications, I could whip my mind back into shape and unsplit any personalities that may have escaped.

But still, the thought that I might have an alter ego that could appear at any time and take over my body is too much for me to handle. How could I ever be certain this other side of me is fully contained?

Either option has ramifications that I'm just not ready to accept right now. There's too much other stuff going on.

"Hey, Ben!" Junior's voice interrupts my thoughts as I walk along the koi pond in the direction of my apartment. "I've been trying to get a hold of you."

"Well, here I am."

"How did it go with the announcement last night?"

"About as well as could be expected."

"People are giving me angry looks."

"Give them some time to adjust."

"Yeah, I'm sure they'll come around," he says. "I have another favor to ask of you . . ."

CHAPTER 21

I can't believe Junior is making me do this. He wants me to take a contractor for the developer on a tour of the premises. I've got to give the guy who's going to bulldoze this place a grand tour. I almost flat-out refused to do it, but then I remembered my promise to my friends. This will be the perfect opportunity for me to familiarize myself with the enemy. Perhaps I'll discover some sort of weakness.

I'm sitting in the golf cart, waiting outside Junior's office. I hope Junior isn't planning on tagging along as well. I don't think I'll be able to stomach that.

As I wait, Frank shuffles by, towing a large black trash bag containing who knows what balanced on top of his walker.

"I heard you're taking somebody from the demolition crew on a tour of the property today," he says.

"Yeah, I'm not too excited about that."

"No, it's gonna be perfect!" He rubs his hands together with glee.

"Why?" My voice turns suspicious. "What are you going to do?"

"Who's it gonna be? The head honcho?" He ignores my question.

"I don't really know. I think it's going to be one of the head contractors."

"Excellent!"

"Tell me what you're going to do."

"No, it'll be better if you're surprised. That way you won't have to act. Just make sure you take him around to the other side of the pond—you know, where that grassy area is with all those trees."

"But there's nothing over there," I say.

"Well, just think of a reason to bring him over there, okay?"

"Okay."

"Promise me."

"I promise."

"Good. How much time do I have?" He readjusts the trash bag balancing on his walker.

"I don't know. Maybe forty minutes."

"Give me an hour. Show him some other stuff first."

"Sure, Frank. Whatever you say. This plan of yours better not involve any firearms."

"Ha! No. That's Plan B."

"Okay. You've got an hour."

"Good. Have you seen Marvin?"

"He's in on this too?"

"Well, I needed somebody's help. Turns out he's not a good-for-nothin' after all."

I'm still waiting. Frank left a good ten minutes ago. This guy I'm supposed to be meeting is running late. My curiosity grows with each passing moment. I wonder what Frank and Marvin have up their sleeves.

"Hi." Lex's voice startles me. "Sorry to sneak up on you like that. I thought you heard me coming."

"Hi." I haven't seen her since the night we played Scrabble.

"How've you been?" she says after an awkward pause. She's wearing jeans, a T-shirt, some old hiking boots, and she's carrying a shovel.

"Things have been a little crazy."

"Well, it's good to see you." She switches the shovel to her other hand. "Sorry, I have to run. I'm late."

"Are you in on Frank's little scheme too?"

"Of course." She hurries off.

I feel an odd sense of sadness as she leaves. Like I'm watching a movie with a tragic ending—the sort of ending where everyone knows how the story should end, but it doesn't end that way. The sort of ending where the characters could have easily made everything turn out differently if only they could have seen it from the audience's perspective. The sort of ending where the audience wants to stand up and scream, "Don't let her walk away, you fool!"

I hate those kinds of movies.

"This is Ben." Junior's voice stirs me from my reverie. He and a well-cut athletic man in his midforties are approaching. I get off the cart and extend my hand.

"I'm John," the man says, crushing my hand.

"Ben knows the property well," Junior says with pride, as if he had something to do with my knowledge of the place. "He'll take us around."

I'm regretting the fact that the cart is a four-seater.

"What would you like to see?" I say as we take our seats.

"I've seen aerial shots of the property from satellite photos, so I have a general idea of the layout, but I need to check into some details such as the location of underground power lines, sewage lines, and water mains."

"No problem," I say as I start driving. "I'll take you around the main building first."

John unfolds a map of the property.

"What kind of a shopping mall is this going to be?" I say.

"I'm not at liberty to say." John studies the map.

I decide to abandon any further attempts at small talk for the time being. As we circle Building C he makes several notations on his map. I try to discreetly read it out of the corner of my eye, but it just looks like chicken scratch. He's probably calculating how much dynamite he'll need to blow everything up.

Eventually we make our way past the koi pond.

"How deep is that?" he says.

"Only two or three feet at the max." I wonder what will become of Marvin's fish. These guys will probably bulldoze a bunch of dirt right into the pond. Marvin's fish will be buried alive.

"Good."

"Oh, that reminds me," I say. "I need to check the pump and filter on the other side of the pond. It will only take a minute." I don't give him a chance to object. I make a quick turn and drive across the lawn, circling the pond. On the other side of the pond there is a small hill—more of a mound—with a gentle slope. A grove of trees is located on the other side. The mound is just large enough to obscure the bottom halves of the trees.

I am headed for the trees. The only thing over there is a small shack containing the pump and filter system for the pond. As we crest the mound, Frank, Marvin, and Lex come into view. Lex is working with the shovel next to a pile of recently unearthed dirt. Marvin and Frank stand next to her, peering into her hole. When they see us coming they begin to wave frantically.

"What's going on?" Junior says.

"I guess we better go check it out," I say. I want to say that I hope it's not his grave they're digging, but I hold my tongue.

When we draw close, we can hear Frank and Marvin arguing.

"I'm the one who found it!" Frank hollers

"I'm the one who recognized what it was. You were totally wrong."

"It don't make any difference what I thought it was, I still made the discovery."

"Only a total moron would mistake a human skull for a dinosaur bone." Marvin shakes his head.

I park the cart next to Lex's pile of dirt. A thin layer of grime is plastered to the sweat on Lex's brow.

"What's going on here?" Junior says. "Did you say human skull?"

"Yep!" Frank says. "And I want it to be clear that I'm the one who found it." He points to a dirty human skull next to the pile of dirt. A fragment of pottery rests on top of it.

Junior takes a step back when he sees the bony eye sockets glaring at him. I steal a glance at the contractor, who is masking a look of concern.

"Frank thought it was a dinosaur fossil," Marvin says. "He was bragging about how he was going to sell it to a museum for twenty million dollars. Turns out all he found was a dead body."

"It might be a prehistoric man," Frank says. "Maybe it's the missing link. I bet I could get eighty million."

"Stop digging!" The Professor is hurrying toward us, slightly out of breath. "I came as soon as I heard." He heads straight for the skull and kneels to examine it. He gingerly picks up the shard of pottery and gives it a close inspection. "Hmmm. Just as I suspected."

"What?" We all say.

"We're standing on sacred ground." He looks at us with a grave expression. "This could be a Native American burial sight—most likely from the Pechanga band of Luisiaño Indians who have lived in this area for more than ten thousand years."

"Holy moly," Frank says. "So you think this whole hill is a burial mound?"

"That would be a plausible theory. Temecula is the only city in Southern California that has maintained its Native American name—I don't see how these bones and pottery could be anything else."

"Holy moly." Frank pauses and scratches his head. "How much do you suppose it's worth?"

"Worth?" Marvin throws his arms in the air. "You can't sell an Indian burial mound."

"Why not?"

"You just can't. It's sacred. It belongs to the tribe."

"Let me take a look at that." The contractor picks up the skull and gives it a cursory exam. Then he takes the shard of pottery from the Professor's hand and taps his finger against it.

"Hey, be careful with that," Frank says. "If I can't sell the bones I might still be able to get something for the other artifacts."

"Where exactly did you find these?" the contractor says.

"I saw the top of the skull poking through the ground where the last rain eroded some of the mound away," Frank says proudly, "so I dug it out. I found this piece of pottery next to it. I think it was right here, but it might have been over there too." He points to a spot of bare earth on the slope about twenty yards away.

"I see," the contractor says. He abruptly takes the shovel from Lex's hand and starts digging in her hole.

"Hey! What do you think you're doing?" says the Professor.

"Seeing if you're right."

"I don't think that's such a good idea," Marvin says. "I think the penalty for desecrating a Native American burial site is pretty steep."

"I think Jerry and Marvin are right," Lex says. "Maybe we should contact the proper authorities before we proceed any further. I don't want to get into any trouble."

The contractor tosses the shovel aside and gazes at the imposing mound. The wheels are turning in his head. The hill is right smack in the middle of the property.

"Hold on a minute, everybody." Junior finally finds his whiny voice again. "Let's not jump to conclusions." He wrings his hands. "In fact, I don't think it's such a good idea to tell any authorities about this. These Indian burial grounds just cause a big political mess. Sometimes it's best just to let the past rest in the past."

"This is no good," the contractor says. "Did you know about this?" His voice turns accusatory.

"No, no!" Junior's face turns pale. "Absolutely not. I swear!"

"We can't develop this land. It's worthless," the contractor says.

"But the papers are already signed!"

Ignoring Junior, the contractor unclips his mobile phone from his belt. "Shoot, no signal." He looks at me. "I need to get to a phone."

"I'll take you," Junior says as he gets into the driver seat of the cart. "Ben, you stay here and handle this. I don't want anybody to leave this spot until I return, okay?"

"Okay, boss," I say.

The contractor takes a seat next to Junior and they speed away. When they are out of earshot, Frank and Marvin burst into laughter.

"That was great!" Frank says, giving Marvin a high five.

"And the academy award goes to Dr. Lex Kentucky, who recited her line perfectly!" Marvin says.

"Where did you get the skull and pottery shard?" I say.

"I know a guy who volunteers at the museum," Marvin says. "He let me borrow them."

I pick up the skull and examine it. A small number etched in dark ink at the base of the occipital bone jumps out at me. Probably the museum's archival numbering system. "Do you think he saw this?" I ask.

"Nah," says the Professor. "We smudged some dirt over it, so it's hardly noticeable. Most people are too shocked by the sight of a human skull to notice a small detail like those numbers."

"It was risky, but it worked!" Marvin says.

"You know what?" I say. "I think you might be right."

We're having a party at Boop's place to celebrate today's victory. The developer wasted no time in pulling out. Even Junior wound up being pleased because he got to keep the deposit—the exact amount of which remains unclear to me. Junior wasn't invited to the party.

But Lex is here.

And so is Hailey.

I want to be happy about today's victory, but I'm distracted by too many other things. I'm sitting in a chair in the corner, nursing a Diet Pepsi. Frank and Marvin are across the room, laughing and joking like old army buddies. The women are gathered around the kitchen table going through one of Boop's photo albums—she has a library of several hundred.

"Which one are you tonight?" The Professor takes a seat on the empty sofa next to my chair.

"Huh?"

"Which Ben are you?" He chuckles.

"That's not funny."

"It wouldn't be funny if it was true, but it's not, so it is."

"I don't see how you can be so certain," I say.

"When are you going to make your decision?" His tone is more serious.

"Decision?"

"You keep acting like you don't understand what I mean," he says. "That makes conversation cumbersome."

"You keep making vague references," I say. "That makes conversation annoying."

"Okay, I'll give you that one." He leans back into the cushion as if settling in for a long stay. "The way I see it, you have three major decisions you are wrestling with. Any one of them alone would be a huge burden. Instead of bringing all three of them up at once, I was trying to give you the option to steer the conversation in the direction of the one that was bothering you the most."

"How thoughtful of you."

"Sarcasm. Another manifestation of your stress."

"Okay, I'll bite," I say. "I'd be very interested in knowing what you think these three major decisions are."

"Crazy versus God, janitor versus doctor, and"—he lowers his voice—"Lex versus Hailey."

I glare at him. I don't know why I'm angry, but I am. I'm about to say something sharp when he clutches his chest, groans, and pitches forward.

"Not this game again," I say.

"Hey, is he all right?" Marvin says from across the room.

"He's fine," I say. "Just trying to prove a point."

"Not—fine," he gasps.

"Seriously, this isn't funny," I say. Frank and Marvin are out of their seats.

The Professor rolls forward off the couch and lays flat on his back on the floor. "Can't breathe."

"Something's the matter with Jerry!" Frank hollers to the kitchen. "Someone call 911! Jeez, Ben, why aren't you doing anything?"

Time stands still as I finally realize this isn't a game. The Professor's eyes roll back in his head. He's no longer breathing.

In a blur I'm by his side. Neon shirt is ripped from his chest. My fingers are on his neck, my ear next to his lips. Then my mouth is on his, trying to force oxygen into his lungs. My palms are on his sternum, thrusting. I don't know for how long this goes on. I hear nothing. Eventually I realize the emergency personnel are by my side. I don't yield my position. They join in. Oxygen mask is on his face, somebody is bagging him now. I continue chest compressions as they load him onto a stretcher and into the ambulance. Somebody tries to take over the compressions, but my palms never leave his chest.

We arrive at the hospital. I continue my task. Somehow the emergency room physician knows I'm a cardiothoracic surgeon; I don't know if I told him or somebody else. He listens to my instructions and takes my advice, but somehow manages to pry me away. I will not be permitted to remain with the Professor any longer. I am confined to a private waiting area. Alone.

God, please help him.

Please help him, God.

God, please help him.

Hours have passed. Everybody is here. I don't know what they're saying, I don't hear them.

God, please help him.

Please help him, God.

God, please help him.

The minutes seem like hours and the hours seem like minutes. All my energy is focused on one task.

God, please help him.

Please help him, God.

God, please help him.

A surgeon enters the room. I hear him say, "I'm sorry to give you this news . . ."

And then I can't hear him anymore. All I know is that I'm running, counting as fast as I can.

The hospital is over five miles from my apartment. I think I ran the whole way. My bronchioles are constricted and clogged with mucous. If I don't use my inhaler, I might suffocate. I'm tempted not to use it.

But I do. I puff on it four times. My airways slowly begin to relax and the air flows into my lungs once again.

Then I burst into tears. I scream and cry until I reach the point where I need to use my inhaler again. Two more puffs, and then the screaming begins again.

When I'm finally exhausted, I lie on my back in the middle of my disaster of a living room and stare at the dark ceiling. The thought, *Why, God, why?* wants to creep into my mind, but I beat it down. It's a stupid question. I already know the answer.

It's a stupid question because it's the wrong question. There is no why. There is no reason. And I'm crazy anyway. I wish my other self would take over now.

"Ben?" Hailey's voice invades my dark apartment. "Are you here?"

"Yes."

"Where's the light switch?"

"To the left of the door."

She turns it on. It's brighter than I remember.

"What happened in here?" she says. And then, without waiting for an answer, "Why did you run off?"

"I can't deal with this right now."

"Well, we're all going to take turns and we want to know if you would like a shift."

"What?"

"Someone should be there around the clock so he's not alone when he wakes up."

"I don't understand. The doctor said he didn't make it."

"He didn't say that." Hailey picks her way through the mess and sits next to me. "Jerry's not dead. He's in a coma. He didn't wake up from surgery."

"But I heard the doctor say—" I sit up. "He's not dead?"

She places her hand on my arm. "No. He's still very much alive."

"So the doctor saved him."

She leans around so she can look me full in the face. "Doctors don't save people or fail to save people. They just do what they're trained to do. They're not God."

I turn my head away. I can't stand to look her in the eye. "Doctors can fail. Don't try to tell me they can't."

She leans forward and grasps both of my cheeks in her hand, forcing me to meet her fierce gaze. "Not any doctor I've ever known."

She manages to hold my gaze for several seconds. When our eyes lock, I feel a vice tighten in my chest. Squeezing, squeezing. Her warm hands are still on both sides of my face. I can feel her pulse through her palms. I finally tear my eyes away from hers. Her lips are parted ever so slightly. And then I look completely away, past her, through my screen door and out to my dark front porch. There I see Lex's unmistakable profile turn and walk away.

CHAPTER 22

His fingers have been moving. Tapping incessantly. I wonder if it's Morse code. He doesn't look right in the bland hospital gown. I brought a neon-green blanket and draped it over the foot of his bed, but it's still not enough.

"How long have you been here?" Marvin says. I didn't realize he was standing in the doorway.

"All night."

"What's the status?"

"They did an EEG," I say. "Lot's of brain activity. He's probably solving the Theory of Everything right now. And as you can see, he's no longer on the ventilator. They extubated him a couple hours ago and he's breathing on his own."

"The TOE," Marvin says. "I saw a special on that on TV. You think there really is a set of physical formulas that can explain everything?"

"Yes. I think everything has an explanation. But that doesn't mean we'd be able to understand it."

"Mind if I sit for a while?" He slides an empty chair next to mine.

"Not at all."

"So you think he's gonna wake up?"

"It's only a matter of time. Knowing him, it will be sooner rather than later."

"You think he can hear us right now?"

"I believe he can."

"Then I guess we better not mention the fact that Frank gave him a sponge bath last night." Marvin chuckles. The Professor's fingers stop twitching for a split second. "Hey! Did you see that?" Marvin says.

"I told you he can hear us," I say.

"The funeral committee's gonna be disappointed." Marvin gives me a wink. "I heard they had a meeting last night just in case." The twitching intensifies and Marvin laughs again. "Sorry, Jerry. I'm just playin' with ya."

"Remember, his heart is weak," I say.

"Ah, he can handle a little jostling. So Ben, why'd you run away last night?"

"I thought the doctor was telling us that Jerry didn't make it. Back when I was practicing surgery, I never started my talk with the family with the words 'I'm sorry' unless someone had died."

"Yeah, I thought the worst had happened when he said that," Marvin says. "Someone should tell that guy to be more careful. But he explained what happened right away. You were still there."

"I guess I didn't hear that part."

"When you didn't come back, Lex and Hailey went looking for you." He jabs me in the ribs. "I can't remember a time when I ever had two women looking for me."

"Do you mind if we talk about something else?"

"Okay. How does it feel to be a hero?"

"I have no idea."

"Oh, come on! You saved Jerry's life! We all saw you do it. It took that stinking ambulance twenty minutes to get to Betty's house. You were doing CPR that whole time. Jerry would've died for sure if you weren't there."

"Yep," Frank's voice joins the conversation from the doorway. "I was a witness. When Jerry wakes up, the first thing I'm gonna ask him is if you're a good kisser."

"Ha!" Marvin slaps his knee. "That's a good one!"

Frank scoots his way across the room, using his walker properly, and says to me, "Are you gonna give up your seat to an old man?"

"Oh, I'm sorry." I yield my chair. "Is your hip acting up again?"

"Nope." He plops down and shoves his walker aside.

Marvin leans over and whispers something in Frank's ear. Frank snickers and then says in a loud voice, "Hey, Jerry. Did you enjoy your sponge bath last night? I made sure I got behind your ears real good. I gave your backside a good scrubbing too. In fact, I scrubbed so hard I got tennis elbow."

Frank and Marvin both laugh.

"Come on, you guys," I say. "He's been through a lot. Take it easy."

"Lighten up," Frank says. "Laughter's the best medicine. Every good doctor ought to know that."

"I'm a janitor."

"Don't give me that crap," Frank says. "I'm never letting you clean my room again."

"Then you really will die from toxic mold," I say.

"I'm not letting you clean my room either," Marvin says.

"That's fine. My job will be a lot easier."

"We're gonna get everybody to boycott you," Frank says.

"Then Peterson will fire me. He'd love that. Do you really want to give him that satisfaction?"

"If that's what it takes . . ." Frank says.

"But after he fires you, I'll be your first patient," Marvin says.

"No, it'll be me. He still owes me for setting him up with Dr. Kentucky. I want that growth cut off my shoulder."

"He isn't even with Dr. Kentucky," Marvin says.

"That's 'cause he's an idiot."

"Maybe he's holding out for Hailey."

"Nah, she's way out of his league," Frank says. "Actually, they're both out of his league." He pauses. "Speaking of idiots going after women who are out of their league, what's up with you and Betty?"

"That's none of your business. What's up with you and Jane?"

"I'll tell you what's up with me and Jane: more than anything that will ever be up with you and Betty."

"Ha!" Marvin slaps his knee again. "That's another good one!"

"I'm going to the cafeteria to grab a bite to eat," I say. "Would either of you like anything?"

"Yeah," Frank says. "Scrambled eggs. I can't remember the last time I had good scrambled eggs."

"That sounds good," Marvin says.

"All right, three orders of scrambled eggs coming up," I say.

Frank and Marvin are finally gone. It's getting close to noon. I'm dozing in my chair. Betty and Hailey called and said they were planning on visiting after lunch, so I'll have a little time to get some rest. I'm not going to leave the Professor alone. None of his family have come to visit. I'm not sure if he even has any. I wonder what went wrong. I know it's not my place to wonder, but I still do.

I slouch down in my chair and rest my eyes.

"Hey, Doc," a raspy voice startles me. The Professor's eyes are open. He glances at the foot of his bed. "Thanks for the blanket."

I lean forward. My eyes well up. I wipe the tears away with embarrassment.

A sly smile is on the Professor's face.

"What?" I say, wiping my eyes again.

"You know that light Frank was talking about? The light everybody's supposed to see when they die?"

I nod my head.

"I didn't see it." His smile broadens.

At first I think it's the pain medication talking, but his eyes are crystal clear. Still, I don't understand how not seeing the light could make him so happy.

Then I figure it out. He's telling me he didn't die. He didn't die because of me. "I didn't save your life, Jerry."

"I know you didn't. I was quite dead."

"Huh?"

"Yes. Quite dead. Very dead. And there wasn't a light."

"Then why are you smiling?"

"Because what I saw was so much better. I suppose I had forgotten . . ." His voice trails off and he closes his eyes again.

Now that I know the Professor is going to be all right, I can go home and get some much needed rest. My mind is fuzzy. I used to get like this back when I was a resident physician working a forty-hour shift without any sleep. After a while, my brain would just stop functioning. That's how I feel now. I could sleep for a week. Before I can face any more of this, I need to get some rest.

For the first time in seventy-two hours, I actually get between the sheets of my own bed. It took me a while to find them before I could do so. Somehow they wound up in my bathtub. After I get some sleep I think I'll start putting my apartment back in order. And if I still have any energy after that, I just might start to tackle the rest of my life.

As soon as my head hits the pillow I'm asleep.

CHAPTER 23

I awake feeling refreshed but anxious. I must have slept eighteen hours straight.

As I sit on the edge of my bed and survey my disastrous room, a sense of panic comes over me. How will I ever get this mess back in order again? I don't know where to start.

I guess my striped shirts are as good a place as any. They should hang on their hangers with their buttons facing to the right. Horizontal stripes go in the first section of the closet, vertical stripes next. After that, my pants should be arranged from lighter shades to dark. Sweatshirts and jacket should follow.

Perfect. I feel a little better. Not much, but it's a start. The panicky feeling is still there, wriggling under the surface, threatening to take over, but it's still contained.

I gradually work my way around the apartment, biting off small chunks of the disaster. Bit by bit, I gain ground. Bit by bit, I realize my life will go on.

I like cleaning. It calms me.

As the morning progresses, I begin to convince myself that perhaps I can get my life to how it was before Betty Boop arrived. Everything was going fine up until then. I was comfortable. I had carved out a good niche for myself. Then she came along—with her picture of Hailey—and ruined everything.

I almost succeed in fooling myself, but I suddenly stop in the middle of organizing my paperclips and gaze around my half-cleaned apartment.

What am I doing?

That's the problem. I have no idea. I'm just making it up as I go. Cleaning my apartment isn't the answer.

I abandon the rest of the mess. I need to talk to the Professor.

"Ben! It's good to see you." He's sitting up in bed, meal tray in front of him, plate piled high with scrambled eggs. "These are fantastic! Want some?"

"No, thanks. Eggs for lunch?"

"Had 'em for breakfast too."

"You look well," I say.

"Not too bad for having my ribs spread. The staples in my chest hurt a little, but my throat is the worst. That breathing tube really hurt." He shovels a large bite of eggs into his mouth.

"Don't overdo it."

"I'm fine. You look pretty good yourself."

"I got some much needed rest."

"Good. What's on your mind?"

"I just came to visit."

"Please, just spit it out. I'm sick of all this beating around the bush."

I glance around the room. The noise and bustle of hospital activity filter through the door. "Mind if I shut that?"

"Go for it."

I shut the door and take my seat again. When I open my mouth, it all comes pouring out. Everything. Starting with how I met Hailey, then moving on to my brother's engagement, and then how he died on my operating table and how I abandoned my life and moved out here. And how I was finally at the point where I was going to allow myself to get involved with Lex, but then my past came rushing back to haunt me.

When I'm finished, his uneaten eggs have grown cold.

"Do you love her?" he says after a long pause.

"Who? Hailey?"

He shrugs. "Either one of them."

"I'm not sure I know what love is."

He sighs and leans back in his bed. "I don't have all the answers, Ben."

"Please, just tell me what to do."

"I don't have the answers. I think you should pray."

I give him a blank stare.

"What's wrong with that suggestion?" He takes a bite of his cold eggs. "You prayed for me when you thought I was going to die, and look—it worked! Here I am, enjoying scrambled eggs that don't taste like they were fished from the garbage disposal."

"How do you know I prayed for you?"

"Sorry, can't tell you that."

"Seriously, Jerry, I need some advice. Out of anybody I've ever known, you seem to understand me the best."

"I don't know what else to tell you, Ben. Like I said before, you need to start putting your faith in something bigger than yourself."

I hang my head and turn to leave.

CHAPTER 24

L ast night I thought a lot about what the Professor said. I decided I'm just not ready to take his advice. I won't deny that I prayed when I was afraid he was dying. That's what people do when they're desperate. I've never been on a plane that's crashing, but if I ever find myself on one, I bet I won't be able to find anybody who isn't praying.

The Professor is coming home later today. Usually people who go through what he went through have to stay in the hospital longer, but since he's doing so well and Building C technically qualifies as a skilled nursing facility, he can return.

This morning I finished cleaning my apartment and then dove right into catching up on my neglected duties around the facility. Frank and Marvin both kept their word and refused to let me clean their rooms. But they've been unsuccessful in arranging a general boycott of my services. These people like having me around.

Right now I'm cleaning Assembly Hall. Earlier, while I was walking the grounds, I noticed that spirits are high even though the future of this place remains uncertain. Junior made the first bank payment with Frank's help, and Marvin has arranged for an appraiser to come take a look at his books. I already did a little research on my own. His signed first edition of *The Hobbit* alone could go for over $100,000. We should be able to stave off foreclosure for at least several months using these resources.

I've pretty much abandoned any hope of finding my winning ticket. In fact, I feel much more at peace not thinking about lottery tickets. I'll just let some time go by and things will get better. Time is a wonderful thing. It dulls the sharp edges of life's problems. What seemed like a calamity yesterday turns into a misfortune tomorrow. Maybe, if I wait long enough, all my problems will fade into oblivion.

The hours pass in a flash while I'm occupied with my work. I can survive the days as long as I keep busy. It's the nights that are going to get me. I need a new hobby. Maybe jigsaw puzzles. I never had the patience for them before. But I need some sort of mindless task to fill the void. Although I don't know if mindless is the right word. I need something to occupy enough of my mind to distract me from everything else, and whatever that something is, it needs to take a lot of time.

Of course, if I do take up jigsaw puzzles I'll need to make a few modifications on how I assemble them. Otherwise they'll be too easy and my mind will start to wander. To make them more challenging I should mix the pieces from two different puzzles together and assemble them with the pictures face down.

I'm so excited about my new idea that the afternoon passes in a flash. Before I know it, I'm at Walmart to purchase my first two puzzles. I don't care what the pictures are. I just pick two random boxes that have fifteen hundred pieces each.

When I get back to my apartment, I waste no time in opening the boxes and mixing the pieces together in a massive pile on my table.

I'm blissfully separating edge pieces from nonedge pieces when my phone rings. I shouldn't have plugged it back in.

"Hello?"

"Hi, Ben, it's Lex."

"Hi."

"Can you come over?"

"It's almost ten o'clock. Is something wrong?"

"I have something to tell you, and I wanted to show you something too." She voices the second part of her sentence with excitement, but the first part sounded strained.

"Is it good or bad?"

"It's good. It's really good news."

"Okay, I'll be right over."

My mind churns with theories as I make the short drive to her place. I could shave several minutes off my travel time if I would compromise and make two left turns, but I'm not in that much of a rush.

A thrill runs down my spine. I want to convince myself it's due to the prospect of good news, but I know that's not what it is. I'm excited to see her. I enjoy her company more than I care to admit. In fact, I enjoy it more than I deserve.

What could her news be? Maybe she found out she inherited a large sum of money and she's going to help Heritage Gardens.

But she said she wanted to show me something. She could have just told me about the inheritance thing over the phone.

Maybe she found a suitcase full of money. That would be something she could show me.

Or maybe her news has nothing to do with our plight at Heritage Gardens. Maybe there was an earth-shattering breakthrough in the world of podiatry—somebody discovered a permanent cure for foot fungus and she wants to show me the journal article.

When I arrive at her place, she's all smiles. "Come on in." She leads the way to her couch. "That's what I want to show you." She points to an inch-thick ream of paper on the coffee table.

I pick up the pages and leaf through the first few. "Okay . . ."

"Do you know what that is?"

"It looks like a script for a play." I have to work to maintain a cheerful tone.

"That's an answer to prayer." Lex says.

"I'm happy for you," I say. "I didn't know you were an actress."

"I'm not."

"Oh. Did you write this?"

"Nope." She's grinning like a kid on her way to Disneyland for the first time.

"So . . . do you want me to keep guessing or what?"

"You'll never guess. I'm just enjoying the suspense of not telling you."

I glance down at the pages again. The title on the first page is *Prime of Life*.

"You know how I have a zillion cousins? Well one of them is a major Hollywood producer and that is the screenplay for her next project."

"Are you going to be in it?"

"No, silly. They want to do most of the filming at a retirement facility and they have a major interest in using Heritage Gardens."

"What's it about?"

"It's a mixture of drama and comedy. It's about a con artist who targets elderly people over the telephone and tricks them into donating money to fake charities. When she's caught and convicted, she's sentenced to house arrest in a retirement facility where she has to perform ten thousand hours of community service for some of the very same people she swindled. At the beginning of the story she's a bitter, horrible person and it seems like it's too late for her to get her life back on track, but as she builds relationships with the people in the retirement home she starts to turn her life around."

"So if they decide to use Heritage Gardens as a location, this movie could potentially bring in a lot of revenue," I say.

"Absolutely." Her eyes sparkle. "I doubt it will solve everything, but it seems like it can only be good."

"How certain is this?"

"The location scouts like what they've seen, but they do have other options. Before they make a final decision they want to come interview some of the residents so they can get a better feel for the personality of the place. That's probably what will seal the deal."

"When will they be coming?" I say. "I'd better try to keep Frank away from them. He'll scare them away for sure."

"The day after tomorrow. And actually, I think Frank is exactly what they're looking for."

"This is really great news." I allow my gaze to linger on her face for a few seconds. I see her eyes shift toward the kitchen. Mine instinctively follow and I notice a pile of empty boxes.

"I'm moving," she says. "That's the other thing I wanted to tell you." She hands me a card with an address written on it.

Speechless, I take it.

"A teaching position suddenly opened up in San Luis Obispo. I've always been interested in academics and it's still close to family."

"When will you go?"

"I'm taking over the classes of a professor who had a major stroke. They want me to start on Monday."

"That's only four days from today!" I say. "What about your practice?"

"My competition will be happy to take over my patients. There's only one other podiatrist in the area. I'm sure he's ecstatic to see me go. His business will double overnight."

We share an awkward silence.

"Well, I'm happy for you." I stand and place the screenplay on the coffee table.

"Are you sad to see me go?"

"Well, yeah, of course. The residents love you at Heritage Gardens. It's like you're part of the community. We'll all miss you."

"I see." She picks up the screenplay and hands it back to me. "Please take this and spread the word. I was hoping to get a bunch of copies made so that any residents who are interested in trying out for parts could get an idea, but then all this came up and I simply don't have time. Do you mind taking care of it?"

"Sure. No problem."

She turns toward the kitchen. I can't see her face anymore. "My cousin is coming to Heritage Gardens tomorrow to take a look around. She wanted to take a look before the other production people come the following day, and she's hoping to stay incognito. I was going to show her around, but I absolutely have to go to San Luis Obispo tomorrow, and I'm not even done packing."

"Are you asking me to show her around?"

"She won't bite." She picks up a box and starts putting some plates in it.

"Do you want some newspaper or something to wrap those in?"

"No. They'll be fine."

"Okay." I'm still standing there with the card with her new address and the screenplay in my hand, unsure what to do.

She grabs another box and fills it with crystal glasses. Still no paper. "Thanks for coming by," she says. "And thanks for helping out with the copies and my cousin and all."

"Yeah. It's good news—the movie, I mean."

"Okay, then." She dumps some silverware in with the glasses.

"Okay. Well, I guess I'll see you later." I turn and let myself out the door.

When I'm outside I abruptly turn and go back in. "Lex?"

Wordlessly she walks out of the kitchen.

"What time is your cousin coming?"

"Eleven."

"Where?"

"The parking lot outside Building C."

"Okay." I turn and leave again. Clutching the screenplay and her card tightly in my right hand.

When I set the script on the seat of my truck, my eye once again catches the title.

Avoiding the fourth gear and any left turns, I drive back to my apartment.

I'm back in my apartment, pacing across my small living room. The screenplay is on the couch. I'm clutching the card with Lex's new address in my right hand, which is trembling. I eye the telephone as I pace back and forth.

I don't know how long I do this. I've lost count of my paces. The card in my hand is getting damp from sweat. I examine it to make sure the ink isn't smearing. I sigh with relief when I see it's still legible. I take out my wallet and carefully place the card inside, next to the wadded up plastic bag containing my losing ticket. Then I head to my bedroom. A tear rolls down my cheek.

CHAPTER 25

Lex is gone. I know where she is, of course, but still, she's out of my life. I've never been to San Luis Obispo. It's not terribly far from here, but it's far enough.

Despite the many distractions of the day, my mind keeps returning to her. As promised, I give her cousin a tour of Heritage Gardens. She seemed highly interested. I'm pretty sure she's going to choose this place to shoot the movie.

My short time with Lex's cousin wasn't enough of a distraction. By evening I'm nearly beside myself. I can't focus. My mind keeps wandering. I need to stay focused enough to break the news about the movie to the others. I head to the cafeteria for dinner. Frank, Marvin, Jane, Boop, and Hailey are sharing a table in the corner. The Professor is resting in his room.

"I saw you joyriding with Dr. Kentucky all over the grounds today," Frank says when I take an empty seat. "What were you two doing? I bet Peterson would have a cow if he knew you were using the golf cart to fool around."

"That wasn't Dr. Kentucky," I say.

"Then who was it?" Frank is gnawing on a large bite of roast beef.

"Her cousin, who happens to be a big Hollywood producer."

"What was she doing here, and how come you didn't introduce me?"

"She's making a movie here and I didn't want her to change her mind."

"A movie?"

"Yep."

"About what?"

I tell them.

"Holy moly."

"How come Dr. Kentucky didn't come with you?" Marvin asks.

"She couldn't because she's in the middle of a last-minute move up north to San Luis Obispo. In fact, I'm pretty sure she's already gone."

"What? She didn't tell me that," Frank says as if Lex runs all her decisions by him. "Who's gonna take care of our feet? Not that McNeil guy, I hope. He's a little odd. He enjoys his job a little too much, if you know what I mean."

"Why so sudden?" Marvin says.

"A teaching position suddenly opened up. I'm sure she'll be back down here to say a proper good-bye. It's not too far of a drive."

"A sudden move like that doesn't sound like her," Jane says. "Are you sure something else isn't going on?"

"All I know is what she told me."

"Well, I want to know more about this movie deal," Frank says. "Do we get to be in it?"

"They want to cast some residents as extras."

"Holy moly, we're gonna be movie stars! I won't agree to do any nude scenes unless they pay me extra."

"I'll pay you not to," Marvin says.

"You could hire me to be your butt double," Frank says to Marvin. "Did you know they have those? If you don't think your butt is good enough, you can hire a substitute. The audience never knows the difference."

"I can't imagine why this movie would require either one of you to disrobe," I say.

"Because it's funny," Frank says. "Every comedy with old men in it features some sort of nude butt scene. I'll bet you any amount of money they'll stick an old man butt scene in this movie too."

"I don't think that's funny," Jane says. "It's crass."

"Sorry, honey, crass sells," Frank says. "Speaking of selling, I bet this deal is gonna bring in a lot of dough."

"I think it's going to be a really good thing," I say. "I have a copy of the script. I'm going to get several more made so people have a chance to take a look at it and decide if they want to audition for any parts."

"Well, what are you doing sitting here?" Frank says. "Go get those copies made!"

"I plan to, but not until after I finish dinner."

The full moon casts enough light for me to see the shadowy forms of the koi swimming by as I stare at the still waters of the pond. I sit on a bench and try to occupy my mind with simple things. I find it amazing how large some of these fish grow. I wonder how old they are. I wonder how large the largest koi on record is. How long do they live? Are they colorblind?

I know surprisingly little about koi. Or any type of fish for that matter.

Soft footsteps approach from behind. Hailey sits next to me on the bench. "Hey there," she says.

"Hey."

She gazes at the water. "The big ones seem ancient." She pauses. "I wonder how old they are."

"Yeah."

We study the pond in silence for a while, then she says. "It's hard to believe that it was only eleven days ago that I showed up for my grandfather's funeral. It feels like months."

"Time is a funny thing."

I feel her eyes on me as she says, "Do you ever feel like you're watching your life like you watch a movie? And you know how you want it to turn out, but you just can't make the characters do what you want them to?"

I nod my head without meeting her gaze.

"I hate those kinds of movies," she says.

I nod again.

"Well, it looks like everything is going in the right direction around here. My aunt is as happy as a lark. I think she has a thing for Marvin." She chuckles then sighs. "Anyhow, I need to get back to my life back home."

"When are you leaving?"

"Early tomorrow morning."

"I see."

She stands. I'm not sure what to do, so I stand too. She's still standing there, not saying anything, so I say, "It was good to see you again." I finally look her in the eye.

"It was good to see you too."

I can't read her expression. She turns to walk away, but halts, turns back, and hands me one of her business cards. "I want you to keep in touch, Ben. Please keep in touch."

"Okay."

"That's how you can reach me. It's right there. Pick up the phone. Or better yet, get in your car and come—and maybe even stay for a little while, or a long while. Just hang on to it. Don't throw it away or lose it or—I don't even know what I'm saying."

"Okay."

"Okay?" she says.

"Okay." I take out my wallet and put the card inside. Next to Lex's. And next to the wadded up plastic bag with my losing ticket.

CHAPTER 26

I t's been two weeks since Lex and Hailey left. I haven't heard from either one of them. I didn't really expect to, but I still rush to answer the phone every time it rings. I thought things would get better with time, but they're only getting worse. I feel ill at ease. Restless. The jigsaw puzzles no longer soothe me. I try to go about my daily routine, but nothing feels right about it anymore.

The other night I almost became desperate enough to follow the Professor's advice, but I'm not that far gone yet. I still think I have what it takes to pull myself back together. I just need a little more time and I'll be able to get everything back under control.

Even though I'm a mess, Heritage Gardens is better than ever. Marvin successfully auctioned off his books and raked in over $300,000. And tonight there is going to be a massive party to celebrate the production company's official decision to film the movie *Prime of Life* here. It looks like we've bought a good chunk of time.

The party starts in under an hour. I feel obligated to come, even though there's going to be square dancing. I wonder if Lex will come down from San Luis Obispo for the party. I wonder what I'm supposed to wear to a square dancing hoedown. Is it truly a hoedown, or is it called something else? I guess it doesn't really matter. My only options are horizontal stripes or vertical stripes—unless I wear my work clothes. I suppose I'll wear horizontal stripes.

I select a purple-and-green shirt and my favorite pair of button-fly jeans. The jeans came with four buttons so I had to rip one of them off to bring the total to an acceptable three. I had to sew the extra buttonhole closed, but it's hardly noticeable.

I promised the Professor I would take him to the party as long as he agreed to let me take him in a wheelchair. He's able to walk just fine and his physical therapy is coming along nicely, but I still think he should to take it easy. I figure if I confine him to a wheelchair tonight he won't try anything foolish, such as dancing.

As I walk to get the Professor, I decide I need to think of a believable excuse for why I can't dance, just in case somebody asks me to. I doubt this will actually happen since there aren't any women my age around here anymore. The only person who might ask me is Boop, but she's been pretty preoccupied with Marvin lately. Hopefully she'll leave me alone. I shouldn't have to worry about Jane either, because she will dance with Frank—unless Frank is doing the calling, but if he is, I'm sure Jane has a substitute. Even so, I ought to have an excuse prepared just in case somebody decides to harass me.

I guess the best strategy would be to pretend I have a bad ankle. It's easy enough to fake a limp. I practice it the rest of the way to Building C.

When the Professor and I arrive at Assembly Hall the party is already in full swing. Frank is at the microphone giving instructions to an array of dance partners out on the dance floor. It looks like they are about to begin doing whatever it is that square dancers do. Chairs are arranged around the perimeter of the room for spectators. A row of banquet tables is arranged at one end with an assortment of finger foods and beverages. There's even a live band on stage—a hodgepodge of residents, including a fiddle player, someone on the banjo, two guitars, a flautist, and to round them all out, bongo drums. I feel a headache coming on already, and the band hasn't even started playing yet.

"Where do you want me to park you?" I say to the Professor.

"Over by the food, of course."

A speaker pops and feedback from the microphone reverberates through the room. Frank bangs the top of the mic, but that only makes it worse. "Sorry folks, sometimes my hearing aids interfere with this gizmo." He adjusts his aids and the noise finally dies down. "There, that's better. Okay, ladies and gents, we're gonna take it slow and easy at first for the newcomers tonight. This first song will just be a warm-up. Then we'll take a break to get some food and do some socializin'. Maybe later on I'll do some more advanced calls so the beginners can see what square dancing is really all about." He turns to the band. "Hit it, boys!"

The band strikes up an indescribable tune. "Partners, square up," Frank says. The dancers arrange themselves in groups of four couples facing each other in a square formation.

I've never actually witnessed people square dancing before. I just assumed it was something I wouldn't like. I was right. I now truly understand how atrocious it really is. I didn't know that the square literally means the shape of a square. What could possibly be worse than four sets of people dancing in a square formation? It's a total nightmare. Triangle dancing would be better. Or even better yet, pentagon dancing. But no, it has to be a square.

Frank rattles off a sequence of dance moves and all the couples obediently follow his commands. "Promenade and take a little walk around the ring . . . Heads lead to the right . . . Everybody touch one corner . . . Pass through with a wheel and deal . . ."

"To tell you the truth," the Professor says, "I'm kind of glad I'm in a wheelchair."

"I hear you loud and clear," I say. "Want some punch?"

"Sure."

I leave the Professor parked at the end of the line of tables and limp over to the punch bowl. As I grab two glasses I see the back of Junior's greasy head. I do my best to avoid him, but he turns and sees me. "Hey, Ben. Quite a party, don't you think?"

"It looks like it's going to be a success."

"I can't believe my facility is going to be in a big Hollywood film!" He raises his glass as if making a toast.

"I know." I do my best to hide my disgust.

Junior leans in. "They agreed to put my name in the credits."

"Wow. That's great."

"I know!" He grabs a handful of shrimp from a platter without bothering to use the serving spoon.

"Well, I've got a drink to deliver." I show him the drinks and limp away.

"I hope that sore foot doesn't get in the way of your work," he calls after me. "We've got to have this place shipshape for the filming crew!"

As I head back to the Professor I see a small crowd has gathered around him. The band is taking a break, so Boop, Marvin, Frank, and Jane are laughing and talking with him. As I watch the scene from a distance, a wave of sadness suddenly washes over me. These people aren't going to be around for very much longer. They're like my family, but the odds are that I will outlive every single one of them.

"There's a part for you in the movie, Jerry," Frank is saying. "It's a kissing scene with two old love birds."

"I can't remember the last time I kissed a woman," the Professor says.

"Sure you do."

"No, I don't."

"But I saw you kissing someone just the other week." Frank scratches his head. He turns to Marvin. "You were there too, weren't you?"

"Yeah," Marvin says. "But that wasn't a woman."

"Oh, yeah . . . that was Ben!" Frank bursts into laughter.

At first the Professor looks confused, but then he gets it. "All right, Frank, I'll have to hand you that one. You had me going for a minute there. You can call it kissing if you want, but that kiss brought me back to life. It's a good thing Ben knows CPR."

"Well, I bet Ben is a wonderful kisser," Boop says. "Women can tell these things just by looking at a man."

"Really?" Marvin says.

"Yep. Why do you think I chose you as my dance partner?"

Marvin blushes.

"I think I'm gonna lose my lunch," Frank says. "I better get back up on stage. It's almost time to start up again."

"I want Ben to dance the next round with me," Boop says.

"I'm sorry, but I have a bad ankle." I point at my foot.

"You don't know what you're missing, hon." Boop takes Marvin's arm and leads him back to the dance floor.

I chuckle and watch them go back out. I can't deny that they all seem to be having the time of their lives.

The evening turned out far better than I expected. I was surrounded by people I've grown to care about. More so than I ever imagined I would. We laughed. We celebrated. We enjoyed the moment.

It's good to care about people and have them care about me.

But now that I'm back in my apartment I feel the loneliest I've ever felt. I can't handle this. I can't live like this. This isn't how my life was meant to be.

I'm pacing again. I take my wallet from my back pocket and peer inside. The plastic bag is still there along with both Lex and Hailey's cards. I finger them, fold my wallet, and put it back in my pocket.

I need to talk to the Professor.

"It's been an interesting ride." The Professor peers at me over his glasses. He's in his usual spot—reclined in his easy chair, hardback book minus its dust jacket propped in his lap. "You're finally leaving us," he says.

He's right, as usual. I made the decision quite suddenly only a few minutes ago. I don't know how he knows.

"What do you plan to do?" he says. "Where will you go?"

"It's come to my attention that there's a national shortage of geriatric physicians," I say.

He smiles with approval. "We need more good doctors." He pauses. "Like you."

I shrug my shoulders. "We need good janitors too."

"That's true, but I'm glad you've finally come to your senses. It took long enough."

"I'm going to miss you, Jerry."

"I'm sure you'll come to visit." He returns his gaze to his book.

"I just wanted to thank you for everything. I feel like you've always been looking out for me."

"No need to thank me." He shuts his book and puts it in his lap. "Have you taken my advice yet?"

I shake my head. "I'm just not sure I'm ready for that yet."

"Well, I hope you get ready soon. You're really missing out on something great."

"Don't worry. I haven't forgotten your advice, and believe me, I've tried to ignore it."

"Good." He smiles and opens his book again.

"I guess I'll see you later," I say as I turn to leave.

"I certainly hope so."

When I'm almost out the door he calls out, "You know something, Ben? I'll never get over the fact that you were holding a winning ticket and you failed to cash it in."

"I lost it before I knew it was worth anything," I say. "Otherwise I would've cashed it right away."

"I'm not talking about the lottery, Ben."

"I'm not sure I follow."

"Sure you do."

I shake my head and step out the door, closing it behind me. As I walk down the hall my shoulders start to feel heavy. The Professor's words nag at me. Why is he always sticking his nose into my business?

I turn abruptly and march back to his room. I fling open his door. "Do you really think any woman in her right mind would want to have anything to do with me? Look at me. I'm a total disaster. Why would anyone want to be with someone like me?"

"What's the danger in finding out?" he says.

I can't think of a good response.

"Take an old geezer's advice, Ben: start cashing in your tickets before you lose them. You're in the prime of your life. Act now, before it's too late."

Without a word I turn and leave again.

Once I'm in the hallway, I grab my wallet and reach inside. I shove the bag with my losing ticket aside and take out the card I'm looking for. I gaze at the address. I don't really need to look at it. I've stared at it so many times these past several days that I have it memorized. But still, it comforts me to see it again. I walk toward the exit of Building C with a new direction in mind. Something has finally clicked inside my head. A world of possibilities lies in front of me. Countless opportunities for the taking. I need to start grabbing them.

EPILOGUE

There's so much more to this story. I could fill several volumes with all that's happened since I left Heritage Gardens five years ago.

San Diego is always nice this time of year. In fact, it's nice every time of year. I need to get back here more often. I miss Southern California. Perhaps I should move my practice here. The nice thing about practicing geriatric medicine is that anywhere I go I'll have no trouble finding patients. I'll have to talk it over with my wife.

We've mentioned it to each other before, but neither one of us ever took the conversation seriously. We both could feel at home here. The move wouldn't be too hard and I bet we'd both be happy. We've come to visit several times. This time I broke down and agreed to go shopping at Seaport Village. I've managed to avoid this tourist trap for years, but I knew that sooner or later I was going to have to come.

The day is turning out better than I expected, thanks to Jake. He's our blond towhead, recently turned two. Everything's an adventure with him. Right now he's examining a blob of seagull excrement on the ground. "Whazz-at, Daddy?" He squats and extends his finger toward the gleaming white beacon on the cobblestone path.

"Don't let him touch that," his mom says, reaching into the diaper bag for a pack of sanitation wipes.

"That's nature's response to this conglomeration of shops marring the beautiful Southern California coastline," I say. I swoop down and pick him up. He giggles as I hoist him over my head and then bring him in close for an Eskimo kiss. "You can put those away," I say to my always prepared wife. "I caught him before he contaminated himself."

"What's that smirk for?" She puts them back in her bag.

"I just love the fact that we think so much alike," I say. "You were amazingly quick on the draw. You whipped those babies out even faster than I could have." I eye the bulging diaper bag. "Do you want me to carry that for a while?" It probably weighs thirty pounds. Our little family could survive in the wilderness for a month using just the contents of that bag.

"I'm fine." She shifts it to her other shoulder.

I admire her beauty for the umpteen-millionth time and wonder again how I got so lucky.

As we stroll along the walkway bordering the harbor, my thoughts drift to the real reason behind this trip and I feel a sudden emptiness in the pit of my stomach.

Lex casts me a sideways glance. "I'm sure gonna miss him."

It never ceases to amaze me how often our thoughts are in sync.

"Just think," she continues, "if it wasn't for him, we probably wouldn't be together."

She's right.

"It bothers me that none of his family was at the funeral." She gives the diaper bag an angry shrug. "He has family, doesn't he?"

"Jerry was always vague about that." I hold out my arm that isn't holding Jake, indicating that she should hand the bag over to me. "I never pressed him for information about his family, and he never really volunteered any. It's funny how you can feel like you really know somebody, but when you think about it, you're only getting one tiny sliver of the whole pie."

She keeps the bag and we continue to stroll along.

The funeral was bittersweet. It was hard saying goodbye to Jerry, but it was great to see everybody at Heritage Gardens again. Frank and Jane tied the knot over two years ago and they still appear to be in the honeymoon phase, which must be some sort of record. Marvin is still around when he's not off in Hollywood. Turns out he's quite an actor. Ever since his small role in *Prime of Life* he keeps getting offers. Last I heard he's appeared in six different films. Boop is still keeping the place alive with her contagious energy. Unfortunately Hailey wasn't able to be at the funeral. I wish she could've been there.

As we continue to walk, Jake starts feeling heavy. It's amazing how fast he's growing. I set him down and slow my pace so he can keep up. He grasps two of my fingers in his small hand. Up ahead I spy a grassy area where several street vendors have set up shop. There's a college kid drawing portraits, a suspicious-looking character selling knock-off Rolexes, and further down the way artists displaying overpriced paintings.

"Whazz-at, Daddy?" Jake points at a bright-blue pop-up tent situated among the vendors.

"I'm surprised they allow camping in this area." Lex shakes her head in disapproval.

A cardboard sign taped above the opening to the tent reads "Storyteller."

"Hey!" I say. "I wonder if that's really him."

"Really who?"

"Jerry used to talk about a character in a novel called *The Storyteller*."

"Oh yeah, I think I remember him mentioning that once. What's the story again?"

"Jerry loved to talk about this guy. I finally picked up the book and read it sometime last year. It's a novel, not a biography, but Jerry always insisted he really exists. He's a homeless man who earns money by telling stories. You can pay him a dollar for an amusing tale, or you can pay him twenty dollars for a story that will change your life. People who pay the twenty dollars eventually find themselves actually living the story he told them."

Lex frowns. "Now it's coming back to me. Sounds creepy. You think the guy in that tent over there was the inspiration for this novel?"

"That's precisely what I intend to find out."

"You're not serious."

"Hey, I've been shopping with you all day and I didn't complain at all. Now it's my turn to have a little fun."

"So you're saying you haven't been having fun?" She puts her hand on her hip.

"You know what I mean. Just keep an eye on Jake for a few minutes, okay?"

I make my way over to the blue tent. The flap is open. I stoop to peer inside. A man with long grey dreadlocks is sitting cross-legged on the far side of the tent. He's facing away from the opening and gives no indication he's aware of my presence, so I clear my throat.

"You may certainly enter if you feel so inclined."

I'm surprised by the tone of his voice. Judging by his thin, bony frame, I was expecting something feeble and whiney.

Still in his cross-legged pose, he somehow rotates his body 180 degrees without removing his arms from his lap. I can now see that during his seventy-some years of life he never bothered to shave.

"If you are going to stay, you must sit."

"Oh, okay." I stoop further. There's only room for one more body in the tent.

"But wait." He waves a bony finger. "If you are going to sit, you must first pay."

I notice another cardboard sign taped above his head and begin to reach into my pocket.

"My fees have changed since the posting of this sign." He reaches up, snatches the sign, and places it face down on the floor.

"What are your new fees?"

"Four dollars for a short, amusing tale. Forty-four dollars and forty-four cents for a story that will change your life."

I stare at his shaggy face. 4444. How does he know? What kind of twisted mind game is he playing? All I want to do is get out of here, but something won't let me move.

"I only accept exact change." He holds out a hand. "Check your wallet."

I reach into my back pocket and pull out my wallet. I flip it open, revealing two twenties. "See? I'm short."

"And your pockets?"

"I don't have four dollars and forty-four cents in pocket change."

He lifts his chin and waits for me to check.

And then I remember my weakness for cookie-dough ice cream. I bought two cones to share with my little family earlier this afternoon. I paid with a ten and then shoved all the change into my front left pocket.

I slowly reach inside and extract the bills and several coins. I count it all and my heart skips several beats.

"Okay." I hand him the money. "You've got my attention."

He transfers the loot beneath his thigh.

"You may now sit." He pauses. "Do you believe in God?"

"I try not to."

"Oh?"

"I thought I was paying for a story, not a religious debate."

"Have patience, friend. You will get your story. But first you must answer a few simple questions."

"Fine."

"Do you believe in angels?"

"Absolutely not."

"Why not?"

I shrug my shoulders. "Because I haven't seen a shred of evidence to support their existence."

"Very well. The story I shall tell you—the story that will change your life—shall be about an angel."

His eyes close and his voice takes on a deeper tone. "Once upon a time, in a land not so far from here, there lived a man whose life was sorely off track. At the rate he was going, he was never going to get back on course. God looked down on him with mercy and sent an angel to nudge him in the right direction. This angel only had one request of God: If he was going to shed his heavenly body and be forced into the limited physical form of a human, he wanted permission to adorn himself in the brightest, most colorful garments created by humankind. God, of course, agreed. And so, ever so gently, this angel-turned-tropical-fish-of-a-man helped the lost human find his way. And this angel told me that when you came to see me, I should give you this." His hand is out again, hovering in front of my face. Between his thumb and forefinger is a folded piece of paper. "Of course it has expired by now and therefore holds no monetary value, but you might like to have it anyway."

I take it and unfold it with unsteady fingers. A tear rolls down my cheek as I study an old lottery ticket with the numbers two, three, five, seven, eleven, and thirteen printed on the front.

As I stumble out of the tent into the bright afternoon sunlight, the ocean breeze collides with my moist cheeks. I look around and I'm stunned. The world looks different. Everything has suddenly changed.

Lex approaches from where she and Jake have been waiting in the shade. "My goodness, you weren't in there more than five minutes!" She reaches up and wipes my cheek. "What happened in there?"

"God cares about us." The tears continue to stream down my face. "He really does care."

"I know, Ben." She shakes her head and cocks her head to the side. "I've been waiting and hoping and praying for this day for years. How in the world did that man in there convince you in less than five minutes?"

I hand her the lottery ticket and sweep Jake up into my right arm. I carry him on my hip and take Lex's hand as we stroll away.

Jerry was right—the sooner we learn who's really in control, the better. Now that I know, everything will be different. And some day, many years from now, I will look back and think how fortunate I was to realize this truth while I was still in the prime of life.

ACKNOWLEDGMENTS

The journey this story took from my head to these pages was long indeed. I was not the only person who went along for the ride. Many others deserve my thanks.

Christy, thank you for your patient support through all the years as I stubbornly pursued my dream to be a writer. This dream didn't come true overnight; it required significant sacrifices of time and finances with no guarantee that any of these sacrifices would pay off. There is absolutely no way this book could have come about without you. I love you.

To my family and friends, thank you for reading drafts (and not just drafts of this work, but of my earliest works—most of which must've been excruciating to endure) and for never failing to encourage me along the way. You have no idea how much your support has meant.

To my agent, Les Stobbe, thank you for fishing my query letter out of your electronic trash bin and giving my writing sample a second look after you had already sent me a polite rejection. Thank you for believing in me. You helped me believe in myself.

Jeff Gerke, when I was desperate for help I sent you a half-written draft of this manuscript for your professional opinion. Without your genuine optimism and encouragement I might never have completed it.

Jennifer Day and Leslie Peterson, thank you for your priceless edits and for patiently walking me through this process. And to the rest of the team at Worthy Publishing, thank you for taking a newbie under your wings. The manner in which you support your authors is exemplary, and your dedication to helping people experience the heart of God is crystal clear.

Jerry B. Jenkins and the Christian Writers' Guild, thank you for giving previously non-traditionally published authors a chance to break into a very difficult market with your Operation First Novel contest. You will forever have my humble gratitude.

And last but not least, dear reader, thank you for spending a few hours with my story. I hope it stays with you a little while longer. I have pledged to use proceeds from my writing to help reduce preventable blindness in developing countries. If you would like to learn how you can get more involved, please visit me on facebook under P. D. Bekendam or on the web at PDBekendam.blogspot.com.

ABOUT THE AUTHOR

Author and practicing eye surgeon, P. D. Bekendam is happily married and a proud father. Proceeds
from his writing go to help bring cataract surgery
to the needlessly blind in developing countries.
Prime of Life is his debut novel. He loves to interact
with his readers on facebook or his blog at PDBek-
endam.blogspot.com.

WORTHY

PUBLISHING

IF YOU ENJOYED THIS BOOK, WILL YOU CONSIDER SHARING THE MESSAGE WITH OTHERS?

- Mention the book in a Facebook post, Twitter update, Pinterest pin, or blog post.
- Recommend this book to those in your small group, book club, workplace, and classes.
- Head over to facebook.com/PDBekendam, "LIKE" the page, and post a comment as to what you enjoyed the most.
- Tweet "I recommend reading #PrimeofLife by @PDBekendam // @worthypub"
- Pick up a copy for someone you know who would be challenged and encouraged by this message.
- Write a book review online.

Visit P. D. Bekendam's blog at PDBekendam.blogspot.com.

You can subscribe to Worthy Publishing's newsletter at worthypublishing.com.

WORTHY PUBLISHING FACEBOOK PAGE   **WORTHY PUBLISHING WEBSITE**